TAKING LIBERTY

THE NEXT GENERATION

RILEY EDWARDS

Taking Liberty
The Next Generation
Book 7

Riley Edwards

Cover design: Lori Jackson Designs

Written by: Riley Edwards

Published by: Rebels Romance

Edited by: Rebecca Hodgkins

Proofreader: Julie Deaton and Rebecca Kendall

Taking Liberty

Print ISBN: 978-1-951567-07-1

First edition – January 2020

To my family - my team – my tribe.
This is for you.

through my skull—I'd be lucky if I got out of this mess with my hearing intact.

"McCoy. Five, five, one—" I started to tell him through the wet towel pulled tight against my face.

Without warning, another bucket of water poured over my face before I could hold my breath.

I tried to close my mouth but it was too late—I couldn't stop the liquid from pooling in my mouth. Swallowing wasn't an option, it was coming too fast. The sensation of being smothered and drowned at the same time was too much. I had no choice but to accept what was happening.

They were in control.

If they wanted to kill me here and now they would and there wasn't a damn thing I could do about it—not restrained and weaponless.

The only thing I had left was my integrity.

I would die before I told them what they wanted.

Embrace the suck, McCoy. My SERE instructor's words played in my head. *Keep the circle and get out of your head.*

My mind drifted from the torture.

What would be, would be. But I would die a proud United States Army Ranger.

Recognizing that I volunteered as a Ranger, fully knowing the hazards of my chosen profession, I will always endeavor to uphold the prestige, honor, and high esprit de corps of my Ranger Regiment.

Acknowledging the fact that a Ranger is a more elite soldier who arrives at the cutting edge of battle by land, sea, or air, I accept the fact that as a Ranger my country expects me to move farther, faster, and fight harder than any other soldier.

"Are you fucking listening?" I tasted blood before the pain registered.

The water had stopped at some point and now the towel was off my face, but even as I blinked the wetness off my lashes, I couldn't see. My eyes hadn't adjusted and the room was dark.

Always fucking dark.

"This would stop if you'd simply tell me what I want."

Never.

Something I'd learned during my incarceration; no amount of training could've prepared me for capture. You cannot simulate real fear. My SERE instructors were the best of the best, they'd pushed us to the brink of breaking. But what happened when that last bit snapped? The part you couldn't train for, when the enemy stripped all of your humanity. When the torture wasn't in a controlled environment. When the only thing you had was your will to survive. When you're faced with death—knowing at any moment your life could end.

One thing I knew for certain was I couldn't control the manner in which these men killed me, but I could and would control how I died—and that would be with my mouth closed. My secrets would die with me. They'd get nothing out of me.

I was yanked from the plank and the room spun from my head being at an incline for however long they had me strapped down, with that goddamn towel over my face.

Stupid idiots should've shoved a rag in my mouth, their waterboarding would've been more effective.

Before my legs buckled two men rushed me, one on either side. Both not so gently held my biceps as a third man stepped in front of me.

"I will break you," the masked man grunted.

Then in a fury of fists he set about breaking me. The first strike to my kidney had me crying out in agony. By the fourth blow, I'd slipped away.

I would never break.

Never shall I fail my comrades. I will always keep myself mentally alert, physically strong, and morally straight and I will shoulder more than my share of the task whatever it may be. One-hundred-percent and then some.

Gallantly will I show the world that I am a specially selected and well-trained soldier. My courtesy to superior officers, neatness of dress, and care of equipment shall set the example for others to follow.

Energetically will I meet the enemies of my country. I shall defeat them on the field of battle for I am better trained and will fight with all my might. Surrender is not a Ranger word. I will never leave a fallen comrade to fall into the hands of the enemy and under no circumstances will I ever embarrass my country.

"Talk, you fucking bitch!"

Readily will I display the intestinal fortitude required to fight on to the Ranger objective and complete the mission though I be the lone survivor.

RANGERS LEAD THE WAY!

I don't know how long my beating lasted, I never did. But the aftermath was something I couldn't ever forget.

Two guards unceremoniously dropped me onto the floor of my cell and slammed the metal bars closed, locking me in. It wouldn't be the first time I'd laid crumpled on the dirty, cool stone. The agony was indescribable—from the soles of my feet to the hair on top of my head, everything hurt. The ache so

cotton would lessen the damage, but mentally it wouldn't have been so degrading.

"I can't think straight," I sputtered when I caught my breath. "Everything hurts. My head's foggy."

"I think your head is just fine," the man returned. "I think that you remember everything. I just haven't found the right motivation. Which is a shame, Liberty, I'd hoped it wouldn't have gone this far."

There was shuffling then the crackling and popping of a stun gun went through the room. Fear slithered down my throat and my lungs seized. I braced for thirty-eight thousand volts to electrocute me but it didn't come.

Instead the man did something far worse.

"Start recording."

My worst fear.

No, no, no.

"What was your mission objective?"

"McCoy. Five-five-one—"

A crack rang out before my body jerked, convulsed, then every muscle painfully tightened.

"This first video will be my gift to your father. He trained you well, I think he should see the fruits of his labor. Levi McCoy and his Ranger daughter. Tell me, Lieutenant McCoy, was he proud of you when you told him you were following in his footsteps?"

Shit, shit, *shit*.

"McCoy. Five-five-one—"

Again my words were cut off, blow after blow connected, until I went somewhere else. Somewhere where these men couldn't hurt me.

I'm so sorry, Dad.

2

"Drake," Matt called from inside the stone house that had been built into the rocky foothills. "You gotta see this."

I didn't move.

Five men from Lieutenant McCoy's squad laid face down in front of me. Their wrists bound at the small of their backs, their ankles roped.

No woman.

Flashes of all the possible ways Lieutenant Liberty McCoy could be suffering at the hands of the enemy made my skin crawl.

Seven days we'd been on the hunt, only to be too late. I ground my molars until they ached.

Five United States soldiers, face down in the motherfucking dirt.

"We need confirmation." A voice I didn't recognize crackled in my ear.

No shit, Sherlock. I locked down my ever-growing annoyance at helmet and body cams that sent a live-stream back to command, where some snot-nosed shithead felt the need to instruct me on how to do my job.

I glanced at Luke who was taking the necessary photos of the men, before we turned them over and prepared their evac.

"You got this?" I asked.

"Check," he answered.

I made my way to the entrance and met Matt at the door with a lift of my chin. He led me through an empty room and down a corridor lined with open doors. Metal bedframes and dirty mattresses filled the rooms but nothing else. When we got to the end, Matt pushed open the door. Trey and Logan, already in the tunnel, had their flashlights on, beams of light scanning the area, giving just enough illumination to see the stone walls and metal bars.

Fucking hell, the stale smell of blood and sweat was enough to make me want to gag. I pulled in a breath through my mouth—it did nothing to cleanse the foul taste of failure. The emotion was not one I was accustomed to. My team didn't fail.

and down the dungeon corridor, Matt already had the TV and DVD player set on the floor and plugged in.

"There's a disk in here," he told me.

"Play it."

He pushed the tray back into the machine and the blue screen on the TV came to life.

Suddenly there wasn't enough oxygen in the room.

Jesus, I'd been right, someone small had been restrained in that fucking chair—Lieutenant McCoy.

Not that I could see her face. She was hooded and stripped. There wasn't a single square inch of her that wasn't covered in bruises. Her bra and panties may've at one time been white, but it was hard to tell, they were soiled with blood and dirt. Her dog tags still around her neck hung between her breasts which struck me as odd. *A Ranger would never wear their tags around their neck. They'd be knotted around a belt loop and shoved in the back pocket.*

Blood, filth, and more blood.

Son of a motherfuckingbitch.

"Have you had enough?" a man in a mask asked.

"He's American," Matt growled. "What the fuck?"

"McCoy—"

Her words were cut short when she got a fist to the face. I watched in horror as her head snapped to the side.

"I know your fucking name, McCoy." The man yanked on the hood, righting her head. "What the fuck was your mission objective?"

"I don't remember."

Three quick punches to her middle had her gasping and grunting.

What the actual fuck? More anger than I'd ever known welled inside of me. So much fury I didn't know it was humanly possible to feel so much hate.

"Fucking tell me!" the man shouted.

"I would rather die than betray my brothers. I *will* die before I embarrass my country," Lieutenant McCoy said, her voice sure and strong. Then she shouted, "*Sua Sponte!*"

"Very well, Lieutenant, that can be arranged."

I braced to witness her murder but the recording stopped and the screen flashed back to blue.

The air in the room had gone electric—I was vibrating with rage and Trey and Matt were equally angry.

I swung my pack off my shoulder, letting it fall to the floor before I took a knee and rummaged through it. I chugged back half a bottle of water before I fished the satellite phone out and made a call I didn't want to make.

Levi McCoy had to be going out of his mind. And as much as I wished this call was to tell the General—who'd personally flown to Israel under the pretense of a US-Israeli training campaign—that we were bringing his friend's daughter home, he still needed an update.

I turned off my helmet cam and made the call.

"Update," General Wick clipped.

I took no offense at the man's tone. Thanks to the live-stream, he'd just witnessed one of his oldest friend's daughter being beaten. That had to be hell on the man.

"Hellraiser-one is still MIA. We need evac for the KIA."

"Ice—"

Hearing my callsign instead of confirmation he had a plan to evac our dead had me seeing red.

"All due respect, Wick. There's no chance in hell we're leaving them here."

A string of expletives rang out and I heard him issuing orders.

"Take them to the checkpoint."

"Come again?"

"Get them to the checkpoint and someone will be there to accept and transport from Bravo—"

"You're shitting me?"

"Ice, it's the only way. We don't have any American assets in the vicinity."

"You're fucking shitting me. The plan is for us to hand our dead over to the Russians? The motherfucking Russians. Call in a nine-line."

"That's the best we got, son, unless you want to sit and wait your ass there for three hours." General Wick expelled a long, exasperated sigh. "UN personnel will be present during the exchange."

"I don't give the first fuck who's present, General. The Pope himself could be there waiting to give the prayer for the faithfully departed and I'll still gut those assholes if they disrespect our men."

"And you'll create an international shitstorm that neither I nor anyone else will be able to contain."

Did Wick seriously think I gave a fuck? Not one time in my nineteen-year career in the military had I turned our dead over to a foreign fighting force.

"Then I suggest you tell the UN forces to keep the Russians nice and friendly."

"You're willing to die to protect bodies—"

down at the two pieces of metal in the palm of my hand and silently vowed—*I'm gonna find you and bring you home, Liberty McCoy.*

3

"This is more fun than I'd thought it'd be." I looked up into a pair of cold, dead eyes.

I fucked up.

In a moment of sheer weakness, I'd gone against everything my father had drilled into me.

I lashed out.

I'd accepted my situation and my loss of control. My mental integrity remained steadfast. I would die knowing I didn't compromise operational security.

But I *would* die.

I'd stayed calm during the physical and psychological torture. I'd played my fear up, I'd never stopped planning escape, I'd never given up hope.

But I'd snapped—mouthed off and broken all of the rules I'd been taught. Not only would my dad have been disappointed but my SERE instructors as well. Of course, I'd been hooded so I had no idea if I'd been recorded or not—but the asshole finally found my weakness. My real one, not me playing to his macho, *I'm a man so I'm bigger, badder, and scarier than you*, bullshit.

I would rather endure any amount of torture than have my mom and dad be subjected to witnessing me being beaten. It would break my dad and destroy my mother. The video would be suppressed, but not before it made its rounds on every YouTube-style website. They would never be able to unsee that.

"This is your last chance." I had no doubt he was telling me the truth.

I was on my back, my wrists shackled to the wall, ankles zip-tied, and he was straddling my hips. Even if I could buck him off, my limbs were useless.

I closed my eyes and prepared to die. Something I'd spent time thinking about—even before my captivity. It had started during OCS, the thoughts morbid but necessary. Sometime in the hours—or maybe it was days since I'd been dragged down a long, dark tunnel and driven to a new torture-location—I'd made peace with my death.

I drew up the memory I wanted to relive as I

In an effort not to cry like a baby in front of my fellow Rangers, my gaze went to the bleachers and landed on the rest of my family. I scanned the crowd, looking for my uncles, Jasper, Lenox, and Clark, but they were not sitting with my aunts and cousins.

A hard thump on my shoulder and cheers of congratulation explained why my uncles were no longer with their families.

"Ranger," Uncle Clark gave me a nudge.

Damn, the sound of that, the pride radiating off of the four most important men in my life filled me with more warmth than I'd ever known.

My mom stepped back and seconds later, my dad and his brothers-in-arms, my uncles, men who had served our country with pride and honor, seen battle and had bested it, taught me, loved me, Rangers themselves before they'd gone on to become Deltas. Men who had walked in my shoes, and I in theirs. Men whom I admired and looked up to. My inspirations. Surrounded me.

"Can't think of a day I've been more proud of you," Dad said and pinned his tab to my sleeve. "And it has nothing to do with this tab." He tapped over the embroidered patch. "And everything to do with your determination."

Uncle Lenox held out his hand and opened his fist. Holy shit—his tab. "May it bring you strength."

With a shaky hand I took his offering. But before I could say anything, Uncle Clark held out his. "May it bring you courage."

"Roman!" someone shouted and the asshole loosened his grip. "Hurry up, we have company."

"Hold them off."

The pressure returned. This time I couldn't stop my legs from kicking out.

Uncle Jasper opened his hand and I held his gaze as he spoke, "May it remind you of those who have gone before you and their sacrifices."

Rangers did not cry, I reminded myself.

"Thank you. I'll cherish these always," *I choked out.*

"Rangers lead the way," *my dad said and smiled.*

"That is until the Combat Application Group gets there, then you step aside, Ranger," *Uncle Clark joked.*

"Love you, girl," *Dad said.*

"Love you, Daddy."

Then there was nothing but blackness.

I'd won.

4

"So much for a UN safe zone," Luke muttered from beside me.

"Safe's a relative term," Trey returned. "I'd rather be lying here with my dick in the dirt than be in Damascus surrounded by Daesh."

It had been three days since we'd dropped off the Rangers at the Quneitra border checkpoint where we were met by a Russian Lt. Gen. who personally gave assurances the men would be handled with respect.

After the exchange, which included me giving him too many hundred-dollar bills—the only bright side to that was I knew the US currency would remain in his pocket for quite some time unless he

enemy never stood a chance. Our formation was tight, our aim true, as we navigated across the expanse as one.

Angry voices came from our nine o'clock and rapid gunfire rang out. Three men ran from the house shooting wildly in our direction. No sooner had we taken out the first three, five more ran out.

I took aim at the man closest to me. He fell before I could get a shot off, so I adjusted my aim to the next target and pressed the trigger. Two down, three more to go. As we were clearing the men in front of us, a car started and a dusty Mercedes accelerated, spitting rocks and debris as it sped down the long dirt road.

Seconds later, it exploded.

"Good splash," Matt whooped over the radio.

Crazy bastard.

"Whelp, if they didn't know we were here they sure as fuck do now," Luke complained.

By "they" he meant the rebel forces, and he was not wrong. The explosion just cut our time in half.

The last of the men in front of us went down and the silence was startling.

Logan and Trey preceded us to the front door, entering the house as Luke and I took up the rear.

"Clear," Logan called out.

"Clear," Trey echoed from a room tucked in the rear.

Luke and I hit the hallway and I felt it—a tingling in my spine so strong I couldn't ignore it. My feet were moving before my mind registered what they were doing, and when I turned the doorknob that I found myself in front of, operational protocol was the last thing I was thinking about.

I needed in that room. I felt it—someplace deep in my gut—I had to get inside, quickly.

Liberty McCoy's beaten body lay unmoving—hands cuffed to eye bolts screwed into the wall, ankles tied together, every inch of her filthy and bruised.

Christ. My body swayed and my breath caught. *Jesus fuck.*

Again I rushed in without a care for the possibility I was walking into a trap or the prospect of unfriendlies in the room.

I was on my knees next to a battered Lieutenant McCoy. I tore my gloves off and pressed my fingers against her throat.

"I have eyes on Hellraiser-one," I radioed. "Unresponsive, weak pulse," I called out and lowered my face to hers and waited. "No breath sounds."

Uncaring her cracked lips were covered in blood,

I tilted her head back and gave her two rescue breaths, checking to make sure her chest was rising, and started chest compressions.

Luke was already working to release the cuffs and Trey had joined us, cutting the zip ties at her ankles.

"We have company coming up the mountain," Matt radioed.

"We can't move her," I responded.

"You have three minutes."

"Come on, breathe, goddamn it."

Two more rescue breaths and I paused when my gaze caught on the fresh marks that circled her throat.

"Drake, grab her and let's go."

I ignored Trey and went back to compressions.

"Drake—"

"Fucking fight, *Ranger*."

Three rescue breaths and I lowered my cheek to her mouth—still nothing.

"Move out," Matt ordered with impatience.

"I'm not moving her until she is breathing," I told the room as I counted my compressions.

"Goddammit, *Liberty*, breathe."

It was as if I commanded it, a barely audible inhale followed by a few more sputtered breaths.

"We're moving," Luke announced.

"This is gonna hurt like a son-of-a-bitch," I warned the lieutenant, as I lifted her into my arms.

Her long, low, painful mew was music to my ears —she was alive.

Thank fuck.

Logan took point leading us back down the hall, Trey took the rear. With the lieutenant in my arms, I was weaponless and had to rely on my team to get us to where we were going.

"You're out of time," Matt grumbled. "Plan B."

Plan B wasn't a great option—that entailed us walking nearly two miles to an abandoned factory we'd already cleared then booby-trapped to make sure no one entered.

"No." Liberty suddenly arched her back, but in her weak state it wasn't more than a slight movement.

"We're here to take you home, Hellraiser-one."

"No," she croaked.

The obvious damage to her larynx pissed me right the fuck off and I hoped that one of the eight men who lay dead in dirt was the one responsible for harming the lieutenant.

My gaze went from the pickup trucks speeding up the dirt road to the woman in my arms. She looked so frail and small, but I knew she was anything but. I heard stories about how fierce Liberty McCoy was. My old teammate and good friend Carter was proud of his cousin and spoke of her often.

I'd only ever seen the lieutenant's official Army portrait. Carter had talked a lot about her, described her attitude and determination, but this woman was not what I'd imagined. Over the years I'd pictured a tall, muscular woman, something close to a German bodybuilder with thick legs, defined biceps, a manly-woman. But there was nothing manly about Liberty.

Her eyelids fluttered as she struggled to open her eyes.

"All you have to do is rest," I told her.

"We've got three more trucks coming in," Trey announced.

If we didn't leave right then, we wouldn't be leaving at all.

"I'm useless," I reminded Trey. "You take point and get us the fuck out of here."

My teammate gave me a sharp look conveying just how stupid he thought my reminder was, then started toward the trail that would take us up the side of the mountain. We needed to hustle, the landscape was sparse—there were only a few boulders large enough for us to hunker behind if needed and not enough bushes or trees for us to blend into. As soon as those trucks got into range, we were sitting ducks.

The loose gravel under my boots gave way and I stumbled. My arms tightened and the lieutenant's low groan of pain pulled my attention down to her face.

I couldn't stop the wince when my gaze took in the angry welts and bruised flesh.

"Sorry," I mumbled. "As soon as we get over this ridge the terrain evens out."

The lieutenant's eyes snapped open and my breath caught in my lungs when her golden eyes locked onto mine. Cat eyes. There was no other way to describe the way the gold gave way to brown the closer you got to her pupils.

Unique.

Beautiful.

Breath stealing.

And pleading.

Before I could further contemplate those unusual orbs, or the fact that the whites of her eyes were not white but bloodshot from being strangled, bullets rang out, slicing past us, kicking up debris as they hit the ground less than a yard away.

"This is gonna hurt. Bear with me."

I took off in a sprint knowing my team would cover us until I cleared the crest. Every step I took drew another pain-filled moan from Liberty.

"Stick with me, we're almost there."

Trey was at my side ready to take out any unfriendlies should one happen to be hiding behind the large rocks as we neared the top.

Gunfire exchanged behind me, our situation was fucked, Liberty was beaten to hell, but I couldn't stop thinking about those astounding eyes and why the moment she looked at me something deep inside of me roared to life—something possessive and over-whelming.

"You two get gone!" Logan shouted and Trey didn't miss a beat running full-out with me on his heels.

The steep terrain was a bitch to navigate, and with Liberty cradled in my arms it was ten times harder. I tried my best not to jostle her but her constant grumbles told me I was doing a piss-poor job. But she didn't utter a complaint.

"Almost at the top. Hang tight."

I chanced a look down at her face—her cracked lips had fresh blood trickling down her chin. I licked my own and tasted the coopery tang of her blood. There was no use second-guessing my lifesaving measures, I knew I hadn't been gentle and I'd probably torn open some of the healing cuts, but it was that or let her die. And that was not an option.

The other side of the ridge was a sharp decline. Trey would have no issue traversing the downward slope. But with Liberty in my arms it made negotiating the angle difficult.

I made a last-second decision, one I knew would cause Liberty agony but it was our best and quickest option.

I went down on my ass, taking the brunt of the fall, and started to slide.

"Shit," she grunted.

"Just hold on."

Our descent was fucking painful—rocks jabbed my ass and hips as I skidded down the mountain side.

"You're doing great," I grunted after she let out a howl of anguish.

A minute later I dug the heels of my boots into the pebbly ground, bringing us to a stop. Liberty's head lulled to the side and she was dead weight in my arms.

Fucking hell.

"She's out," I told Trey who was behind me helping me to my feet.

"Probably for the best. All that knocking around has to be painful as fuck."

He wasn't wrong, but I still didn't like that she'd lost consciousness.

With a battle raging behind us, I followed Trey down into a rocky valley that would lead us to the factory.

An hour later we were coming up on the building we'd secured last night. The two-mile walk normally would've taken us forty minutes at most, but Trey had wisely taken the long way. With my arms full of Liberty I wasn't exactly the best battle buddy.

"She awake yet?" Trey asked, and I glanced down at the woman in my arms.

Thank God, her eyes were still closed because I couldn't conceal my cringe as I took her in. Nor could I contain my fury. The impulse to kill thrummed through my veins. The urge to exact revenge pulsed through my body the longer I stared at her marred flesh.

I felt powerless. The emotion was foreign and unwelcomed—but overwhelmed me nonetheless.

"Negative," I finally answered when Trey cleared his throat.

With a sharp jerk of his chin, he knelt in front of

the door and cautiously brushed dirt and debris off the thin piece of scrap wood before he gingerly picked it up, exposing the four-inch-deep hole he'd dug.

"It ain't high-tech but damn if it doesn't work," Trey joked as he continued to disengage the cartridge trap he'd set last night.

He wasn't wrong, there was nothing high-tech about a hole in the ground, a firing pin, and a .308 round. But damn if it wouldn't blow a hole in your foot if you stepped on it.

The trap wasn't meant to kill, or Trey, the explosive genius he was, would've rigged the building to blow. The only purpose of the primitive device was to ensure no one had entered the building and set IEDs. With this being the only entrance, and the .308 cartridge still intact, we were safe to enter.

Trey pocketed the bullet but still checked the door for a charge.

"Boy Scout," I jabbed.

"Boy Scout my ass. More like bacon saver."

"It's a good thing you're pretty, brother, because you have the shittiest comebacks," I unnecessarily informed him.

Trey's lame retorts and failed attempts at verbal retaliation made for hours' worth of fodder.

"Fear not, friend, I've never needed a snappy quip to get a woman into my bed. And you can trust and believe they always want to come back."

"Yeah, you need to work on your delivery, too."

The banter halted as Trey slowly opened the door. The feeling of worthlessness swamped over me. Normally when we breached, it was all hands on deck and weapons were trained on any possible unfriendlies, but with the lieutenant in my arms I was useless. The alternative would be setting her down and leaving her exposed—and that was not going to happen.

"Where are we?" Liberty slurred and I glanced down to find her awake.

"Hey." I tried to give her a reassuring smile but damn if it hurt to look at her. "Welcome back. We're stopping here and waiting for my team to catch up. Then we'll get you home. You need to sip some water."

Trey quickly pulled his canteen from his pack and pressed it to Liberty's lips.

"Ouch," she protested and he pulled it back.

"Shit. Sorry. Let's try that again."

This time Trey tipped the opening to her mouth and poured slowly. Water trickled down her chin washing some of the blood and dirt away, reminding me I needed to get her cleaned up and clothed.

"Lieutenant?" I called when Trey pulled the canteen away after she'd successfully taken a few swallows. "I need to look you over."

Panic flared in her eyes and she started to shake her head.

"I'll be gentle, but I have to clean some of these cuts."

"I don't..." Her scratchy voice made me want to kill someone. "I'm fine."

"You're not fine," I told her as I surveyed the room.

"Nothing's broken."

Fucking hell, she needed to stop speaking. Every time I heard her scratchy voice, disgust and anger swirled together making my head throb.

I found a fifty-five gallon drum and set Liberty down.

"Sorry it's dirty," I mumbled.

"Right, because I'm so clean."

Once I had Liberty settled, Trey handed me a canteen before he produced a second one and started sprinkling water over her feet.

This was the first time I'd had more than just a moment to take in her injuries and there were many.

So many, I didn't know where to start. Bruises of all shapes and colors—some fresh, some in various stages of healing.

"You did good, Ranger," I croaked, unable to hide the fury in my tone.

"Don't look at me with..." She trailed off and tried to clear her throat.

The movement brought my eyes back to her neck and the swollen flesh circling the long, delicate column of her throat.

Son of a bitch.

"Look at you with what? Respect? You're fuckin' tough, that's for damn sure."

"My team?" she asked.

I didn't want to tell her, not now, not when she was vulnerable and raw, but I wouldn't insult her by dodging her question.

I gave my head a shake in the negative and her bloodshot eyes closed. She took a moment to compose herself before she asked, "Anyone?"

I knew she was inquiring about survivors so I gave her another swift head shake and moved on.

"I'm gonna clean your face while Trey's finishing with your feet. After that, I'll check your back."

"What's your name?"

I couldn't help it, I chuckled. Here I'd given her

mouth-to-mouth, carried her damn near two miles, and told her she'd lost her entire team, and I hadn't introduced myself.

In my defense, when my team rescues a hostage there are no introductions. We were typically masked, used call signs instead of our real names, and we didn't make small talk. Our job was to secure the package, deliver it safely, and leave with our identities safely concealed.

But the rescue of Lieutenant McCoy was anything but typical, and in an effort to keep emotions in check and detached, I dismissed giving her my name. I wanted the distance the uniform code of military justice could provide.

Fraternization between officers and enlisted was strictly prohibited and by my reaction to Liberty I was glad for it. Frankly, I needed a reminder when everything inside of me was telling me that this woman in my arms was more than an Army Ranger we'd been sent in to save.

"Master Chief Hayes," I answered.

Trey chuckled, then he started in with the jabs. "How long have you been waiting to finally introduce yourself as master chief?" He shook his head then continued. "Don't let him fool you, Lieutenant, he just passed his E-9 test a month ago. Drake's like a baby master chief. I'm Trey."

"Drake?" she asked.

"That's my name."

"Like the duck?"

Trey roared with laughter, his hands shook with hilarity as he splashed water over Liberty's ankles and calves.

"Let's just announce our location," I scowled. "It's not like every fucking household doesn't have a rocket launcher or anything."

My sarcasm was met with a soft, husky laugh and I wondered what Liberty sounded like when her windpipe and vocal cords weren't crushed and damaged.

What the fuck is wrong with me?

She was not Liberty—she was Lieutenant McCoy.

5

Every. Single. Part. Of me was in agony.

There wasn't an inch that didn't ache or hurt.

But somehow, I was alive. I'd take the pain over death any day.

"How'd you find me?" I asked and regretted each word that came from my sore throat.

"How 'bout you let me finish washing your face, then we'll talk," Drake told me.

No, he's Master Chief Hayes.

I knew why I was feeling emotionally connected to the man—his had been the first friendly face I'd seen in weeks. He was the first person I saw after I thought my life was over. That was all this was—hero worship. He'd saved my life and now I was clinging to him. Actually, I wasn't clinging to anything, he

"Sexual assault?" The blunt question had me involuntarily stiffening.

Drake's body had gone solid and I felt his gaze burning into my skin. That was just about the only question he hadn't asked when going over my injuries. Though he also hadn't asked what kind of torture I'd endured, he kept his questions mostly about pain level and if I had any signs of infection.

"Matt," Drake's angry rumble vibrated through my body.

"Brother, you know you can't wash…"

"I wasn't," I cut in.

"Ma'am, there's no shame in telling us. But we need to preserve evidence."

"Matt, right?" The man nodded and I continued trying to sound stronger than I felt. "Look at me. Do you think I have any embarrassment left? They did their best to strip me of my dignity. They humiliated me and took everything they could from me. But they did not rape me. I have no shame, I know I did what I had to do to survive and I did it without disgracing my oath."

Matt's face had gone from matter-of-fact to pissed right the hell off and I wasn't sure what had made him so angry. What I did know was my throat felt like I'd swallowed nails.

"May I have some more water?"

"Just a few sips," Drake told me and lifted the canteen.

My hands wrapped around his as I brought it closer to my mouth so I could drink without it being poured down my throat.

I'd had enough water being forced on me to last a lifetime.

"Easy," Drake cooed, and I realized I was shaking so badly the water wasn't making it into my mouth.

"I... I'm sorry."

"Don't be. Just relax and I'll pour."

"No!" I snapped and Drake froze.

Maybe I still had some shame left because I had to close my eyes to block out Drake's concern.

"Talk to me. Tell me what it is you don't want."

"Don't pour it in my mouth. They... I can't have the water poured."

Drake let out a long string of colorful words, some I'd never used myself, and I was known for my potty mouth.

"Waterboarding," he surmised.

"So many times I lost count."

"You wanna try to put it to your lips? It might sting a little but you'll be able to drink without pouring it in your mouth."

"Yeah."

Our combined hands brought the metal to my lips and Drake allowed me to take over, tipping the canteen back. When I was done, I noticed his thumb was gently stroking mine. The contact barely registered beyond the fact Drake was being nice.

It was odd how detached I felt from the whole ordeal. It was like the last few weeks had happened to someone else. Sure I was sitting in a dilapidated building with crumbling walls and it smelled like death warmed over. I had all the physical reminders it had indeed happened to me, but emotionally I'd completely closed down. My thoughts and feelings were well out of my reach even if I wanted to access them.

I'd lost my entire team. Kirby, Pritchett, and Ball would never go home to their wives. Their children now fatherless. Perez and Martin would never jackass around again, they'd never tease me and poke fun at my painted toenails. The world had lost five great men and I couldn't find more than a transient thought of sadness.

I was going home and they weren't. There was something disgustingly wrong about that. And for a moment I wished Drake and his team hadn't found me.

Overwhelming anger coiled in my stomach, it seeped into my bones, it infected my blood.

"Liberty?"

"What?"

Drake's gaze slid over my face and I watched his Adam's apple bob.

God knows what I looked like.

If the throbbing was anything to go by, I had to look like I'd gone rounds with Conor McGregor and lost.

"Settle, Liberty."

"Don't tell—"

My skin was suddenly burning and becoming tighter by the second, I wanted nothing more than to shed my broken body. I didn't want to ever be Liberty McCoy again.

"Settle," he demanded.

Matt abruptly stepped back and I glanced around the group of men who all stood with their arms crossed over their chests wearing identical scowls.

Fuck it.

Fuck them.

"Don't tell me what to do, Master Chief."

"Breathe, Ranger."

"Stop... Stop... Fucking..."

I couldn't catch my breath, my chest labored to suck in oxygen, my lungs burned, and my vision started to swim.

No, no, no.

I didn't want the darkness.

Not now.

No more darkness.

6

"Jesus Christ," Luke growled.

"I've never seen someone turn so fast," Trey added.

Neither had I and it scared the fuck out of me.

The episode came on so quick I didn't think Liberty understood what was happening. One second she was drinking water, the next she was shaking so violently she looked like she was having a seizure. Her face had gone pale and she was in the throes of a panic attack. The episode had snuck up on all of us and had her so entrenched there wasn't time to stop it before she fainted.

And just like the first time she'd lost consciousness, maybe it was for the best to give her mind a moment to rest.

"Grab her uniform out of my pack, will you?" I asked Logan.

There was no doubt each of us was feeling our own level of anger seeing Liberty beaten. No man wanted to see a woman harmed. But for men like us, it ignited something dangerous. However, Logan was feeling something different. He had three sisters, and I'd bet he was seeing each of them in Liberty as she laid limp in my arms.

"Logan—"

"I'm fine," he clipped unnecessarily, verifying I was right.

"If you need—"

"I said I was fine, Drake. Leave it."

I heard Matt sigh—another indication Logan was not fine. But we all knew him well enough to know, when the man didn't want to talk—he wouldn't.

Logan set her folded uniform and a blanket on the barrel Liberty had been sitting on and asked, "Do you need help?"

"No."

I grabbed the items, stood, and walked us to the far side of the room to preserve what was left of Liberty's modesty and fanned the blanket out the best I could before I gently laid her down. Nausea crept up as I took her in.

Good Christ.

The sight of her was like a knife to the heart. Every cut a twist of the blade. Every bruise salt to the wound just looking at her injuries caused me.

Unable to look at Liberty's abused body for another second, I got to my knees and as carefully as I could, I started to dress her. I didn't know for sure how long it had been since she'd been stripped down, but since we'd found her uniform trousers and blouse as well as her boots in the first house we'd hit, which wasn't too far away from where she and her team had been ambushed, best guess was from day one.

I lifted her hips and slid the pants under her ass, doing my best to advert my gaze yet needing to watch what I was doing. Never had I been so sick to my stomach as I tended to a wounded soldier. Never had my hands shook with anger. As I buttoned Liberty's pants, I tried but failed not to think about her bloodstained panties. She said she hadn't been sexually assaulted, and I prayed she was telling the truth. There was more than enough blood that had leaked from her nose, mouth, and lacerations on her abdomen to explain the stains. But my heart still throbbed in my chest at the mere prospect that it *could've* happened to this strong, brave woman.

"Lieutenant, wake up." I brushed some of her

matted hair away from her face and once again winced at the contusions.

Proof of what she'd endured.

No, that wasn't right. Proof of what she'd survived.

"Liberty," I called again when she didn't rouse. "Wake up, Ranger, we have to get you dressed."

Her eyelids started to flutter, then they shot open and fear-filled eyes met mine right before she started to struggle.

"Easy, Liberty." I backed away enough that I wasn't crowding her but close enough to restrain her so she didn't hurt herself. "You're safe, remember? We got you out."

"No!" she shouted a struggled plea. "Don't."

"Focus, Liberty. No one's gonna hurt you."

My gut clenched when she scrambled to sit upright and let out a painful scream.

"Look at me, Liberty, and focus. Breathe. You're safe."

Finally her wild eyes started to relax and she blinked a few times.

"Drake?"

"Yeah, I'm right here. I thought you'd like to get dressed."

"Dressed?"

Why did she look so damn adorable when she tilted her head and wrinkled her forehead in confusion?

"We found your uniform," I told her. "Your socks and tee were missing, but at least you'll be covered up."

And that was when Liberty McCoy's armor cracked. I saw the tears pool in her eyes before they started to fall. I sat back on my knees with my ass to my heels, completely frozen as I witnessed this resilient woman's pain. She made no move to wipe or hide her tears—heat raced up my spine and settled so deep I knew I'd never forget this moment. Lieutenant Liberty McCoy was giving me the greatest gift I'd ever been given—her trust.

When she spied her camouflage top still folded on the floor next to her, she snatched it so quickly she swayed.

"Whoa. Careful. I'll help you put that on but I need to check your back first."

She ignored me and continued to shake the blouse until it was unfolded. The sound of Velcro ripping open echoed in the cavernous room. I wasn't sure what she was after but whatever it was it must've been important because she was on a mission to retrieve it even though her hands shook and chest heaved with exertion.

"Thank God," she whispered. "Thank you, God."

She pulled her hand from her breast pocket and opened her fist, palm up to show me her treasure. Four scrolls from the 75th Ranger regiment.

"Your dad's?" I surmised.

"Yes," she sobbed. "And my uncles—Jasper, Lenox, and Clark."

I smiled at her obvious relief. I couldn't say it was unusual she'd keep something so special to her while she was on a mission. Most men I knew always had *something* with them. A photo, a charm to bring them luck, a letter, a pocket bible, a cross. We were a superstitious bunch and used anything and everything to get us through deployments.

"I thought they were gone. My dad... he taught me this trick, when the pain got to be unbearable I slipped away into a memory. The last thing I was thinking about when I was dying was my graduation. That's where they gave me their scrolls. I saved my favorite memory for the end. I wanted that to be the last thing I thought about. I thought maybe somehow they'd know that everything they taught me meant something. It got me through without breaking. I didn't... I didn't give them what they wanted."

I didn't think she had and I thought she deserved to know so I told her.

"Didn't think you did, ma'am."

"Liberty," she reminded me.

Now more than ever I needed the professional distance our ranks provided but I found I couldn't deny her.

"Your dad's worried sick—everyone is. We'll get you to a phone as soon as we can so you can speak to them."

In an instant her face closed down and the tears that had been flowing stopped as if the faucet had simply been turned off.

"Liberty?"

"Would you mind checking my back so I can get dressed?"

"Sure, as soon as you tell me what's wrong."

"Nothing's wrong."

"Um, hate to tell you this, but you're not fooling me. I witnessed it. The moment I mentioned calling your dad, you shut down. You know how proud your family is, right? I'm sure by now your dad's been notified you've been rescued..." Liberty flinched and her lips flattened into two thin lines that had to be extremely painful. "Right there, why the scowl?"

"I'm not scowling. I'm in pain, Master Chief. Forget it, I don't need my back checked."

She started to swing the blouse so she could dress herself but I caught the material and took it from her before I moved behind her.

"You know, it only gets harder. And the more you try to fight it, bury it, pretend it didn't happen, deny the fear and helplessness, the worse it is. Advice, Ranger—deal with it now. Acknowledge what happened, admit you were scared, process that you were held captive against your will and tortured. Because until you concede, you cannot begin to recognize your strength.

"Now comes the hard part, the part they don't teach you in SERE school, the part that cannot be taught because until you've truly lived it there are no words for it. This is where you learn to rebuild. Starting right now, is when you realize you will never be the same and that is okay. This is where you fight *again* to regain the control you lost. But you do that by letting it all hang out. Open those wounds and let them bleed. Purge all the poison polluting your soul. Allow it all to hemorrhage because if you don't, you'll be stuck here, in this fucking shithole building in Syria, for the rest of your life."

My gaze hit her welted back and I was happy she couldn't see me. There was no way I could hide my disgust at what they did to her.

"Before you put that on, I need to dress this," I told her and stood. "I'll be right back."

Liberty didn't utter a word as I stomped across the room. There was no other way to describe my pounding footsteps.

Where in the hell is my professional detachment now?

"How's she doing?" Logan asked when I made it to my team.

"She's shutting down."

"You need to—"

"I know what needs to be done," I snapped, cutting him off.

I didn't like the looks my team exchanged and I braced when Luke pinned me with a knowing stare.

"You want me to take over?" he asked.

"Absolutely not."

"Brother, you sure you know what you're doing?"

Hell no, I don't.

"Yep."

"Drake. Be smart."

"I am."

Since when had I started to lie to my team? I wasn't being smart—not even close. Getting attached to the lieutenant in any way was the stupidest thing I could do. Yet the thought of Luke or anyone else dressing her wounds or helping her had me seeing red.

I grabbed my pack and stalked back to Liberty—her face blank, and staring off into space.

"Liberty?" Her torso jerked and her eyes swung to me.

She started to speak but had to stop to clear her throat. "Have you been..."

Liberty let her question hang and even though I knew what she was asking, I was going to make her say it. I didn't lie when I told her she had to start dealing with the repercussions of being taken and held captive now. The longer she let it fester, the worse it would become.

"Have I been what?" I pushed.

"Held hostage."

That was a start.

"Yep. Thirteen days."

She fell silent, and sensing she had more to ask but didn't want to look at me while she did, I moved behind her. I set my pack down before I

7

There had never been a point in my life when I'd felt lost. I'd been blessed with two great parents, a loud, fun, loving extended family, cousins who were my best friends, teammates who had never seen me as anything other than an equal.

But right then, I was lost. I was falling into an abyss and I didn't know how to stop it—or even if I wanted to.

I was numb. Not physically—I could feel every cut, welt, and bruise. But emotionally I felt nothing.

Shouldn't I feel something?

Gratitude my life had been spared. Anger toward the men who'd captured me. Something? Anything?

"Here," Drake said from behind me. Before I

could question what "here" meant, he shoved a t-shirt over my head and helped me push my arms through the openings. "It's about five sizes too big but the cotton will feel better than the nylon of your blouse against your back."

I glanced down at the overly-large, sand-colored shirt and he was correct; it was five sizes too big. The extra material bunched at my waist and the sleeves nearly went to my elbows.

"Thanks," I muttered as Drake took my ACU top and continued the process of dressing me.

I felt like a helpless child, unable to perform the simplest of tasks—I hated being weak and I should've cared—yet that was another emotion I couldn't summon up.

There was rustling behind me, a zipper sounded, and I felt Drake move before he appeared in front of me. I hated he was now standing, looking down at me, arms crossed over his chest, a fierce look of disappointment clear.

That was when I took him in. He was huge. Vaguely, I wondered if he would look so big and broad without all his gear on. I could see brown hair peeking out from under his baseball cap. In the low light I couldn't see the color of his eyes, but I didn't need to to know they were expressive. He was seriously good-looking even with several days' worth of stubble and grime coating his face.

Of course, I'd be rescued by the world's hottest warfighter.

He looked menacing and mean looming over me and I had to fight the urge to shrink back.

What the fuck was wrong with me? I didn't cower. I also didn't sit on my ass and stare up at pissed-off men. I didn't wait around for orders. I was the leader. I *gave* the orders.

I started to get to my feet, determined not to let the pain stop me, and sweet Jesus it was excruciating.

"There she is," Drake mumbled.

"There who is?"

"*Ranger* McCoy."

Drake didn't offer his help as I made it upright and nearly cried out as my weight settled on my abused feet.

I wanted to remind him to call me Liberty. I wasn't a Ranger, not anymore. I failed. I left a fallen comrade—five of them. I didn't complete my mission. I had not displayed the intestinal fortitude required of me.

"Tell me, Ranger, what's got you so pissed off?"

"You," I snapped.

"Me?"

"Stop looking at me like that."

"Like what?"

"You're glaring."

Drake's deep chuckle filled the space and I was stunned. I wanted to ask him to do it again.

I wanted to close my eyes and bask in the warmth of that rumble. I wanted to pretend I wasn't in Syria. I wanted to pretend my team was still alive. I wanted a lot of things that I couldn't have because they weren't real. I *was* in Syria, my team *was* dead, and I had let everyone down.

"Stop," Drake growled.

"I'm not doing anything." And I wasn't. I was literally standing statue-still because I was afraid I'd fall on my face if I tried to move.

"Sure you are. You're in your head beating yourself up. There's plenty of time for that later. Right now, we need to get moving."

"So let's move."

"I'm waiting on you."

His glare said it all. The bastard knew why I hadn't moved, yet his smug ass stood a few feet away, the picture of impatience.

Fuck him.

I took a tentative step, stumbled, and gritted my teeth in an unsuccessful effort not to howl my pain.

"Are you enjoying this?" I asked.

"Not even a little bit."

"Then why are you standing there watching me?"

"What should I be doing, Ranger?"

"Stop calling me that."

"Would you prefer Lieutenant?"

Asshole. He was enjoying this. Poor, weak, Army officer struggling to walk.

"I'd prefer if you just left."

"Not gonna happen."

"Just go, Drake. I'll be ready in a minute. I don't need you watching me, waiting until I fall down so you can laugh at me."

Welp, that was the wrong thing to say. In two long strides, Drake was in my face more pissed-off than I'd seen him.

"Is that what you think? I'd fucking laugh. There's not a goddamn thing funny about you being injured. Ask for help."

Was he insane?

"I'm not weak and I don't need your help."

"You're damn right you're not weak. But what you are is stubborn. I don't take you as stupid, Ranger. Don't know what they teach you in the Army, but in the Navy, on the teams, we know our

Before I could explain to him why, he swept me up into his arms and I let out a surprised gasp, which was akin to razor blades slicing my throat.

With me in his arms, he knelt to pick up the blanket I'd been standing on and I was seriously impressed with his lower body strength.

"Thanks," I grumbled, remembering my manners.

"You're welcome, Liberty."

I was too busy trying to figure out why sometimes Drake called me Liberty, but others Lieutenant, ma'am, or Ranger. The name distinction was confusing. I'd missed Drake walking us over and rejoining the men, but then was pulled from my thoughts when I heard my name.

"I'm sorry, I missed that," I said.

"I was asking if you were ready or if you needed to hit the head before we left," Logan repeated and my face heated.

Thankfully my bladder was empty and I didn't need to go to the bathroom—the mere thought of working out the logistics of that while my feet were in the condition they were in was enough to make me hold it for a hundred hours.

"I'm ready."

But before we left, Drake did as he said he'd do

and set me back down on the drum while he squatted in front of me. He taped my feet and dug out a pair of socks from his pack.

"Do me a favor and stand. I wanna make sure it's not going to be too painful for you if I have to set you down."

Without argument, I took the hand he was offering and gingerly got to my feet.

"Can't say it feels good, but it's better than it was when I was barefoot," I told him. "If need be I can fight, I won't hold you back."

Drake swung his backpack over his shoulder, adjusted his rifle, then picked me up.

"Counting on it."

"Trey, you and Luke take point. Matt, cover Drake and the lieutenant, I'll take the rear," Logan barked orders.

"Just the way you like it," Matt said and the guys all chuckled.

Something about the normalcy of joking with the team soured my stomach. I'd never get to exchange light-hearted jabs with my comrades again.

"Where'd you find my team?" I finally found the courage to ask after we'd been walking a few minutes.

"The second house we hit," Drake told me.

"When was that?"

"Yesterday."

I wondered if he was being intentionally short or if this was just the way he was.

"Were they..."

I couldn't finish my question. Not only couldn't I utter the words but I was regretting asking in the first place. I didn't want to know. Not right then while Drake was carrying me. It would be easier to learn about my teammates' demise during the debriefing, where after I could hide away in my bunk and no one would see me break down.

"By the looks of it, you caught the worst."

"That's not true, they're dead and I'm not. I'd say their price was higher than mine."

"Didn't say they didn't make the ultimate sacrifice, what I said was, you caught the worst of the torture."

"Did you get them home?"

That earned me a squeeze from Drake. "Of course we did."

"Thank you."

"You don't need to thank me for that. We never leave a man behind."

"Like I did."

Whoa. Why the hell had I let that slip out?

"You didn't leave anyone behind, Lieutenant."

I was too tired to figure out why I was Lieutenant again instead of Liberty. The man made me dizzy.

Silence fell and I didn't try to fill it. Instead, I pressed my ear as hard as the pain would allow to Drake's chest and tried to feel his heartbeat but nothing registered through his plate carrier. So instead, I settled on listening to his slow, steady breathing. I was not a small woman, yet Drake lugged me around with ease.

My eyelids got heavier and heavier until finally I couldn't keep them open.

I just wanted to close my eyes and never open them again.

Unfortunately, I did wake up to the thrum of helicopter blades slicing through the air.

Panic invaded so quickly I choked on it, coughing and sputtering. Drake's arms tightened and somehow he lifted me higher until we were face-to-face.

"Breathe, Ranger." I sucked in a lungful of oxygen that did nothing to stop the fear from spreading. "Focus on me. Nothing else and slow down." I was ruined, so totally broken I couldn't stop the flashes of memories that were playing in my head. "Goddammit, Liberty, focus." Drake gave me a bone-

seat next to me. But damn if I could let her go—she'd be taken from me soon enough.

She'd go home, and I'd go wherever I was needed. That was the way this worked—yet, I didn't want her to leave.

And that was a problem.

The pilot's voice crackled through the headsets telling us we were two minutes out. I glanced at Luke and fuck me, he was staring, too. Not at my face but at my hands where I stupidly held Liberty's.

So much for professional detachment.

I gave her hand a squeeze and her eyes came to mine and once again I was struck with their uniqueness. Even bloodshot, they were stunning.

"We're landing," I shouted over the noise in the cabin.

She nodded and went back to staring off into space.

A minute later we touched down and I knew we had seconds before all hell broke loose. The whining of the rotor blades started to wind down and my team started to move. It was now or never and I needed a word with Liberty before she was swept away.

There were a hundred reasons why this wasn't a good idea, but right then, not a single one of them mattered. I caught Luke's attention as he slid open the helicopter door and gestured for him to give me two minutes. With a disapproving scowl, he jerked his chin and jumped down.

Liberty stirred in my lap and I tightened my hold, trying not to, yet failing to think about how right she felt in my arms.

"Do you understand what's getting ready to happen?" Her wide eyes locked on mine and she nodded. "You're gonna be okay."

Her gaze started to slide away and without thinking, I cupped her cheek and she flinched.

Fucking hell.

"I'm not going to hurt you."

"I know."

"Everything's gonna be okay," I semi-repeated.

I knew she didn't believe me and I also knew there was nothing I could say right then to convince her she'd make it through.

Once the silence stretched to awkward and I couldn't bring myself to say what was truly on my mind, I leaned forward and gently kissed her forehead.

"You're damn strong, Ranger."

"I'm not—"

"The fact you're sitting here proves otherwise."

"Thank you for... Everything."

Normally this was where I'd give the textbook response of "just doing my job" but saying that to Liberty felt wrong.

"My pleasure."

"Will you do me one more favor?"

"Anything."

And surprisingly I meant those words. I'd do anything she asked.

"After you help me out, will you let me walk?"

Pride filled my chest and I couldn't stop myself from smiling.

"Sure will."

"And stick close, just in case I start to take a header."

"I'd never let you fall, Liberty."

Christ, she smiled.

And when she did, the warmth in my chest turned to a burn.

Suddenly I needed to get away from the pretty Army Ranger, far away where I could have my head examined and shake these crazy thoughts.

But before I could stand and exit the now stifling cabin, Liberty brought our hands to her lips and pressed a kiss to the back of mine.

And fuck me, I felt that kiss like a shot of adrenaline.

"I won't ever forget what you and the guys did for me. Not ever, Drake. Thank you."

Shit yeah, we had to get the hell out of the helicopter before I made a complete fool of myself.

I exited as gently as I could but her mew of discomfort told me I didn't cushion the hop down as well as I'd hoped.

"Ready?"

"Yeah."

I set her sock-covered feet down on the tarmac and waited until she was steady before I stepped away so Ranger McCoy could walk to the briefing room under her own power. And damn if she didn't hobble on bloody soles all the way to her commanding officer.

Not only did she walk but she did it with her head held high.

Goddamned magnificent.

"WE NEED TO TALK," Trey said as soon as Liberty was whisked away.

"I need to call Carter first."

"Drake, don't fuck with me. How bad?"

"Brother—"

"You know what's going through my head right now. Don't treat me like I'm some green team, wet behind the ears asshole. Just put me out of my misery and tell me."

I glanced around ensuring I was still alone and told Carter what he wanted to know. "We didn't talk about much. For certain she was waterboarded, her back's a mess from being strapped down, she's gonna have some issues from that. Even though her lips are cut to shit, she insisted on sipping water instead of me pouring it in. She's...damn, Carter, she looks worse than you did after our incident in Africa. Head-to-toe covered in cuts and bruises.

"But the thing you need to focus on right now is, she's tough. The woman's a warrior, no other way to describe her. We touched down and she insisted on walkin' across the tarmac. Don't know if that's something that your uncle instilled in her, don't know if she was taught that shit, or if she was born with a determination I've only ever seen in my teammates. However that came to be, she owned that shit—head held high, every bit of the Ranger she is. Don't forget that, Carter. Not now as you pull yourself together and not when she gets home."

"Is that pride I hear comin' from Drake Hayes?"

"Hell, yeah, I'm proud."

"Well, damn. From the man who's never impressed, I can sleep tonight knowing my cousin's coming home and she's doing it not broken."

I didn't say she wasn't broken.

"I'm sure they'll have her on a transport after she's been debriefed."

"And her team?"

"KIA."

"Fuck. That's gonna hit her hard."

"Already is. My advice, watch for survivor's guilt."

"Copy that. Thanks for everything. We can't ever repay you enough for bringing her home."

"Sure you can. Bring that wife and daughter up to Virginia and buy me a beer."

"I'm not bringing my wife anywhere near you swine. The last time, I caught every single one of you fuckers checkin' her out."

"Man, she was nine months pregnant and none of us knew breasts could—"

"Right now, I don't care that you just saved my cousin's life. You talk about my wife's breasts again, I'll kick your ass."

"Damn, you're easy these days. I remember

when none of us had anything to yank your chain about other than the fact your poor dick never saw the inside of a woman."

"That's because none of you knew about what I had waiting for me at home."

"True story."

Carter Lenox had kept Delaney Walker a secret from all of us. None of us knew he had a woman at home—his childhood sweetheart. After months of watching our new team leader turn down every woman who approached, we thought he was gay but not ready to come out. We spent the next few months trying to tell him that none of us cared. His abstinence earned him the nickname Church.

"As fun as this chat was, I'm gonna go grab a shower. And see if there's something to eat around this place other than a gut-busting MRE."

"Ten days... I'll never forget what you did, Drake," he croaked.

I cleared my throat, battling the emotion that had lodged itself there. "I'd say anytime, but I hope like hell we never have a repeat."

"Hear that. Talk to you soon."

9

"Lieutenant," General Wick sighed.

I knew I'd pushed him to the brink and I was being unfair using a familiar connection to manipulate the man. Under normal circumstances I would've felt bad—hell, I wouldn't have used my father's name at all. However, there was nothing normal about me being taken hostage, my team being murdered, and my target still alive and breathing.

"You know I'm right," I whispered and tried my best to look contrite.

"You're not wrong," Wick begrudgingly admitted. "But it will not be you who goes back out."

"With all due respect, General—"

"Liberty, I know this is not what you want to hear but it's impossible."

"Are you saying it's impossible due to your relationship with my father or as a general? Because you know the major gave me the green light. His recommendation was a few days' rest then I was good-to-go."

I was seriously testing my boundaries. I'd known General Wick my whole life. He was a good friend of my dad's. They were so close there was a framed photograph in my father's office of five young men; General Wick—then Captain Wick—with my dad and uncles after a successful mission in Bosnia. But even with the friendly and informal relationship I was extorting, I'd gone too far. I knew it when Wick's eyes narrowed and his graying eyebrows pinched.

"Lieutenant, at this juncture you're skating damn close to an article 89," he grunted. "The major assessed your physical wounds, not the psychological effects of your capture. You're being debriefed and sent home."

"Why?"

"Why?" Wick repeated, stunned I'd dare to prod him further than I had.

"Yes, General. Why would you send me home when my team was so close? I know Lore better than anyone. It would take months for a new team to get up to speed."

Before the general could give his rebuttal, a loud rap on the door made me jump. Unfortunately Wick didn't miss my regrettable reaction to the noise. It certainly wasn't helping my request to be sent back out on a mission by responding like a scared kitten.

"Come in," Wick boomed.

Drake stepped into the room followed by Logan, Matt, Luke, and Trey. Suddenly the TOC seemed much smaller than it was. Wick had cleared the tactical operations center of all personnel when I was brought to him.

The center, normally a hub of commotion, now sat eerily empty. The computer screens dark, the make-shift war room devoid of the constant chatter as the battle captain and his soldiers collected, consolidated, and scrutinized real-time battlefield information.

Their latest mission was complete, I'd been brought home.

The area of operations map was still tacked to the plywood wall, complete with my team's pictures printed out and thumbnailed beside the charts. Seeing the pictures of the men who'd lost their lives was too much—after a cursory glance I'd had to turn away.

"Sir." Drake's deep voice jolted me from my thoughts.

"Job well done," Wick praised.

"Easy day," Trey muttered, and I wanted to roll my eyes at the use of the SEAL motto.

That seemed to be their answer to everything.

"We'll get this debrief done and get you boys home." Wick gestured to the folding banquet table in the middle of the room.

"Sir?" Drake's eyes sliced to me in question before they went back to the general.

"I've asked the lieutenant to be present. In the interest of time and the ongoing mission I felt it prudent to have all the players in the same room."

"Ongoing mission?" Drake inquired.

"My mission is incomplete," I informed Drake.

"Come again?"

"In...com...plete." I enunciated the word. "My target is still alive."

Drake's forehead wrinkled and the general let out an exaggerated sigh.

The man was beyond annoyed with me, but in my current state I didn't give the first fuck.

My team was dead, I'd been captured, and Lore was still making bombs that were killing US and allied service men and women. So, incomplete didn't begin to accurately describe my mission—more like total failure. But that was mine to process later. There was no way I was admitting my shortcomings in a room full of men who had been sent in to come to my rescue.

"Who's the target?" Trey asked.

General Wick's intense stare told me I was getting closer to that article 89 he'd threatened earlier.

But to my surprise, he answered Trey. "Flip the white board."

Trey ambled over to the free-standing, reversible board and flipped it, revealing the map and intel reports.

"Lore?" Trey whistled then turned to face Wick. "What was a Ranger squad doing tracking Lore?"

"I expect this to stay in this room," Wick snarled. "And before one of you pops off with some sort of GOFO snappy comeback—I'll make myself crystal clear. This is not a need-to-know situation. This is a no-one-needs-to-know operation. Not anyone, am I clear?"

I'm not sure what I was more shocked by; Trey knowing who Lore was or the general getting ready to impart intel that very few people knew.

"Clear," Drake grunted.

It didn't take a rocket scientist to see none of the men appreciated the reminder to observe operational security. And I was fairly sure none were impressed with Wick's *grasping of the fucking obvious* acronym either. Wick was treating the men like they were POGs instead of SEALs.

"Lieutenant McCoy took an ODA tactical team on a special purpose extraction operation."

"I'm sorry," Drake cut in. "Did you say, the lieutenant took a special forces team on a mission?"

"Yes," Wick replied.

"Why would a Ranger lead the Operational Detachment Alphas tac team on a mission?"

"Because McCoy is SF."

Drake's angry eyes swung to me, his glare cutting me to the quick. "If she's SF then why wasn't the rest of her team sent in for the extraction?"

"Given the circumstances, we felt your team was the best option given who we're dealing with."

"Let me see if I'm understanding this. You know who took her?"

"We had a good idea," Wick confirmed.

"So you know he's an American?"

My head spun with this new information.

Had I told Drake the voice of my tormenter had spoken perfect English?

"How...how do you know that?" I stammered.

Drake pulled his backpack off, slammed it on the table, unzipped it, and rummaged around. Then much to my horror he unwrapped a DVD.

Of course I knew there was a possibility my interrogation had been recorded—I'd been told it was —but I was hooded at the time and couldn't be sure if it was real or a form of physiological torture.

"Was that released?" I was acutely aware I was panting in fear. "My dad."

The vein that had been throbbing in Wick's neck now looked like it was ready to explode.

"Give me a minute." Wick took the DVD and left the TOC, the door slamming behind him leaving me with six angry SEALs.

"I'm sorry, I couldn't correct you," I told Drake.

The jerk of his chin told me he understood what I meant. But he was nowhere near accepting my apology for not correcting him all of the times he called me Ranger.

"I take it your family doesn't know?" Trey cut in.

"They don't," I confirmed.

"Must've sucked going through SFQC and having no one there on graduation day."

"I didn't go through the standard qualification course. There was...a handful of us that went through a modified program. Same phase structure, same physical training, different training location and specialized tactics."

"What does that mean, exactly?" Matt asked.

"Officially, it means I'm a tabbed Ranger, but not assigned to a regiment, therefore I did not earn a scroll. I'm an intelligence officer under the Army's psychological warfare division. Off the books I'm the Special Forces Officer in the 8th Special Forces Group."

"Why off the books?" Matt pressed.

"I'm not at liberty to say."

"Cute," Drake sneered.

"Excuse me?"

"The I'm not at liberty bullshit."

Why was he being such a dick? Drake of all people should understand the need for specialized units. Our best assets should be kept hidden from both the enemy and the public.

"Seriously, Master Chief? You of all people are going to be an asshole about this? Tell me something, how many times have you and your teammates watched some news network plaster your work all over the evening news and wish they'd keep their traps shut about your missions? Missions that are supposed to be classified and not for public consumption. How many times has the media put good men's lives in jeopardy as they report outside of Dam Neck? And, really, I'd love to know your opinion on our vice president outing DEVGRU after UBL was put to ground. How did it make you feel when the wives and children of teammates had to go into hiding out of fear of retaliation?"

"Drake, brother, what the fuck?" Logan stepped back from the whiteboard and looked at his teammate.

"I don't like mission specifics being withheld," Drake defended. "And this has bullshit written all over it."

The door slammed open and one look at General Wick told me any patience he had when he'd left the TOC had taken a hike. The man looked positively undone. Not something you'd expect from a career military man. Wick was the picture of propriety—a battle-hardened warrior. *Except when I pushed him to the brink.*

"Sit the fuck down—all of you," Wick barked, and tossed a thick file folder down on the table. "We have a problem."

"What kind of problem?" I asked as I moved slowly to a chair and gingerly sat.

My gaze went from Wick to Drake. Even

"Was the lieutenant targeted?" Drake inquired and dread started to swirl in my stomach.

I wasn't sure if I wanted to know the answer to that.

"Yes."

Shit.

"Because she's a woman?"

"Because she's a McCoy." General Wick's tone held an edge I'd never heard before. One that was not indicative of a fierce general but of a man who cared a great deal.

I was speechless, my words were caught in the firestorm that burned my throat as Wick's declaration settled over me.

"What aren't you telling us, sir?" Logan asked the question I wish I could've.

"A lot."

A deadly silence fell over the TOC, electricity sizzled in the air, so much anger was radiating off the general I was surprised he hadn't combusted.

What in the world was going on? Why would I be targeted because I was a McCoy? Nothing made sense.

My team had been closing in on a known Lore hideout when we'd been ambushed and overtaken. No one knew we were in the area but the Lieutenant

Colonel in charge of the 8th Special Forces Group, my company commander, and General Wick. The squads were compartmentalized—I didn't know what the other team's objectives were and they didn't know mine.

That was how the Hellraisers worked—we had anonymity and invisibility even within our group.

And if I was specifically targeted, that meant five good men died because of me—not the inherent danger of the job.

It was all my fault.

10

We were losing her.

Liberty sat in the seat next to me and what had started out as a shiver was now a full-blown quake. She was putting pieces together and coming up with the truth. She was also taking on misplaced guilt. It was not her fault her team had been killed—but she wouldn't see it that way. Hell, if the roles were reversed, no one would ever convince me the death of my teammates wasn't on me.

General Wick was taking his happy-ass time filling us in, and I couldn't help wondering why that was. The man wasn't looking at Liberty like a soldier under his command, he was studying her with what I could only describe as fatherly concern.

I did a quick mental scan and tried to remember

everything I knew about General Wick. He was former SFOD-D which meant there was a chance he served with or at least knew Liberty's father Levi McCoy. The Special Forces Operational Detachment, better known as Delta, was a small community, much like the SEAL teams.

"You mind filling us in or are we gonna hunt and peck for information?" I tried to hide my irritation but when Trey cut his eyes my way and shook his head in censure I knew I'd failed.

"Roman Bolick was CAG."

Christ, the Army and their unit names. They couldn't just have one element distinction, they had to give it multiple names—Combat Application Group—SFOD-D—Delta Force—ACE or Army Compartmented Element—The Unit, and of course Task Force Green. All the same group, just different acronyms.

"Was?" Luke asked for clarification.

"Roman was part of the 707..."

Wick let that bombshell hang and the color drained from Liberty's face.

"I don't understand why his son would want me dead. Did he serve with my dad and uncles in the unit?"

"Carter Lenox Senior took Roman Senior out

her cousin. Which meant she'd be a hellion to control.

"The mere fact you have intel on Roman Junior means he's been on radar, why hasn't he been taken out?" Luke asked.

"He's connected."

"What the fuck does that mean?" Logan scoffed.

"His mother, Annelise, is Ukrainian. When her father was alive he was the Don of Nova."

"Goddamn perfect," Matt muttered. "A piece of shit traitor for a father and a Ukrainian mob princess for a mother. It's no wonder the kid turned out to be such a piece of shit. He had no chance. But the grandfather's dead, so who's he connected to that shields him from a bullet to the face?"

Wick sighed, clearly uncomfortable with Matt's question. And as much as I wanted to hear Wick's reply, I needed more from Liberty.

"Did Roman say anything else to you?"

"Yeah. Roman called my dad a piece of shit—he said the thought of sticking his dick in me was repulsive."

The tingle of worry I'd felt moments ago, morphed into blinding anger.

"He said what?" I whispered, well aware I was

showing my hand and not giving a fuck. "Did he try—"

"No. I told you, no one touched me like that," Liberty cut me off and placed her palm on my chest. "The only thing he wanted to know was how long my team had been on patrol. That's weird, right? He asked over and over. And he knew my name and rank. My full name. Wait!" Liberty's hand on my chest fisted my shirt and she jerked me forward. "He knew me. Wick's right—I was the target. Hundred percent."

Of course he knew everything about her—she was the target—but fear and panic were muddling her mind and she wasn't thinking clearly.

Anxiety had taken over, and by the way she was staring at me, I knew that for her the rest of the room had faded away. In her mind it was just the two of us and she was using me as a lifeline.

Why the hell does that feel so damn good?

"Roman called me Moira. No one's called me that since grade school. He said it was a shame my dad would never know who took his precious Moira's life. I was fading in and out, his hands were around my throat and all of his weight was on my chest. I couldn't breathe. I was trying so hard to stay still and not beg him to stop. I think he said something about them taking something important from him."

Jesus. I hated she had to relive this, but we needed every piece of intel we could gather. Roman would pay for what he did to her, but first we needed to find him, and if he said something to aid in that, we had to know.

"Who is *them?*"

"I think my dad and uncles. Roman said he was taking one of theirs. An eye for an eye." Wetness started to well in her eyes and Liberty did her best to blink it away. "He told me my death was on them. The last thing I remember was him saying, the sins of the father. Then I may've passed out or I was able to slip into my mind and block him out. I'd come to terms with dying, but everything hurt, I was so tired I just wanted it to happen fast so I could..."

"Hey." Liberty's gaze came back to me and I gave her what I hoped was a reassuring smile though I was sure it looked more like a grimace with all the fury that had built in my chest. "You did great, Liberty."

The general cleared his throat, the sound reminding me we had an audience. Not only that, but it was highly inappropriate for me to address an officer by her first name. Forget the fact she was holding on to me and at some point my hands had found their way to her hips. Yeah, I was breaking all sorts of rules but couldn't bring myself to care.

"What are we gonna do about Roman?" Luke asked.

"If we can find him, you're gonna take him out."

Liberty stiffened, then she exhaled and relaxed.

"I'm going with," she announced.

Someplace deep, a switch flipped—it was instantaneous. It was like I was having an out-of-body experience as a ball of possessiveness grew. It wasn't protective as such, more like—primal. There was no way in fuck Liberty McCoy was going on the hunt for the man who had hurt her—tortured her—held her captive.

Hell to the no. Liberty's sweet ass was getting on a transport and going home for some R and R. She needed to heal and she needed her family to aid in that.

But before I could answer, Wick did. "If you can pass your psych eval, I'll approve your request."

The man had lost his fucking mind.

Liberty was in no shape to go back out. She'd lie her way through the eval, it was easy to do. After every stressful mission, part of the debrief was seeing the shrink, and all of us knew what to say and how to act to bullshit our way through.

11

This was exactly what I needed to get my head right —a mission—a clear objective and intel. For the first time in what felt like forever, even though it had only been ten days, I felt human. Useful. This I could do, plan, plot, execute.

We'd been tracking Lore for months, and before my team came on board, there'd been analysts tracking and scrutinizing Lore's purchases and movements. He was predictable, but still remained elusive. He, like most bomb makers, had a certain signature.

I suppose they couldn't help themselves. The cowards hid in the darkness, yet still needed praise and celebrity for their work. Lore especially loved to give the double middle finger to allied forces.

"May I?" I asked Wick.

Funny, I was asking for permission now after I'd trampled all over protocol and military courtesy.

Wick gave me a sharp nod and faced Drake and his men.

"As you know, Lore is a Syrian born bomb manufacturer. His IEDs are credited for sixty percent of the American and Allied deaths in Afghanistan and he's the number one supplier in Somalia and Iran. Our objective was to capture Lore and extract intel needed to shut down his network. My team was closing in but each place we'd hit, we'd just missed him."

"Did it ever occur to you it was a set-up?" Luke asked.

"How do you mean?"

"From a tactical standpoint, if you keep *just* missing him, then he knew he was being tracked. Wouldn't be the first time a terrorist laid a trap."

How the hell did we miss that?

"So, Lore knew, and led the squad into an ambush. Doesn't explain how Roman, a man with a personal vendetta, was there to take Lieutenant McCoy and her team."

Why did my heart clench hearing Drake call me lieutenant instead of Liberty?

"Best guess, Roman's part of Lore's network," Wick replied.

"Best guess?" Trey muttered and tilted his head in question. "What does the intel say?"

"Loose connection," Wick admitted.

"How loose?" Trey pushed.

There was something in Trey's tone that garnered my full attention and I took in the operator who had assisted in saving my life before my gaze skidded across the other men. Logan, Matt, Luke, and Drake all looked menacing—but not Trey. He looked as if he belonged in a major Hollywood production. Not an action adventure war movie, no, a romantic comedy. He certainly had the looks and smooth voice for a leading role. Extremely good-looking if you liked the over-the-top handsome type.

I did not. I preferred my men to have an edge to them, I liked them rough around the edges—kinda like Drake. Actually, there was nothing *kinda* about it—Drake fit the bill to a T. A man like him... What the hell was I doing daydreaming during a debriefing —or briefing as it were?

Pull it together, McCoy.

"Recently, Roman has been moving large quantities of citric acid, food-grade hydrogen peroxide, and hexamine fuel tabs."

"Lore's signature," I blurted out. "Three out of the four ingredients needed to make HMTD. That's Lore's favorite charge."

Trey's eyes narrowed as he studied me. "You seem to know your demolition recipes."

"I'm no expert but I know Lore. I know he's a narcissistic, egomaniac. There are easier ways to construct just about every IED, EFP, and explosive device he manufactures, yet he likes to flex his skills. For instance, HMTD is heat sensitive, it has to be kept cool and has a short shelf life, yet that's his *thing*. I would imagine during the hottest months in the desert it's damn hard to get his mixture in an ice bath—but somehow he does. He also charges top dollar, keeping his explosives in the hands of only the top tier of the terrorist shitbags."

His devices also had caused the most casualties mainly because they never failed. Unlike the roadside bombs and IEDs made by amateurs that thankfully didn't detonate a hundred percent of the time— Lore's did. He gloated incessantly about his discharge rate.

"What I know about Lore," Trey started, "is he always has a secondary power source."

"Correct. His devices are redundant. Part of why they never fail. Just because the man is a scumbag

doubt wasn't the best combination, especially if I had to pass an eval bright and early tomorrow morning. If I didn't get my head right there was no chance of me fooling whichever shrink the Army sat me in front of. And knowing Wick, he'd handpicked the doctor.

The phone in my hand became heavier and heavier the longer I procrastinated. My dad would be relieved, overjoyed even to hear my voice. He loved me, my mom did, too. Being an only child meant I'd grown up with my parents' undivided attention. They were the best parents anyone could ever hope for. My mom had supported my military career even though she hated it.

Not because my mom didn't like the military— on the contrary, she'd supported and respected my father's career. But my mother had firsthand knowledge what it was like for a woman in the boy's club. She'd been in the CIA then worked directly for the Director of National Intelligence. She'd been in the field for many years and only stopped after I was born.

Yet, she'd still supported me. If my father had taught me about military tactics, my mother taught me how to navigate my way through a man's game with humility and grace. She showed me I could be strong and capable without turning into an aggressive bitch like Major Wilbanks. I could earn respect if I didn't demand it just because I was a woman.

Her lessons had been just as valuable as my dad's.

Screw it.

I dialed my dad's cell and listened to it ring.

Maybe I should've called my mom. No, it was better to let my dad handle her. She had to be going crazy.

"Hello?"

"Hey, Dad," I croaked and cleared my throat. "Sorry it took so long to check in."

"*Moira.*" The relief I heard in my big, strong dad's voice made my heart squeeze. "Jesus, it's good to hear your voice, even though it sounds like hell. Where are you?"

"You know I can't tell you that."

"I'm gonna meet you in Germany."

Oh, shit.

"Mission shift, Dad." I tried to keep my tone even though there was a lump in my throat and my heart was beating double-time. My dad could sniff fear out a mile away, and yes, that included over the phone.

"Come again?"

"You know the drill, Sergeant Major, mission before self."

"Don't be cute, Liberty."

Unexplainable irritation slithered up from my belly and threatened to spill out. That was the second time in the last few hours someone told me not to be cute. First, Drake when he was acting like a butt-hurt asshole, and now my over-protective father. He wouldn't say that to one of the men he employed at Triple Canopy nor would he have given Carter a hard time if he was in my place.

"I'm not, Dad. I'm reminding you of my duty to serve. I took the same oath you took. I have a mission to finish."

Why was I getting so upset? Shouldn't I be thrilled to hear my dad's voice—he was always my touchstone. Mom was the listener, Dad was the fixer. Maybe that was my problem—Levi McCoy was getting ready to launch into his Mr. Fix-it mode and I didn't want any part of it.

There was nothing he could do. Nothing anyone could do.

"Ten days!"

I felt the pain in my dad's words straight down to my bones.

become—the warrior you grew into. As your dad, I want you home so I can see for myself you're okay. As an operator, a fellow Ranger, a man who's been in battle and knows the deep-seated need to complete a mission—I'm so goddamn proud of your bravery and determination."

My dad had no idea how badly I needed to hear that. Though I didn't feel brave—I felt numb. Which was a good thing. Feeling nothing at all would help me get through the rest of the mission. I could fall apart later after Lore was taken out of commission and Roman was dead. For now, I just had to put on a brave front and get through it.

"Thanks, Daddy. I can't wait until this is over and I get to come home and see you."

More lies.

I was scared to death to face my father, he'd see straight through my bullshit. Maybe I wouldn't go back to Georgia. Thankfully, I was stationed at Fort Lewis, on the other side of the country where I could hide from my family.

"When are you headed back out?"

Even if I knew, I couldn't tell him.

"Not for a minute. I'll call again before I head out. Please tell Mom I love her."

"You could call her now."

No freaking way am I speaking to my mom right now.

"I don't want her to hear me like this. I'll talk to her after I've gotten some sleep and my throat doesn't feel like I've swallowed rocks."

"Make sure you drink a lot of water, dehydration's a bitch. A protein bar with a spoonful of honey every few hours will help you get your strength back up. And your feet—the major should have Epsom salt. You need the magnesium, it will help with swelling, too."

My cracked lips tipped up; typical Levi McCoy, a vat of knowledge and combat healthcare.

"Will do, Dad. I love you."

"Love you so damn much, Moira. Call me when you can."

"I will. Tell everyone I said hi and I love them, too."

"Sure thing."

I quickly disconnected and pocketed the phone, uncaring if I was supposed to keep it or not, it was now mine.

I scrubbed my hands over my face, praying the headache that had started would hold off long enough for me to get to the quarters Wicks had assigned me.

Being alone in a room didn't appeal to me, but my body was protesting its upright position.

I had one more thing to do, then I'd go find my bunk.

12

I kept to the shadows in the hangar and watched Liberty as she stood in front of five flag-draped pine boxes with her head bowed, noting the statue-still Marine keeping watch over the men.

My hand went into my pocket and found Liberty's tags. My thumb skimmed the bumpy metal. Something that had already become an obsession. It was a compulsion—the need to stroke the discs—a sick reminder of where I'd found them.

"I know you're there," she mumbled, her voice still scratchy.

"I didn't mean to disturb you."

I made my way to her and stopped a respectable distance away even though the urge to pull her into my arms was damn near overwhelming.

Liberty McCoy was all contradictions. It was hard to reconcile this small woman with a tough warfighter. She looked fragile standing in front of her fallen teammates—yet I knew she was far from weak.

The woman was damn beautiful even with bruises on her face, her long brown hair pulled back in a severe bun at the nape of her neck, and wearing a now-clean uniform. Never in my nineteen years in the military had I ever found a woman in uniform sexy—not once had I ever been tempted by a woman I worked with. But there was something about Liberty McCoy that called to me on a different level—it was primal, instinctual, primitive. My head cluttered with all sorts of inappropriate shit when I got near her. And when she'd been taken from me at the airfield, I wanted to rage and fight to keep her.

The fuck of it was it wasn't purely sexual. Sure, she was attractive—extremely so. But what I felt for her was fundamental—a base need—she was intrinsic.

"You didn't disturb me." Liberty's sad tone wrapped around my heart and squeezed. "I wanted to say goodbye."

"Were you close?" I asked, then immediately wanted to kick my own ass for being so insensitive.

What did it matter if they'd been close? Five men were dead.

"Yeah. We went through Ranger school together. The six of us were pulled for SF at the same time. I don't think I would've made it through the first day if it wasn't for Perez. He had a way about him. He could laugh his way through anything. He saw the bright side. Him and Martin always had a joke about the suckage that was our daily life. Kirby, Pritchett, and Ball were stoic. Maybe because they were older, married, and fathers." Liberty's voice hitched and she covered her mouth with her hand to stifle a sob.

Without a thought, my hand shot out, tagged her behind the neck, and pulled her close. Her face went to my chest and my arms wrapped around her.

I didn't offer any platitudes; not only would they not be welcomed but they'd be insulting. She lost her team—men she was close to—but more than that, men she'd led into battle. That responsibility was formidable—losing those men, devastating.

"I don't know...I can't...What am I supposed to do?"

"Do?"

"Do. Say. Face their families. I can't ever make this right."

No, she couldn't make it right. That was the fuck

of it. There was nothing anyone could do to give the families back their loved ones. A gamble we all took every time we entered the theater of war. Unfortunately, the chances we took had far reaching implications—repercussions that we ourselves didn't have to live with. A dead man didn't pay the consequences, those who loved them did.

"You offer them the only thing you can—your support."

"Tell me, Drake, how am I supposed to offer them support when I can't even... never mind. Support. Right. I'll do that."

The first crack in the hard shell she'd coated herself in since we'd come back to post. In the field after her rescue her reactions were raw and real, she couldn't hide her fear and pain. But in front of Wick, she'd built a façade of false bravado—which was dangerous.

"Tell me, Liberty, what can't you do?"

"Nothing. There's nothing I can't do."

"Nothing...except admit you need help."

"I don't need help." Liberty struggled to pull away and I tightened my arms around her.

"You know, it doesn't make you anything but human to need to talk about what happened."

"I don't—"

"I warned you not to bury this shit. Deal with it now. If you don't, when it finally overtakes your life, it will take years to dig it all out."

"I don't know what you want from me, Master—"

"Drake," I corrected. "Don't hide behind ranks and paygrades. Right now, it's just you and me. Liberty and Drake. Two people who share something in common. What can't you do?"

The rise and fall of her rapid breaths quickened and her arms that were trapped between us shook. I hated her reaction to being pushed, but damn if she didn't need to let go and get it out. More than likely she'd be pissed as hell at me for not allowing her to continue under the sham of rightness. There was nothing all right about Liberty. She'd lived through one hell of an ordeal, and I wasn't lying when I told her if she didn't purge this shit she'd be stuck in a cell in Syria for the rest of her life.

"What do you want to hear? How scared I was? That I thought I was going to die? That I was so afraid I didn't once try to escape or save my men? That I choked and gagged and threw up when I was waterboarded? That I was fucking weak and cried? I fucking failed, Drake. Failed. I should be charged with dereliction of duty, stripped of my commission, and sent home."

"That's a stretch, isn't it? I mean, an article 92 is a little dramatic—you didn't willfully and willingly disobey an order or regulation. Don't manufacture trouble where there isn't any."

"You don't—"

"I don't what, sweetheart, know what it's like to be scared? Told you already, I was held for thirteen days. I know the clench of fear. Those thirteen days are burned into my memory."

"I was gonna say, you don't know what it's like to be a disappointment."

"Huh?"

Liberty mumbled softly against my chest and I missed what she said entirely.

"Look at me and repeat that."

She shook her head, burrowed in deeper, and those feelings of rightness once again filled all the dark recesses of my soul. Yearning and hunger mixed —consequences be damned. There was no denying Moira Liberty McCoy did it for me. I'd known the woman under twenty-four hours but I was experienced enough to recognize how different she was. I'd never met anyone who made me come alive. Not my body, not my libido—though she certainly did that, too—but *me*. My heart, my mind, my very being.

Everything about her called to me on a level I'd never thought existed.

And the fuck of it was—I'd have to let her go.

"I'm tired, Drake. I don't want to talk anymore."

Of course she was tired and I'd been a dick for trying to push her into talking.

"I'll walk you over. Where are you staying?"

"A-co."

Officer barracks—*fuck*, if that reminder wasn't like a wet blanket I didn't know what was. My arms fell away and I took a much-needed, giant step back, putting the appropriate amount of space between us.

I was enlisted, she was a commissioned officer and I'd do well to remember that.

Fuck.

Liberty swayed at her swift departure from my embrace but she quickly recovered and gave me a tight smile. I wasn't sure if the look was relief I was no longer holding her or if once again she was trying to pretend everything was situation normal.

Silently, we walked out of the hangar and made our way through the maze of buildings. The struggle not to slide up next to her and toss my arm over her shoulder and pull her close had become damn near impossible to ignore the longer I was near her.

"Have you been here before?" she asked.

If anyone else had asked me that I would've thought they were fishing for information and wouldn't have answered. Talking about my deployments and training outside of the team was a no-go. But there was something in the wobble in Liberty's voice that told me she needed a distraction, therefore I indulged.

"Golan Heights? Or this post?"

"Both, I guess."

I glanced to my side and her gaze remained firmly fixed on the A-co barracks in front of us.

"Then that would be a yes—to both. We've trained here many times. Is this your first time here?"

"Yes."

"Was this your first operation out with your squad?"

"Second," she whispered.

Fuck, that was a bum deal. It also explained her enthusiasm to get back into the field. She hadn't learned the importance of patience—waiting until the time was right to strike. Her goal was singular— take down the enemy. When she should be focused on recuperating. But now was not the time to tell her she needed to rest and heal, I'd poked and prodded her enough.

We stopped in front of the 1960-era Quonset

hut, the door proudly displaying the insignia of the 88th Armored Brigade. I took in the surrounding barracks and couldn't contain my snort-of amusement.

"What?" Liberty asked, her head cocked to the side, one eyebrow raised in question, and damn if she didn't look cute as hell.

"I was just thinking this set-up reminds me of an episode of Gomer Pyle."

"Gomer who?"

Now it was my turn to stare at her in curiosity.

"You're shitting me? You've never heard of the TV show Gomer Pyle: USMC?" Liberty shook her head and I smiled. "Seriously? Great show."

"Nope. Never heard of it."

"*Go-o-o-o-llee.*" I did my best Jim Nabors impression of his famous catchword—which admittedly sucked, and didn't do Gomer's ability to stretch *golly* into five syllables.

"Still a no." Liberty chuckled. "But you should definitely say that again."

"No way. Not until after you watch an episode. Only then will you be able to appreciate how damn badly I butchered Gomer's famous line."

Liberty's face fell and the light dimmed. All

humor fled. But instead of sadness creeping back in, she looked angry.

"Can I tell you something?"

"You can tell me anything."

Her gaze sliced to the door, eyes narrowed, and her lip curled in disgust.

"If I tell you the truth you won't think I'm weak?"

"Fuck no." My heated reply caused her to flinch before she recovered and squared her shoulders.

"I'm more tired than I've ever been in my life but I'm too afraid to close my eyes. I'm scared the last twenty hours have been a dream, and I'll wake up to find I'm still stuck in that goddamn dirty cell, with my next interrogation looming. Or I'll close my eyes and I'll be right back there with Roman strapping me to a board. Either way, it's a no-win." She paused to scrub her hands over her face, then I watched her press her fingertips into her forehead and I was done.

"Come on, let's go." Her hands fell away from her face and her eyes shone with hurt. *Fuck.* She misunderstood. "You're not going in there. You're coming with me."

"Wh...where?" she stammered.

"To sleep."

I tagged her hand and started to lead her away

from the officer barracks before she had time to protest. We passed two more huts, the showers, and the latrine when she finally found her voice.

"Drake?"

"Yeah, babe?"

Babe? Christ, I need to chill on the cutesy nicknames.

Liberty didn't have a chance to answer. I opened the door to Delta hut, and with a gentle tug, I pulled her into the room.

"Lady present," I called out, hoping none of my teammates were undressed.

Luke, Trey, Matt, and Logan all simultaneously turned their heads in our direction, and matching looks of 'what the fuck?' greeted us.

"Liberty's staying in here tonight," I informed them.

"Um..." Liberty mumbled.

Before my team could protest or point out my stupidity, I launched in. "On this next mission she's one of us. That means, we train, we eat, we workout, we live—together. We learn to move as one. We only have a week. It starts now."

My excuse was bullshit. I knew it, my team knew it, and likely Liberty knew it. But it was the best reasoning I had for my temporary loss of sanity.

I glanced around the room noting there were only five beds, four of which had been claimed by the other guys.

"Last rack in the back corner is yours." I gestured to the open bed.

"What about you?"

"I'll take the floor."

"You can't—"

"Thought you said you were tired."

Weary eyes met mine and the wetness I saw gutted me. Liberty quickly blinked it away and gave me a half-hearted, wry uptick of her lips. The grin was forced but I'd take it over the sadness.

"Thanks."

Liberty silently made her way across the room, not speaking to or even looking in anyone else's direction. If she had, she would've seen the unsettled looks my team was giving me. I wish I could say it was my call and my ass on the line—but the truth was, I'd put my teammates in jeopardy. My bringing Liberty into the barracks had crossed so many lines, it wasn't funny. I could face articles and a court-martial, yet I couldn't bring myself to give a shit.

"I'm gonna hit the head," I told no one in particular. "Have a care." I jerked my chin toward Liberty and left before anyone could give me the dressing down I deserved.

What in the actual fuck am I doing?

It hadn't taken long for the nightmares to start. The first I'd heard Liberty moan in her sleep, she'd been able to settle herself. The last two had required me to get off the floor and shake her awake.

But this time, no amount of jostling her was pulling her from the grip her mind had over her. Doing something I'd never attempt with a male teammate, I lifted her off the bed, shaking her awake in a violent jolt. Liberty's eye popped open—wild and raw. Fight or flight took over and she struggled like a hellcat in my arms.

"Stop," I grunted as her small fist made contact with my jaw.

"No."

"Dammit, Liberty, stop before you hurt yourself."

I started to lower her feet to the floor when the hand she'd just punched me with went to my throat and her nails dug in and clawed down to the collar of my shirt.

Fucking shit, that hurt.

"I'd rather die." Her hoarse rumble sounded feral.

Nowhere near awake, I gave her another jerk. "Wake up."

Liberty's eyes snapped to mine, unseeing, eerily blank, wide discs of nothingness. She was mumbling something that sounded like her name, rank, and serial number but the words were slurred and soft.

"Come on, Liberty. Wake up."

Her lids drifted closed, then they opened and she began to rapidly blink. Finally.

"There you go. Focus. You're safe. Wake up."

"Oh, God," she groaned.

"Everything's fine. I'm gonna put you back in bed."

I hefted her into my arms and turned to lower her back onto the mattress when her arms tightened around my neck and she anxiously shook her head. *Fuck.* Not able to deny her unspoken request, or maybe I was being completely stupid and reckless, reading more into a head shake. *Maybe she wasn't asking anything at all, dumbfuck.* I slid in behind her, tossed my arm over her, and pinned her to the bed.

Seconds ticked into minutes and she finally relaxed. Her soft hair tickled my nose and I nuzzled in closer and inhaled. Totally inappropriate but necessary—I needed to be as close to her as she'd allow. I needed to breathe her in. Remind myself she was safe. Feel her heartbeat pounding.

This was dangerous. She was dangerous. I was too close to her in every sense. But I was desperate to steal as much from Liberty as I could. The days would pass, the mission would end, and she'd be once again taken from me—this time for good.

"Go to sleep, sweetheart. I'll watch over you."

Liberty's swift exhale and wiggle to nestle closer was her only response.

I didn't shut my eyes again that night. I did as I promised. The added benefit was I didn't miss a second of Liberty sleeping in my arms.

13

With my psych eval behind me, I sat in the far corner of the DFAC slugging down the worst cup of coffee I'd ever tasted in my life. I was sitting in the corner because I was hiding. I hadn't seen Drake or the guys since I'd slunk out of their barracks. Okay, I didn't slink, it was more like a covert operation as the men worked together to provide a distraction so I could sneak out unseen.

Slink...sneak...not much of a difference. Both cowardly.

I'd showered, given myself a stern lecture about my embarrassing and spineless behavior, vowing never to be weak and stupid in front of Drake and his team again. Then I stared at myself in the mirror until I didn't flinch when I looked at the bruising on my face. With my game face securely cemented, I went in search of Wick. He'd promptly taken me to see Colonel Sykes, a no-nonsense, stern woman who'd been flown to Golan Heights from Germany specifically to see to me. Personally, I thought Wick had lost his mind. Disrupting someone's practice seemed overboard at best and borderline crazy at worst.

For two hours, Col. Sykes put me through my paces. I couldn't say it was fun, but it wasn't as painful as I'd thought it would be. Something that stood out, the woman treated me as an equal—a colleague. She'd asked tough questions, expecting my answers to be thorough, she pushed me to talk about my *feelings* but not once did the colonel talk down to me. It made me want to open up to her. Which I did just enough to get her to approve my active duty status. A deadman's profile would sideline me, most likely indefinitely.

Once someone is marked as mentally unstable or labeled with PTSD, especially in the spec ops community, they're put under a microscope. I didn't want the hassle or the attention.

So now, I was hiding.

I was holding it together but barely and I wasn't ready to face Drake and his scrutiny. Maybe I was being paranoid and he didn't look at me like I was a ticking timebomb that was nearing zero. But it felt like it. And it wasn't just him—all of the guys had eyed me with concern when I'd woken up.

I needed a few more mugs of sludge and time to fortify my defenses before I faced them. I only had one shot to convince them I was mission-ready. Which, after last night's nightmare debacle, would be hard enough to do. If I went into the war room with the slightest hesitation or weakness, they'd nix me from the team.

I beat back the urge to lower my head in shame and continued to focus on the empty chair across from me. This was not how I'd pictured my life—my service wasn't supposed to be tarnished with failure and defeat. I was meant to carry on my family's legacy. I'd believed that my entire life.

How selfish had I become? Men were dead, and I was worried about some stupid, perceived tradition I'd obsessed over. Children no longer had fathers and I was sulking. One thing was for sure—God had made a mistake. He'd chosen the wrong soldier to live. I should've died so my men could've lived.

The taste of blame and burden coated my tongue. Bitter acid churned in my stomach, threatening to expel the hate fizzing out of control. I wasn't sure who I hated more—myself, God, Roman Kush-nir, or his parents for breeding and producing such a vile creature.

I couldn't begin to wrap my head around the trio and their connection to my family.

Sins of the father...

A price I should've paid—not my men.

"Ma'am?"

My head jerked to the side and a pimple-faced corporal stood at attention next to my table before his left foot smartly moved, his arms went behind his back, and his movements stopped when he'd executed parade rest. I didn't have to look at the floor to know the kid's heels were lined up evenly and they were the proper ten inches apart.

"Yes?"

"General Wick would like to see you, ma'am."

My gaze slid from his face down to the name tape on his chest—Usilton.

Well, Corporal Usilton, I'm not fucking ready to face the firing squad, so too goddamn bad for you.

"Thank you, Corporal."

The kid didn't move, still standing awkwardly at rest when he informed me, "I'm to personally escort you, ma'am."

My jaw clenched and in an effort to hide my

now-shaking hands, I balled them into fists. I wasn't ready, dammit.

I had a plan.

I needed more time.

"My apologies, ma'am."

I plastered on a fake smile and stood. "Nothing to apologize for."

Thankfully, the walk from the DFAC to TOC was short, because it was done in an awkward, uncomfortable silence. I wasn't sure who was putting out anxious vibes more—me or Usilton. Unfortunately, the walk was short, because that meant we arrived before I was ready.

Three sharp knocks, then the corporal opened the door, took three steps in, snapped his heels together, and saluted. "Lieutenant McCoy reporting as requested, General Wick."

The general returned the gesture, and without preamble, dismissed the corporal. The poor kid couldn't scuttle out of the room fast enough.

"Thanks for joining us, McCoy."

Like I had a choice.

What in the world was wrong with me? I was normally a very polite and respectful person. I didn't give lip, not even in my head to my superiors. Never had I treated an enlisted soldier to attitude—silent or otherwise. This wasn't me. I knew it, yet I couldn't stop it.

Frustration had completely taken over. I had no control over the mounting irritation.

I gave the guys a tight smile and looked around the room. Today we had an audience—the room was bustling. Screens were active, personnel at work stations, the clicking sound of keys being stroked, and the low murmur of conversation.

But all of that fell away when I felt Drake's eyes on me. And just as I expected, they were assessing.

"Sykes gave me her report," Wick started and my attention snapped to him.

"That was fast."

"We're on a clock," he reminded me. "She cleared you for duty."

That was good news but the general didn't sound convinced. As a matter of fact, he sounded down-right angry. No doubt the man would like nothing more than to send my ass back to the States. Or better yet, personally deliver me to my father.

"Great. Then let's get to it."

"Not so fast."

I held my tongue and my smartass reminder we were on a clock, something that Wick himself just stated. We didn't have time for "not so fast." Lore was on the move, and with Roman entering Lebanon, we needed to be quick—two birds, one stone.

"The guys have asked for a few days."

"Sir? We don't have a few days."

"Operational security and success of this objective rests solely on me. That includes the lives of the tactical element. The team has asked and I agree, not only do you need time to recover, but an opportunity to train with them."

My temper skyrocketed. I couldn't believe this shit. Train with them? That was total and utter bullshit.

"You mean, they want to make sure I'm not a liability." My gaze sliced to Drake and his stone-faced stare pissed me off even more. "You don't think I'm good enough to go out with you and your team."

It wasn't a question and Drake didn't take it as such. He didn't even blink when he turned his big body to face me, didn't show a single inkling of remorse he'd offended the shit out of me. No, instead he stood taller, stone-faced turned into a vicious stare, and Drake transformed into a deadly combatant ready to battle.

Two could play this stupid game. I might not ever be able to best him physically, but I was more than competent, more than capable of completing this mission. I didn't work my ass off to cower. I didn't sweat and bleed to be benched because some asshole thought I wasn't *good enough*.

"I don't know, Lieutenant, are you?"

Ass.

"Hell yes, I am."

"Then what's your problem?"

"*My* problem? I don't have one. *The* problem is, we don't have time for games. We have a shot to take out Lore and we need to move. Not in a few days when you're done with your assessment and evaluation. If you're curious about my training and skillset, I'm sure the general can fill you in. We can't afford—"

"We can't afford to go in weak," Drake cut me off and before I could stop it, my torso jerked back, giving away too much. "Unprepared means we're dead. Unrehearsed means we're compromised from the start. Rushed means the mission fails. Before every operation, we train, we practice, and we run then rerun every possible outcome. It's what we do, and no disrespect, ma'am, but if you're taking my six, your ass will be training with us."

My face heated, not from anger but from embarrassment.

I knew.

I was better than this.

My bad attitude was going to rightfully get me cut. As pissed as I wanted to be at Drake, he was right—a rushed mission meant people died.

"There's an active R and S unit in the area of interest," Wick cut in. "As soon as they report in, we'll begin planning. Until then, we don't have enough to send you in."

"When do you expect the team to report in?" Trey asked.

"First check-in, five hours..."

General Wick said more but when Drake caught my eyes, all thoughts about the recon and surveillance unit and the check-in times fled my mind. All I could do was stare at the man—he was an anomaly. Kind and caring then cold and calculating. Conventionally good-looking in an all-American badass kind of way, yet unconventionally dangerous.

Drake Hayes was a riot of opposites. He ran the gamut from one extreme to the other and for a brief moment I wondered what it would be like to have all that intensity under my palms. What would it be like to touch him—attempt to harness all his focus from his action-hero to lover? What would that type of power feel like?

14

There was something seriously good going on in Liberty's mind. Whatever she was thinking about, it wasn't the mission, terrorists, or intel reports. There was a sexy as fuck blush painting her cheeks and I wanted to rip her uniform top off to see if it covered her chest. I also wanted to pin her down and demand she tell me her every thought because she was looking at me like I was her next meal and I was a-okay with that.

"Will the team be ready?" Wick asked.

I didn't have the first clue what he was asking about, thankfully Logan did.

"Depends on where Lieutenant McCoy's at."

Liberty's eyes cut to my teammate and my gaze followed. Only, Logan wasn't looking at Liberty, he was staring at me. He knew I'd zoned out and he was covering my ass.

Shit.

"We'll start with the range," Matt added. "Give the lieutenant some time to rest physically before we start doing mockups."

"Range hours are sun up to sundown. IDF has offered to take you out if you'd like to do some field work," Wick returned. "McCoy, go to medical. I want daily progress reports on your recovery. The rest of you, dismissed."

Wick turned from our huddle and made his way over to the TOC battle captain.

Dismissed.

Then why the hell were we all standing around? I jerked my chin to the door and moments later, we were all outside.

Logan's loaded stare was burning a hole in the side of my head. First Trey, now Logan. I had no doubt as soon as Liberty headed to medical my team was going to light into me. They'd been on a low simmer all morning just waiting to pounce.

"Do you know where the range is?" I asked Liberty.

"Yeah."

"When you're done with the major, come find us."

"Do I need to go to the armory first?"

"Armory?" Matt asked.

"To check out weapons."

"Honey, you ain't in the regular Army. There's no checking out firearms," Logan huffed.

Logan's bad attempt at a joke fell flat. Liberty had no idea what his jab at the regular Army meant, mostly because she'd never been in the regular Army to begin with. She'd graduated college then joined—she'd never been enlisted. Never had to work alongside the unmotivated leeches that were in the military to collect a paycheck, free housing, and medical insurance.

Fucking hell, Liberty McCoy was still a baby—four years in and most of it had been spent in schools and training. No deployments, two missions. One successful, one fucked.

"What does that mean?"

Her question hit me and I wondered if this was the real Liberty McCoy. Not the lieutenant, the Ranger, the Special Forces Operator. Just her. And make no mistake, there was a difference. Everything about her had changed. Her voice had softened, her

"Don't look at me, I didn't say anything." Trey put his hands up and snorted. "As you said, we're a unit, we don't need words, we read each other's body language, expressions, hell, most of the time I think we have some sort of telepathic connection we're so smooth. If that wasn't enough, you bringing her into the barracks with some bullshit about her staying to learn to move as one with us. Then through the night she wakes up with nightmares, you coax her awake, get her through, *then* you get into bed with her and wrap her up like you can physically absorb her demons. None of us are stupid, but you sure as fuck are if you don't think we don't know what's going on."

There it was—I was officially fucked. Everyone knew. Though I didn't know what they exactly knew because I didn't understand it myself. There was so much shit swirling inside my head, I couldn't keep it straight. And damn if Luke wasn't right—one second I was pissed as hell that Liberty had been sent out before she was ready. The next I was impressed by her determination and proud at what she'd accomplished. Then I slipped into a savage role and wanted to drag her back to a cave, protect her, provide for her, and make babies with her.

What in the hell was wrong with me? Babies?

Protect and provide? When the fuck had I turned into a caveman? The woman drove me to distraction and that made me furious with *her*. It was her fault I couldn't get my shit sorted.

"Then tell me, Trey, what's going on?"

"You're gone for her." He smirked.

"What the fuck does that mean?"

"I agree," Logan put in. "He's got that same look Church had when he finally brought Delaney around."

Now, that was impossible. Carter Lenox was a man in love and there was no missing it. Not from the first time we'd all sat down together for dinner to all of the subsequent times they'd come up to Virginia Beach to visit. Carter looked at his woman like rainbows shot out of her ass. He was a different man when Delaney was around. In all the years I'd known him, the only time I'd truly seen him happy was when she was with him.

"You're so full of shit."

"Logan's right." Matt entered the conversation. "The look's not quite the same but close enough."

"Why try to hide it?" Luke asked.

"Hide what?"

"Dude, seriously?"

"Yes, seriously." My hands went to my face and

the heel of my palms pressed against my eyes. I felt a headache coming on. All this junior high shit made me queasy.

"Let him be," Trey snickered. "It'll be more fun watching him muddle his way through it."

"Agreed. Let's roll out." Matt flashed me a snide grin and strolled away patting the concealed firearm at his hip. "The day hasn't dawned until gunpowder's filled my nostrils."

"Christ, sometimes I think Kessler thinks he's starring in a major motion picture of The Life and Times of Matthew P. Kessler: Billionaire Turned Team Guy," Logan jabbed, causing the rest of us to chuckle.

"That's millionaire, actually," Matt shot back. "And am I sensing some jealousy?"

"Jealousy? Brother, with you being rich and Trey looking like a GQ model, you make my life easy. The bitches sniff that shit out, swarm, and all I gotta do is ride your wave until they fall on my dick. Easy day."

That was not a lie. That was exactly what Logan did.

"Logan's over there talking about riding a wave like he actually gets pussy." Luke chuckled. "Lefty Lucy don't count, friend."

"That's Righteous Rhoda, asshole. Do I look left-handed?"

Matt's ridiculous comeback was too much. I had to stop walking so I didn't trip and fall on my ass as my head tipped back and all five of us roared with laughter.

THERE WERE no two ways about it—Liberty was a damn good shot.

Offhand, kneeling, prone, running, standing still, on her back through her cocked spread knees. She nailed every shot from fifty yards to five-hundred. And it didn't matter the optic—iron sights, red dot, laser aiming, or scope. The woman had shot everything we handed her and she handled each weapon with practiced ease.

"Goddamn, dead eye, is there anything you can't hit?" Matt's brow was cocked up and he was smiling.

Big praise from the sniper.

"Not much at sighting in beyond five-hundred yards," Liberty told him. "Spindrift is not my friend."

Sweet Christ, hearing her utter the word spindrift while she was on her stomach in the dirt, her hand still stroking Matt's prized Barrett, with a spent

.50 BMG cartridge at my feet, had to be the sexiest fucking thing I'd ever heard.

"We can talk about aerodynamic jump over dinner." Matt winked, Liberty giggled—fucking *giggled*, and jealousy pierced my gut.

The fuck Matt would talk about anything with her over dinner.

"How ya' feelin'?" I asked Liberty.

"My muscles are a little sore, but in a good way." Fucking shit, why did she have to say that? "It feels good to sweat and move around."

I swallowed a groan at the mental images her words flashed in my mind and wordlessly turned to the wooden bench that displayed all of our hardware.

I did that to conceal the fact my dick was getting hard. No, scratch that, there was no getting, it was there. Hard as a rock and ready to pound nails. I'm not sure which is worse, being seventeen in math class popping a hot-for-teacher boner. Or now, with a throbbing erection hot-for-the-lieutenant. Neither were good, both painful, and unfortunately, just like the first the second would be taken care of manually —alone with my hand.

"You okay, buddy?" Matt choked on his words as he chuckled.

Fucker.

"I think he's ignoring you," Trey jabbed. "Bet his mind's on that tower of power."

Stupid fuck.

"Tower of power? Where's that? I didn't know there was a rappel tower."

Christ. That was fucking hilarious until it wasn't.

"N...n...no," Trey stuttered. "T..t...tower of power is a—"

"Shut up," I growled and turned before Trey could explain he was talking about my fucking hard-on.

I locked eyes with Liberty's—hers were bright and warm and happier than I'd seen them. Jesus, she was goddamn beautiful. Her eyes dropped to my chest before they flicked lower. There was no hiding the tent in my pants and any move to cover my obvious reaction to her would only draw further attention. Her gaze snapped back to mine, wide in shock, then her lips curved up into a seriously wicked smile.

"Oh." She drew that one word out, making it last three seconds instead of the half-a-second it would normally take and she finished with, "I get it."

Yeah, I bet she thought she did. She just had no clue what I wanted to do with it.

15

Three days of training with the guys and muscles I didn't know I had ached. No, they didn't ache—they were screaming at me to wave a white flag and admit defeat.

Damn, I feel great.

During the day, it felt good to not be wallowing in guilt, self-loathing, and worry. I didn't have time for any of that. Not when Drake, Luke, Matt, Logan, and Trey were keeping me busy. Each of them taking their time to impart tidbits of wisdom. So much so, they'd inadvertently shown me reality. I didn't know jack shit. Which pissed me off.

Don't get me wrong, I was a Ranger. A special forces soldier—I knew my shit, I just didn't know *shit.* I was book smart, I studied, learned, trained,

trained more, but I didn't have practical, real-life knowledge that was born from experience. I still didn't, but being shown what I didn't know made all the difference.

But at night, lying in what was supposed to be Drake's bunk, I felt that guilt, self-loathing, and worry. And when it started it hit me like a Mack truck. Drake and the guys wouldn't have walked into that ambush. They would've seen it coming. All the signs had been there, signs that I didn't recognize—that my team hadn't—and they were dead because of our combined lack of skill.

That was the hardest part to swallow. Even harder than knowing that ambush was sent to capture me. But the more I thought on it, the more nothing made sense.

I shifted to get comfortable knowing that after my last nightmare I'd never get back to sleep, then I froze when my ass rubbed against Drake. I held my breath, praying he'd fallen back to sleep after he'd once again had to get off the floor—where he started every night—shake me awake, put me back to bed, crawl in behind me, and pin me down. Only then did the nightmares stay away.

"Settle your thoughts, woman." His voice was rough and thick with sleep.

An involuntary shiver took over my body. No matter how hard I tried, it still happened. Every time he was close, but especially when his big body was curved behind mine, his arm heavy across my ribs, his lips close to my ear. Those times when he spoke and the rumble vibrated over my neck made it way worse. Those times, I didn't just shiver, the area between my legs quivered.

He was being nice, or more to the point, trying to get some shuteye without me thrashing around, knowing the only way for him to get that was to get into bed with me—so he did. I was not being nice, I was behaving like a cat in heat, wanting to rub my ass against his crotch until he filled me up and made me forget every guilty, self-loathing, worrying thought.

"I can't," I whispered, not wanting to wake up the rest of the team if I hadn't already.

"What's on your mind?"

I didn't hesitate. "How did Roman know where to find me? I understand why he wanted me but not how he knew where I'd be. And another thing, why did he keep asking me how long I'd been on patrol and what I was doing, if he knew? Why ask me anything?"

"To fuck with your head. Half the torture is psychological."

"I guess," I mumbled, still not convinced.

"Liberty," Drake sighed. "Babe, he was playing with you. Wanted to see if he could get you to break. He knew what you were doing, where you were going, and how long you'd been out there. For someone like him—sick and twisted—it's a game. That's the why of it, no other reason but to play."

"Why not just tell me who he was? He had a reason to beat the shit out of me, he didn't need to pretend."

Drake made a low sound in his throat. A cross between a growl and grunt. It sounded angry but still caused another quake between my legs.

"We'll find out who tipped Roman off. Hate to say it, hate to even think it, but it was an inside job."

I nodded because I thought that, too, but really couldn't get myself to verbally agree. That meant someone back home at the 8th Special Forces Group sold me out. It shouldn't take the CID special agents who'd been sent to figure it out long—once they cut through all the red tape that was put in place.

"Do you think Wick has enough pull with the commanding general of CID and my chain of command that an agent would be allowed to investigate?"

"In your group? No way. No one's going to admit

shit to a CID agent, they'll start with the support staff. Black ops is not off-the-books ops. Someone had to get you on a plane to Israel, there'll be a record of that. The transport into Syria will be harder to trace, but again, your objective won't be listed, but your movements will. Wick's not gonna rest until someone tells him how Roman found you."

That, I believed. Wick was an honorable man, he would not want a traitor in his Army. But he also cared about and considered my father a brother, he'd find the person who sold me out for those reasons alone.

"He said he wanted Carter—"

"Babe." Drake pressed into me tighter. "You're tying yourself up into knots for no reason. So the fuck what. Roman wanted Carter. He didn't get to him. Whether it was lack of opportunity or he saw him in action and realized he could never best him, it doesn't matter. Carter's safe."

Roman couldn't best Carter.

But he could me.

Because I was a woman.

"Liberty?" Drake gave me a jerk and lowered his mouth closer to my neck. "Don't go there."

"Go where? To the truth? Because I'm a woman, I was easier prey."

The next thing I knew I was on my back. Drake was looming over me and I couldn't breathe. My lungs were trying to suck in air but nothing was happening.

"Beat it back," Drake whispered. "Look at me. Remember where you are and beat it back."

I tried to focus on him, but the swift movement had all sorts of wires crossing in my head. I knew it was Drake. I knew he wouldn't hurt me. But I couldn't *see* him.

Drake's hand went to my face, I felt his calloused thumb as it swept across my cheek, but I still couldn't break the spell. Then his lips brushed my forehead, my nose, my lips and when he got there he paused before he spoke. "Come on, Ranger, beat it." I felt his words against my mouth, my tongue came out to lick my dry lips and I was unable to focus for another reason. The tip of my tongue grazed his lips and my heart seized.

No, that wasn't right, it was still thundering in my chest until I felt Drake's tongue meet mine in a soft touch—*then* my heart seized. His tongue speared into my mouth and with what was left of my brain cells I was just cognizant enough to catch the moan that almost slipped out and swallow it. Or maybe when Drake took over the kiss he shoved it back down my throat as he kissed me so thoroughly, so fervently, so overwhelmingly fantastic I'd never experienced anything like it.

Then his mouth was gone, but not his hard-on pressing against my thigh. Not his intense eyes that I knew were the color of caramel even if I couldn't see their color in the dark—studying, scrutinizing, assessing me. Just like they always were, but this time, it was different. This time, I didn't mind, because I hoped what he was reading was to not stop and to give me more, much, *much* more.

"Lib—"

"Shh. Please don't say it. Don't tell me that was a mistake. Let me have it and keep it unpolluted. I want to remember it for exactly what it was—the best damn kiss of my life."

Drake went solid and he emitted that sound he makes from the back of his throat. The one that's part-growl, part-grunt, and my pussy spasmed. Damn, did I want to hear that sound when he was filling me full.

But I never would, not if the look of regret he was giving me was any indication.

And that sucked.

Sucked so bad my insides shriveled up and died.

Drake remained silent as he rolled slightly and

tucked me to his side. The bed was small, really small, so I hitched a leg over his thigh and ended up mostly on top of him. This position was dangerous, it also wasn't conducive to stopping any further wetness from drenching my panties. But there I was, acting a fool and enjoying the feel of his big, hard body under mine.

"Did you know my name means fate?" I asked for some asinine reason.

"I didn't. You have a beautiful name." My lips brushed against the fabric of his t-shirt when I smiled and I wished he was bare-chested. "Why do you go by the name Liberty?"

"Because when I was in school, a substitute teacher couldn't pronounce it. After that, kids started making fun of it. About a year later, and three suspensions for fighting, I started having everyone call me Liberty. My mom and dad still call me Moira sometimes. But mostly they call me Liberty, too. Unless they're mad, then it's always Moira."

"Suspensions? For what."

"Fist fighting."

"You got suspended three times for fighting?" The shock in his voice made me laugh.

"Actually, no. But only because my cousins beat me to it. Ethan, Carter's brother, got busted once.

And Jackson, my baby cousin, twice. Now Ethan sticking up for me was one thing. But Jack being younger than me, I didn't appreciate. Though he'd established early on that no one could mess with him which turned out to be a good thing. Him and my cousin Quinn have been BFFs since the womb, and Quinn grew up to be seriously beautiful. Jack had his hands full beating back every asshole in high school who wanted a piece of her. Of course he had help from my other male cousins."

"It must run in the family."

"What does?"

"Seriously beautiful women."

Say what?

Whoa, Nelly. Drake Hayes thought I was seriously beautiful? I knew I wasn't butt ugly but I wasn't supremely beautiful like Delaney with her dark hair and blue eyes. And Quinn, she was like a triple threat with her shiny black hair, green eyes, and long-ass legs. Then there were the Walker twins, Hadley and Adalynn. Those two took stunning to a whole new level. That left me, the average one, brown hair, brownish eyes, normal height, boring figure. I was too muscular to be womanly. Plain, nothing, standard issue—that was me.

"So, um, what about you, do you know what

the region. Every terrorist on the CIA's watchlist wanted him—not to harm, but to employ.

So five days were five too many for him to be walking around Beirut.

"Romeo-one-sierra, challenge," the battle captain asked for verification.

"Screwdriver. Indian. Thirteen."

"Authenticate."

"Background."

"Confirmed. Romeo-one-sierra go for TOC-one."

My gaze went from the map we'd been studying to Liberty. What a difference five days had made. Most of the bruising on her face had faded. However, the deep red circled by a yellowish-green mark around her left eye remained a constant reminder of what had happened to her.

I hadn't seen her torso or legs since the day I'd dressed her, nor had I asked if those bruises and contusions were healing. The way she kept up with us on runs, workouts, and training, I figured they were. Either that or her determination to go after Lore didn't allow her to complain.

One thing was certain, Lieutenant Liberty McCoy was one tough chick.

"Target one is confirmed. Prepare to copy."

"Go."

"Thirty-three degrees, fifty-four minutes north. Thirty-five degrees, thirty-two minutes east. How copy, TOC-one?"

"Thirty-three degrees, fifty-four minutes north. Thirty-five degrees, thirty-two minutes east," the battle captain repeated. "Target two?"

Hell yeah, the recon and surveillance unit found us a location.

No one spoke other than the battle captain but that didn't mean the room wasn't full of soldiers pounding away on their keyboards gathering every bit of data they could find about the surrounding area.

"Frequently visits target one at that location. Can't get a lock on target two's residence. He's vapor."

Fuck. R and S had a solid location for Lore but not Roman.

My eyes shifted to Liberty, and as expected, she was scowling. She wanted both men and it looked like she was only going to get Lore.

The battle captain looked at the General and waited.

"Tell him the team's going in. I want target two found."

"R-one-S, company's coming your way. QRF-Alpha. Prepare to copy," the battle captain relayed the general's orders.

"Go."

"Linebacker. Complete. Five. Authentication: aftershock. How copy?"

After the R-one-S radioed back they confirmed the new codes, the battle captain ordered the unit to find Roman.

My eyes were glued to Liberty and Liberty's were stuck on Wick. My team was in my peripheral and they were hunched over the large map of Beirut. I didn't need to huddle to know they were locating the coordinates the unit had called in.

"Wheels up at zero hundred," Wick barked and Liberty flinched.

"Roman?"

Yeah, she wanted the man who'd captured, beaten, and killed her squad, arguably more than she wanted Lore. Not that I blamed her, but our mission objective was Lore—not Roman.

"You have thirty-six hours. If target two becomes available, I'll give the order."

I knew she wanted to plead for more time. When she opened her mouth to protest, the battle captain spoke.

"Satellite up on screen one."

And so it began, the TOC was buzzing with intel.

Infil and exfil plans and backup plans were made. Different fallback points, transportation, weapons, threats identified, and again more contingencies. We continued until we had everything down to minute detail. We aimed for flawless, but being in the game for as long as I'd been, I knew the reality was that shit happened. Flawless sometimes turned into fucked-up. And when shit hit the fan all you had were the men at your side. On that thought, I looked up to find Liberty's brows pinched, studying a street view image of the apartment building Lore was staying in.

"What are you thinking?" I asked her.

"We have to hit him on the street." She looked up and held my stare.

"Elaborate," Matt ordered.

"No doubt he'll have his apartment rigged."

"Agreed. We've been over that. Trey will take point to disarm—"

"That won't be enough. He'll have it rigged. Not just the doors and windows. The whole apartment. It will be a minefield once we enter."

The more I considered what Liberty suggested,

jutted out and her eyes narrowed into slits. She was fighting a losing battle keeping her temper in check and I knew she indeed lost that fight when she opened her mouth.

"All due respect—"

"Right." Wick cut her off and chuckled. "Respect." He shook his head, softened his gaze, and lowered his voice. "I'm not asking as your commanding officer, Liberty. I'm asking as a man who watched you crawl on your father's lap when you were in diapers. A man who was at your fifth birthday and placed your ass on a pony and led you around your family's backyard. A man who was at your high school graduation. And finally as a man who fought beside your father. I don't want your respect, young lady. I want your goddamn promise I will not be accompanying a condolence officer to deliver a crushing death notification."

Jesus, I had no idea how close Wick was to the McCoy family. I knew they had ties but not a clue how deep they ran. Neither Liberty nor the general had let on to their profound connection. Which actually impressed me. Liberty could've used the bond for special treatment and she had not, nor had Wick allowed her to bypass evaluations.

"I promise," she whispered.

Wick's body relaxed a tiny fraction and his nose twitched before he sniffed. "Be safe. All of you."

And with that, the man turned and went back to the large screens mounted against the back of the room.

We made our way outside. The fresh air filled my lungs and I took a moment to enjoy the quiet. It was late, most everyone who wasn't on duty was asleep and the ones who weren't knew not to make a ruckus. In a few hours' time, gone would be the fresh air and quiet. Neither of those things would exist while we were in Beirut. It would be noise, pollution, and people.

We made the short walk back to the barracks in silence, each of us lost in our thoughts. This was not unusual, if we had a few hours before we loaded out, we always took that time to get our heads straight.

Trey let us into the hut and went straight to his bunk. The others did the same, leaving Liberty and me alone by the door.

"What's on your mind?" I asked.

Her eyes came to mine and my first instinct was to pull her close.

Now was not the time.

Actually, never was the time. But after our kiss the other night, never was getting harder and harder to accept. For five nights, she'd slept in my arms. Five. And I was addicted. Tucking her close and feeling her strong, lean body pressed against mine was a rush. The same kind I used to get when I jumped out of the back of an aircraft at thirty-thousand feet. Her fingers laced with mine as she fought her way back from a nightmare felt like a gift. Breathing her in, holding her, but most especially kissing her, was the best fucking feeling I'd ever experienced.

And soon it would be gone.

A woman like Liberty made a man reevaluate his life. Reprioritize what was important.

All of that from five nights and a kiss.

I've had women in my bed who were masters of manipulation. They'd tried and failed to lock their chains around my neck. Fronted, schemed, and straight-out lied to get me to commit to them and the fantasy they had about marrying a SEAL. None had tempted me. None had interested me. And none had succeeded in making me fall for them.

But Liberty had.

And she'd done it in less than a week.

"Just running the op in my head," she answered.

"You wanna talk it through?"

"Not right now. We'll run it again when we get there."

"Yeah. About a hundred more times."

"Okay."

There was something working in that pretty little head of hers but I couldn't get a clear read.

"What's really going on, babe?"

"I made myself a promise." When she said no more, I patiently waited, giving her time to gather her thoughts. Something was weighing heavy on her and she needed to get it out now before we boarded a helicopter. Once we were in the air, there was no more time for idle chitchat. "When I decided to go to Ranger school, I promised myself I'd never be the weak link."

"Liberty—"

"No, Drake. Please listen. It was important to me. I swore to myself that if I couldn't keep up with the men, I'd quit. I didn't need to max out the pull-ups or beat their run times, but I couldn't come in last and that is *not* because I wanted to be some trailblazer. It's *not* because being a woman in Ranger regiment was some lifelong goal to move the sisterhood forward. I had to know that me being there and my personal accomplishments were not ever going to put lives in danger.

Trey was gasping for air and coughing, he smiled and said, "And don't be a hero."

"Do we get to enjoy the little things?" Liberty asked with a broad, bright smile.

"Rule number eleven." Trey beamed. "Hot damn. Woman, you're all right."

Matt clapped Liberty on the shoulder as he walked past her on the way back to his bunk muttering something about her being a cool chick. I agreed she was but I didn't like hearing Matt's compliment. I also didn't like seeing Matt touch her.

Where in the actual hell did that come from?

"You trust us?" I asked.

"Yes. Do you trust me?"

"Absolutely."

"There's no hard feelings if—"

In two strides, I closed the distance between us, my hands went to Liberty's hips, her words died, and I hauled her closer. "Straight up truth, when my life is on the line I'm not concerned about hurting feelings. I'm concerned about the job. I'm concerned about my objective. I'm concerned about the good guys coming home and the bad guys dying. At no time during a mission am I worried about offending someone. Hard feelings or not, if I didn't believe you were capable you wouldn't be going with us. And now I know that has less to do with *me* asking for your removal and more to do with *you* asking to be removed. It's good to know your limitations, your strengths, and how to work around weakness. The mere fact you're thinking about these things and they're weighing on you tells me your head's where it needs to be. What you can't do is crumble under the weight. Check your ego but keep your confidence. They're two different things. One gets you dead, the other will keep you alive."

Liberty's hands had made their way to my chest and her tiny palms were burning through my tee. I wished her handprints would forever be blistered on my skin. Tangible marks I could look at, physical reminders of what she meant to me.

"Confidence. You're right," she mumbled.

"Always am, baby."

Liberty's lips tipped up and her eyes lit. Fucking hell, she was something else. Bright—so bright my skin warmed. Unless it was the middle of the night. Then she was filled with darkness and that shit cut me deep. It hurt like a bitch to see her wounded eyes search mine as the remnants of her nightmares tore her apart.

But what hurt worse was soon she'd be dealing with that on her own. I wouldn't be there to hold her hand and help her beat back the demons as they viciously tried to pull her under.

"Can you say arrogant."

"Arrogant?" I shook my head. "I'm unfamiliar with that word."

"Right. You should look it up. The dictionary defines the word as Drake Hayes. There's even a picture of this really hot guy for those who can't read."

"Hot guy?" I teased.

"*Really* hot guy."

Fucking shit.

I lowered my mouth to her ear knowing that the guys were listening in, therefore they'd already heard enough—too much, in fact. No one needed to worry about Liberty's performance on the battlefield. They needed to worry about mine. I wasn't a hundred percent sure because I'd never tried it, but I didn't think running and gunning with an enormous hard-on was recommended. And if we didn't cut this shit out now, hours from now when we landed in Beirut, my dick would still be throbbing.

"You're hell on a man's control," I whispered.

"How so?"

"Just you standing close breathin' is enough to make me want to tear your clothes off. You being cute and funny, admitting you think I'm hot... now that makes me want to tear your clothes off and play with you until you're screaming my name."

"*Really* hot." Her breath fanned across my neck and I was holding on by a thread. "Don't forget the really."

My body made the decision. The decision being, I pressed my hard-on against Liberty's stomach, ignored her body when she softened into me, and growled, "You're playing with fire." My brain finally caught up and I stepped away. "Seriously, Liberty, there's only so much I can take before I *really* take. I think that's what we both want, but I'm playin' it smart. Help me with that, babe, and don't push it."

I took a moment to memorize the pout on her lips and blush on her cheeks. Then I turned and left. But not before I remembered how fucking great she tasted.

17

Beirut was bustling. Even in the wee hours of the morning.

We'd arrived at the apartment we were staying at for the next couple of nights. I wasn't hip on real estate in Beirut but the space was surprisingly modern. It wasn't lost on me the three bedroom, three bath apartment was in an expensive building with spectacular views of the Mediterranean Sea. We were on the top floor and a balcony stretched the length of the apartment on the sea side. Spacious living room, huge square kitchen, gleaming white marble floors with veins of gold running throughout. And it was fully furnished—two black leather couches facing each other in the living room and a four top, round table in the breakfast nook with a view of the Mediterranean. Two of the three bedrooms had that same view.

All in all, the place was swank. I could almost forget we were there on an op and not a vacation if it wasn't for the five sea bags, gun cases, and backpacks strewn about.

Upon our arrival we'd swept the entire apartment before the guys got down to the all-important task of assigning bedrooms. Which is what they were doing now—arguing about who got which room. I was staying out of it because I didn't care. I'd be happy sleeping out on the balcony, the view was that good. Though there wasn't any patio furniture out there which I thought was vaguely odd.

That's what I was contemplating when I heard my name.

"What about me?"

"Only three bedrooms," Matt told me.

"So? I saw two beds in the room I searched. Three rooms, two beds in each, that's six. What's the problem?"

"Five beds," Luke snickered. "Master has a queen, not two singles."

"Oh. Well, I'll take the couch."

"No. You'll take the master, I'll take the couch," Drake shot back and I glanced at the leather sofa.

"Right." I laughed. "Sorry, big man, but you're not fitting on that thing. Not sure if that's some European style I've never seen before, but it's way too small for you. The only person fitting on that couch is me."

"I'll take the floor."

"Told you, brother, I'll take one for the team. You take a single, I shack up with the lieutenant," Trey joked.

And I knew he was clowning around, pushing Drake's buttons, when he flashed me his Hollywood smile while trying his best to beat back a laugh.

"You try that and you'll find your ass over the balcony, pretty boy."

At Drake's outburst, Trey lost the battle and burst into laughter. The rest of the guys weren't far behind, chuckling and making jabs.

They all had great laughs. They were tough as nails when they needed to be. Hard, rough men who carried a heavy load. But when they cut up, they were hilarious together.

Friends.

Brothers.

Teammates.

My smile died, my heart pinched, and bile swirled in my stomach.

Teammates.

Mine were gone—because of me—and there I was, smiling and joking about who was going to get which bed.

Breathing.

I was breathing and they weren't.

How could I forget? Even for a second, how could I joke and smile and enjoy the comradery of the group of men who'd rescued me and not them?

I didn't have the right.

"Come on." Drake's hand snagged mine and then he was dragging me out of the room, up the stairs, and before my brain reengaged, we were in the master bedroom.

"What's wrong?" he barked.

"I don't know. You tell me. You're the one that drug me up here."

"Don't try to bullshit me, Liberty."

My temper rose, and the bile that'd been swirling in my stomach turned into the fuel I needed. I couldn't forget my place. I couldn't forget I was the lone survivor in a murder attempt that should've ended with me dead, not my team. I pulled up all the memories of that day, the day we'd been ambushed. I remembered the look of shock on my teammates' faces. I remembered the anger in Perez's normally happy face. And finally I remembered Ball's prone body next to mine in the dirt. Our wrists and ankles zip tied, our eyes locked, and his last whispered words to me, "Stay strong."

Then I was separated from my men, their angry protests rang out as I was thrown into the bed of a pickup truck and a masked man climbed in behind me. I'll never forget the flash suppressor of his rifle jabbing me in the back as we bounced down the bumpy road. Visions of the man accidentally shooting me as the truck hit pothole after pothole.

I wish I would've died in that truck.

I wish my team had lived.

Five good men died and I'd had five good days breathing, laughing, and joking.

Wrong.

It was so wrong I couldn't find my breath.

"Liberty," Drake snapped.

"I'm unclear what your issue is, Master Chief."

Drake did a slow blink, then his eyes narrowed into two dangerously, pissed-off slits. The corners of his eyes wrinkled, his lips pressed together, and his brows pinched. His face as a whole was a mask of fury.

"Drake," he barked.

"What?"

"My name is Drake."

"So, you brought me up here to tell me your name."

"Say it."

"Say what?"

"My fucking name."

"Why?"

"So you'll remember who the fuck you're talking to. I see you've slipped back into that fucked-up place in your head again. You're putting up walls. But what you still don't get is, those walls, they're not keeping others out. They're keeping you trapped inside. Inside a place that's totally fucked-up."

"Good to know you think I'm fucked-up."

"Babe, your head's a mess. And I keep telling you it's gonna stay that way until you deal with it. What happened to you, to your team, was not your fault. Don't take that on. You have enough weighing you down. Trust me, you don't need that, too."

"Right," I bit out sarcastically. "Roman's vendetta against my family is what killed those men. That means it is absolutely my fault."

"No, Liberty, it means it's *Roman's* fault. His father was a piece of shit, he needed to be put down and Lenox made that so. Your uncle made the world a safer place. One less arms dealer roaming the planet. Junior doesn't see it that way, thinks dear ol' dad was a saint and wants retribution, that's not your fault either."

"You don't understand."

"No, honey, I don't. I've never experienced survivor's guilt and I pray to God I never do, because that would mean those men downstairs would be dead. But I do understand misplaced guilt. I do understand the aftermath of captivity. I do understand the effects of torture and how it twists and poisons your insides. Been there, done that, more than once. I know what you're going through."

"And yet you're still standing there passing judgement."

"Judgement?"

All right, that was a stretch. I knew it was but couldn't stop the anger. My vision blurred with it. Everything was jumbled in my head. It wasn't even so much the guilt as it was the anger. I was so mad it had consumed me to the point I was irrational. I knew it but I couldn't stop it. I wasn't even sure if I wanted to stop it. I wanted to bask in it. Bathe in it until it seeped deeper so I wouldn't ever forget.

"Judge-ment?" Drake repeated, breaking the word into two enunciated, enraged syllables.

I couldn't think of a retort so I remained quiet.

My silence meant Drake got even more annoyed and he took the opportunity to further tell me how annoyed he was.

"Get over yourself," he growled and my breath froze in my lungs. "Woman, you wanna be pissed that Roman took you, beat the shit out of you, mentally tortured you, hurt you, scared you, treated you like a goddamn animal—do it. Be fucking angry. You have every right to be. You wanna hate the son of a bitch who killed your team, I'll stand next to you and curse his very existence. You wanna put two between his eyes, I'll help you load your magazine and try my best to provide you the opportunity. But don't you ever tell me I'm passing judgement on you. Not a man in this house has done a goddamn thing but support you. I'll repeat a-fucking-gain, deal with it."

"I can't!" I screeched.

"You can."

Drake closed the distance, his arms went low around my waist, and what did I do? I lost my ever-loving mind. Or what was left of it cracked open and out poured crazy. So much crazy, I balled my fists, clenched my teeth, and started pounding on his chest like, yes, a crazy person.

"Harder, baby," he encouraged. I did what he

told me to do and hit him harder. "More," he grunted. And I did that, too.

I slammed my fists as hard as I could against the solid wall of muscle until my arms shook with exertion. I could feel the wetness leaking from my eyes and rolling down my cheeks.

"Now tell me, what happened downstairs?"

"We were laughing," I croaked. "Laughing and joking and smiling. My team was laid to rest today and there I was, smiling."

Suddenly my arms were trapped tight between us and Drake shoved my face to his throat and held me so tight I couldn't escape if I wanted to.

My irrational Jekyll and Hyde mood swing concluded and I was close to coming back to myself when Drake whispered, "Baby."

The tears that had already started came faster and Drake held tighter and for the first time since I'd been taken, a sob escaped and I came apart. Everything I'd been holding inside just came spilling out. I couldn't lock it away anymore.

A long time passed, Drake just holding me, letting me take what I needed from him. Then he let me go and stepped back, not far, but enough for him to kneel in front of me. He unlaced my boots, pulled them off, stood, and divested me of my pants.

He wasn't undressing me like a lover, his movements weren't hurried or sensual. They were slow and careful like I was made of glass. Like I was precious. Then he helped me into bed and quickly pulled his clothes off, leaving on just his boxer briefs.

Drake turned off the light, climbed in next to me, and rolled us so his chest was pressed to my back. His strong arm pinning me to the mattress was familiar and comforting. His embrace was so comforting I'd become addicted to it.

That was a problem.

"Wanna tell me about them?" he asked.

I didn't need to think about my answer, it was a no. I didn't want to talk about my team in the dark the night before we were starting our op. I didn't want to think about anything.

"No."

"You should—"

"Please, Drake. Please give me this. I can't do it. I need to clear my mind."

With a heavy, disapproving sigh, he let the subject drop.

"Thank you," I whispered into the darkness, wishing I could say more to express my gratitude.

I snuggled back, forgetting that for the first time there weren't multiple layers of fabric between us.

Just my panties and his boxers. Gone was the heavy material of our uniform pants, leaving only thin cotton. And sweet holy hell, I could feel the outline of his thick dick against my ass.

Not good.

Feeling him, my mind started to wander.

It was going places it shouldn't go, but the more I tried to stop it, the less I was able to. That's because I was telling myself to stop thinking about his dick. And every time I thought the word 'dick' I wondered what it would feel like to have it in my hand. And when I scolded myself for thinking that, I wondered what it would feel like between my legs. On that thought, I squirmed uncomfortably because my panties were now soaked.

Drake's body went still behind me, his arm clamped down, and his growly, rough voice skidded across my neck. "Stop movin'."

That made me shiver, which I reckoned would be considered moving but I didn't ask. I couldn't even if I wanted to because I was sucking in oxygen, trying to stop myself from panting. I could still feel the outline of his dick, but the contour had grown— longer, thicker, harder.

"Serious as fuck, honey, you have to stop squirming. Warned you once about testing my control."

"And what if I want you to lose it?"

I was playing with fire with no comprehension of what I was asking for. I wasn't a virgin but I wasn't experienced enough to know what it meant when a man like Drake lost control. I had a few men in college but none since I'd joined the Army. There'd been no time between basic, AIT, Ranger school, and SF training. I'd been surrounded by men, a lot of them good-looking, but none who were available to me, and if they were, I still hadn't been interested. I hadn't been looking for a man or sex. I'd been laser-focused on being the best I could be. But right then lying in that bed, I was interested in Drake and what it meant for me if his control snapped.

"Trust me, you don't."

Just to test this theory, I wiggled back and turned my head so we were face-to-face. It was then I realized I should've played it smart. I shouldn't have tested anything and I certainly shouldn't have poked the beast because, holy fuck, the beast had awoken and he looked beyond hungry.

The warm brown eyes I'd found solace in glittered with something wild. Drake looked like he was moments away from proving to me not only did I lack the experience needed to take a man like him, but I lacked the skill to give him what he wanted.

"Um..."

"It sinkin' in yet?"

He asked a question but didn't wait for an answer. His palm went to my belly and pressed down, and at the same time the tips of his fingers skimmed the skin above my panties, he flexed his hips.

"Yes."

I thought at my admission he would've stopped but he didn't. I was trapped—his dick was nestled tight against my ass, his hand was dipping lower, but still very far away from where the ache throbbed.

Neither of us said a word as we stared at each other in the minimal light the floor-to-ceiling windows provided. I wanted to turn on a light to see him better. His hand had stopped going down but hadn't stopped moving—his fingers were gently gliding back and forth and they were driving me insane. I needed him to do something. Stop or move lower.

I communicated this by rubbing my bottom on his erection.

"That an invitation?" Unable to speak, I nodded. "I need words, baby."

"Yes." My answer came out in a whoosh.

"Need to know what exactly you're inviting me to do."

"Touch me." Again my words were barely more than an exhale.

"With what?"

"Huh?"

In our current position, I didn't think my answer required an explanation. I certainly wasn't asking him to touch me with some inanimate object he could uncover in the bedroom.

"Lots of ways I can touch you." When I still didn't respond, he continued. "I could use my mouth between your legs. I could get you off with my fingers. Or I could give you my cock. What I'm asking is, which way do you want it?"

This time I answered, though I was so turned on by the buffet of pleasure he'd laid out I was shocked I could speak.

"Hand."

Drake didn't have to be told twice. His hand dove lower, skimmed over my clit, causing my pussy to flutter. And before the flutter had subsided, a long, thick finger plunged inside. My back arched, my bottom hitched back, knocking into his hard-on, and a low moan slipped out.

"Christ," he grunted.

The man wasted no time. He didn't play around, fumble, flounder, or struggle. Drake had found my sweet spot and with extraordinary proficiency, exploited it. He had the perfect rhythm and before I knew it, I was on the edge. Then I lost his finger.

"Not so fast."

"Wh-what? Why'd you stop?"

"Trust me."

Trust him? Was he crazy? I was on the verge of an orgasm when he left me hanging. That didn't instill trust, it inspired sexual frustration.

Drake's hand was back, two fingers this time, and with a twist his thumb was circling my clit.

My hips jerked. His fingers speared in, setting a different pace than he had before. This time he was building something and he did it with deliberate, measured thrusts. Dragging the pads of his fingers over my g-spot, perfect pressure on my clit, and that something he was creating was going to be spectacular.

I knew because I was again close. Drake's eyes hadn't left mine and that was hot. Almost as hot as his dick moving against my ass as he grinded himself into my backside.

"I want you inside of me."

"I am."

"No. I want your dick inside of me."

"No."

"No?"

"You said you wanted my fingers, baby. So my fingers are what you get."

Was a girl not allowed to change her mind? And if I'd asked for his dick from the beginning would I not have gotten anything but?

"I want more."

"Trust me," he repeated. "I'll get you there."

"I want more."

"Right now you do because I've got you close to coming on my fingers. But a minute ago when you were thinking straight, you weren't ready for my dick." Drake put more pressure on my clit and my vision started to blur. "Turn your head more and get ready to give me your mouth."

I kind of understood what he said but mostly I wasn't paying attention because the biggest orgasm I'd ever experienced was barreling down on me. My legs trembled, one hand fisted the sheet, the other found his hip, and my nails dug in there.

Then it hit me and my mouth opened to verbally express my pleasure when Drake's lips hit mine and he swallowed my scream. I wasn't entirely sure if I kissed him back or if I lamely laid there. What I did know was it felt fucking great.

All of it.

His fingers between my legs. His dick grinding. His tongue in my mouth. But most of all my pussy spasming around his fingers in the best orgasm I'd ever had. As in—*ever*.

"Jesus." Drake tore his mouth from mine. His hand came out of my panties. Then I felt it moving behind me. "Fuck."

My mind caught up and I realized what he was doing. That was hot, too, so hot I pushed my ass back in another invitation.

"Babe," he groaned.

"Finish, Drake."

"That's a given."

I wasn't sure how to ask for what I wanted, again my lack of experience meant I wasn't sure about how to say the words. So I decided to both show him and say it. I wiggled my panties down as far as I could get them, pulled the t-shirt Drake had left on me when he put me into bed up enough that my butt and lower back was on display.

"I want to feel you on my skin."

His hand slowed. "Need more than that, baby."

His voice was tight and strained and God if that wasn't off-the-charts sexy.

"I want you to finish on me. You got to feel me. I want to feel you."

Drake didn't move, he didn't speak, and for a moment I regretted my request. I probably sounded like some sick sex freak.

"Jesus," he bit out. There was a rustle of movement behind me, then I felt the smooth head of his dick hit my lower back.

I closed my eyes. The smell of Drake and sex filled my nostrils, my body sated, my mind at ease. And just like all of the other times I was in his arms, I felt safe.

"Wish you'd let me help with that," I muttered.

"Make no mistake, baby, you're helping."

Seconds later, there was a warm splash on my back. It was hot. It was sexy as all get-out. The only thing better would've been if I could've watched.

and Logan would have his hands full. But it was better than her getting dead.

"Like riding a horse," Wick grumbled and I fought back a groan.

The last thing I needed to be doing was thinking about Liberty riding anything—and when my mind went there she wasn't riding a horse. The setting sun over the Mediterranean suddenly vanished and my vision filled with the exquisite memory of Liberty's bare ass, the curve of her hip, and her smooth skin. Soft, silky flesh I'd tarnished with my seed. The image was raw, and damn if it didn't make me an animal, but I wanted to mark her again and again and again until there was no denying she belonged to me.

More than that, I wanted her to mark me. I wanted her scent to linger and leach into my skin. My addiction had turned into an obsession—a dangerous fixation that would end in the worst kind of way.

She'd be gone and I'd be fucked.

But for some Godforsaken reason, even knowing I'd never see her again, I couldn't resist her pull. She was under my skin and I'd decided not to fight it, I liked her there.

"Anything new for the R and S team or were you just checking on Liberty?"

He met my question with silence. I knew why—I'd screwed up. The general didn't miss much, therefore he would not miss the informality.

"Right. Target is still in the proximity and you have the green light," Wick returned.

Excellent.

"Good. Then we're going huntin'."

"Aim true," Wick grunted then disconnected.

Game on.

"Yo," I called out when I entered the apartment. "Let's roll."

Luke and Trey stood, Matt and Logan stopped rummaging through the kitchen cabinets like something in the form of food would magically appear and they moved swiftly to the living room.

Liberty remained seated. Her pretty face turned in my direction and an even prettier smile aimed my way.

Damn. I had approximately two minutes to stop thinking about that smile before I needed to get my head right and get out the door.

Apparently, I'd miscalculated. "You two done making googly eyes at each other so we can bounce?" Trey asked.

"Fuck off."

"Guess not." He chuckled.

Liberty's smile grew and it was painful to see for a variety of reasons. The first being I only had a limited number of them left. The other reason had to do with the fallout when she realized she'd allowed herself to feel something other than grief and anger. Last night, hearing her beat herself up was agony. She was on a dangerous road—porpoising, unsettled, volatile. It wouldn't take much for her to break apart.

And I wouldn't be there.

Matt, Logan, Trey, and Luke were strapping on gear, chuckling amongst themselves at my outburst. Liberty wasn't laughing but she was up out of her chair moving to her kit so she, too, could get ready— she was also grinning.

Time to get a move on. I grabbed my vest, slid it over my head, fastened the Velcro tight around my ribs, and went for my holster. All of this mindless— having done it hundreds of times, I could do it in my sleep. That left room for me to think about Liberty and what it was about her that was so different. I'd shared my bed with plenty of women, done a fuckuva lot more than just put my hand down their panties, yet Liberty coming apart in my arms was hotter, sexier, and more of a turn-on than any other woman had been.

I couldn't figure out how it was possible but there it was. I'd take jerking myself off on her ass over fucking someone else.

If the guys knew my thoughts, they'd likely think I was the one who needed a psych eval.

"You got something to wear over that vest?" Matt asked Liberty.

"My shirt."

Her response had me taking in what she was wearing. Loose-fitting tee that wouldn't conceal her tact vest, jeans, and a pair of Oakley boots.

"Those jeans give you enough room for an ankle holster?" Matt continued.

Liberty raised her right pant leg, exposing the compact .9mm. She dropped the material and moved to the left, repeating the process. A fixed, sheathed blade was strapped around her calf.

"Lose the knife," I told her.

"Why? This is my normal carry."

"You ever run in jeans with that strapped on?"

"No."

"Trust me, you'll thank me later. Big difference between jeans and ACUs. The nine's fine where it is

Until now.

Knowing he was right but hating the fact he was, I agreed. "Me and Matt will take point. You and Liberty in the middle. Trey and Luke take the rear."

With a jerk of his chin, Logan went back to sorting his kit. Minutes later, Liberty came back with my navy blue button-up on. She was swimming in it, but had the tails tied in a knot that somehow made it look fashionable.

Boots, jeans, men's shirt, and Liberty McCoy was still sexy as fuck—knowing what she had on underneath her clothes—that being a tactical vest and multiple weapons, was hot, too. The woman was badass yet somehow she remained feminine.

"You straight?" I inquired and bit back asking more, like if she had extra magazines on her. Something she'd find annoying and frankly patronizing. Especially since I wouldn't be asking the rest of my team if they had extra ammo.

"Yep."

Top to toe—sexy.

Top to toe—a warrior.

Fucking hell, it was seriously gonna hurt when she was gone.

19

Thankfully, the temperature in Beirut dropped as it got closer to nightfall. Logan and I were sitting in the back of a taxi on our way to the port and I was sweating like crazy—any hotter and I'd soak through Drake's shirt. I was actually fighting the temptation of wiping away the rivers of perspiration dripping down my chest. The only thing stopping me was Logan pressed up against me like we were a couple vacationing in Beirut.

The thought was so asinine it was laughable. But that's the impression Logan had given the driver when we'd gotten into the car and told the man to take us to some restaurant a mile's walk from the area in which Lore had been spotted.

As soon as we'd walked out of the apartment building, Drake and Matt had split right and without a backward glance, started down the street. Logan had waited for us to get into a taxi until Drake and Matt had found one themselves and drove off.

We'd left Trey and Luke on the street corner as they pretended to look at a map. They looked every bit the tourist, if tourists looked like large, menacing men.

"Relax," Logan whispered, then his hand picked mine up off my lap and he threaded our fingers together before placing our combined hands on his thigh.

I stared at our hands thinking how wrong they looked. I knew it was fake and part of our cover, but I wanted to snatch my hand away and scoot over. Funny, a few weeks ago I wouldn't have thought twice about holding a good-looking guy's hand. But that was before Drake.

Before my heart had stupidly picked him.

When we arrived at the restaurant, Logan paid the driver, helped me out of the car, and placed his hand on my lower back, giving me a tiny shove forward.

"Babe, you gotta relax."

real. Eyes open—always. Every person is a possible target. Don't dismiss anyone, not women, not children."

"Right."

A nasty feeling slithered down my spine.

"Don't look at the AO as a whole. Break it down into micro-environments. Streets, alleyways, buildings, targets, civilians—they all present challenges. You need to break those down on the fly."

"Okay."

I scanned the area, taking in the water to our right, the busy street we were walking down, the people moving about, tall buildings to our left—some businesses, some apartments, some a mixture of both. Between them, alleys that, when the sun set fully, would be dark. Hidey-holes everywhere. Innocent people going about their lives who could easily be used as human shields.

"And remember these people know the city better than you do. We can study the maps, have the latest satellite images, we can even have scouted the area and the bad guys will always know it better."

Logan was painting a grim picture and the more he talked the more I realized how inadequate I was.

"Last thing. You don't leave my side. Doesn't matter what you see, who you see, what's going down around us, you're my shadow. We work as a team, you and me. And if you've got something to say, say it. You got a question, ask. You're unsure, you get a feeling, your gut clenches, speak up."

"Got it."

"Good." Then his hand went to his wrist. He hit the button to turn on his mic and spoke again. "Bravo in place."

"Check. Alpha in place," Drake returned.

"Charlie one mike out," Trey added.

A slight breeze blew off the Med and I inhaled. The salty air filled my lungs as I tried to control my heartbeat. Logan looked completely unaffected. As a matter of fact, in all the time I'd known him, this was the most relaxed I'd seen him.

He was in his element and I wondered if Drake felt the same thing. Then I wished I could see what he looked like. Once again I scanned the area—Beirut had come a long way since the eighties. The waterfront was beautiful and filled with equally beautiful people, beautiful cars, expensive restaurants, complete with an art gallery, and a music hall.

We stopped at an overlook and I leaned against the railing hoping I was pulling off the tranquil pose Logan had taken.

"See anything?" he muttered.

"Parking lot is full. There must be something going on at the art gallery."

"What makes you think that?"

"Music hall is at the end of the pier. The location of the parked cars suggests art gallery."

"Agreed."

A pinprick of awareness skidded over my skin and my scalp started to tingle.

"We're being watched."

Much to Logan's credit, he didn't move. The picture of professionalism.

"Flip your mic on," he said but still didn't look at me.

My shaking hand slowly went to my wrist and I did as he instructed.

"This is Bravo. We have eyes on us." Logan looked down at me and smiled. His brow went up in a reminder—*oh, right*, we were a vacationing couple. I returned his grin and he winked his approval.

"Bravo, this is Charlie, move to your secondary, we have your six."

Without a word, Logan offered me his hand. I took it and we were off on a lazy stroll down the busy pier.

"Where's it coming from?" Logan inquired.

"What?"

"Who's watching?" he clarified. "Where's it coming from?"

There were too many people, too many obstacles, too many places to hide. I had no idea who or where, I just knew the pinprick had turned into something bigger. The same feeling I'd had right before the ambush.

As if reading my mind, Logan squeezed my hand and said, "Here and now, darlin'. Push all the mental clutter away."

Then my eyes landed on a man, average height, average build, casual dress, baseball cap on. *Baseball cap.* I gazed around the crowd, nicely dressed, expensive, not a single man was wearing a cap.

"Our two o'clock. The man with the hat. He's looking down, head to the side. I can't see his face."

Not only was he too far away to clearly make out his features but he was actively trying to shield them.

"Good job," Logan mumbled. And as if the man heard, his head snapped up and his gaze locked onto mine.

Fuck.

Lore.

I didn't need to be any closer to know it was him.

"I have visual on the target. We've been made," I broadcasted.

Logan kept our slow, leisurely pace like I hadn't just announced that not only was Lore less than fifty yards from us but he knew he was being watched.

My hand started to move to my hip but Logan pulled me to a halt, spun me so we were face-to-face. His arms went around me and he shoved his face into my neck. "Slow your roll, darlin'. Not now, not here. We need him off the pier and away from all these people."

"But he knows we're watching."

"Yep."

"That's it? Just yep."

"That's it. Trust your team."

Trust my team.

"Bravo, you need to move." Drake's angry growl sounded in my ear which meant he was watching.

Logan ignored Drake's biting order. Instead, he stood to his full height, brushed the end of my ponytail over my shoulder, and smiled down at me. Teasing. Flirtatious. Stupid.

"Charlie, this is Bravo, advise when the target is street side."

"Copy, Bravo. He's giving you a wide berth. Coming straight to us."

"We're gonna let him walk right past us. Charlie's in position."

Something ugly grew in my belly as Logan spoke. We had multiple versions of the same plan. We had multiple versions of a backup plan. All of them involved Lore either being captured or killed, preferably captured, detained, and questioned. Multiple exfil locations. We had eyes in the sky, and God forbid, air support if needed. We were covered, we had good intel—as Lore was less than a few yards away and strolling right by us. We'd gone over every scenario the six of us could dream up.

Yet my belly was tight and was screaming at me that something wasn't right.

"R and S didn't see any guards?"

"Negative and as expected. He's never had an entourage."

No, he hadn't. Lore was a lone wolf.

"This is Charlie. Target is on the street. We're in position. You're good to move."

"Bravo-Four continue," Drake barked and it took me a moment to remember I was Bravo-Four.

"This is Bravo-Four," I returned. "Please repeat."

I was looking up at Logan, not understanding what Drake was asking.

"He wants you to continue your line of thinking," Logan whispered, which was pretty much useless because the mic on his throat was meant to pick up the slightest of sounds.

Drake obviously heard Logan's explanation therefore didn't repeat his request. With a nod of encouragement, Logan broke our embrace and started to move us in the direction of the street.

Not following protocol or answering Drake's inquiry, I spoke to Logan.

"Something feels off. He came out of a classy restaurant. One where the other patrons entering were dressed to the nines, and he's casual with a ball cap on. That doesn't fit. Next to that restaurant is an art gallery with what looks like some fancy show going on. The pier is jumping with people. That worries me. He's about splash and headlines."

Drake muttered a curse. Then in his strong, resolute way, he reported in. "TOC-one this is sierra-tango-one."

"Sierra-tango-one, challenge," the battle captain asked for verification.

"Linebacker. Complete. Five."

"Authenticate."

"Aftershock."

"Confirmed. Sierra-tango-one go for TOC-one."

"TOC-one this is Alpha-one actual. We need R-one-S at our location."

I quickly clicked off my mic and turned to Logan. "What's he doing?"

"Calling in backup."

"Why?"

"Because you just informed us Lore's gonna blow the pier."

Logan picked up the pace and I fought the urge to puke. *Oh, shit. Oh, no.* I'd fucked up.

"No, I didn't. I was just talking out—"

"You talking it out was informing us. That's how this works. Remember this, darlin'—always trust your gut. Always. Guns, tanks, airstrikes, those don't win the war. Information does. Knowing how to receive, process, and extrapolate that intel is what bests your enemy. That's what just happened, intel was processed and now he's calling it in."

"And if I'm wrong?"

"Then no one dies and it's a good day."

"...EOD. They go in soft." I caught the tail end of Drake's order.

"Copy that."

We were moving at a fast clip and once we cleared a gaggle of people, I saw him. Lore. I had him in profile—head still down, cell in hand, beelining it toward a junked-up, red Mazda. Totally out of place. I scanned for Trey and Luke, they were supposed to

in pain and my mind quieted. Training and discipline took over.

We were out in the open, exposed on the street, two men down, two more working on our wounded—visible, therefore in danger.

"We have less than a minute to move," I told the group, noting the sirens were getting louder. "Bravo-One, check for distal pulse and get ready," I instructed Liberty and scanned the area.

"You keep your eyes open and on me," Liberty commanded and from the corner of my eye, I saw her left hand reaching toward Trey's ankle while keeping her right on the tourniquet near his groin.

Shit, motherfuck.

"Pulse absent," Liberty informed me and without me needing to tell her, she stood to take my place, standing watch so I could get to Trey.

Her face was carefully blank. No signs of distress or unease. Her mask of indifference was damn impressive and settled an ache of worry I didn't realize had coiled in my gut.

But there it was, in the shitshow of a situation I was worried about Liberty—her response to the stress, her state of mind, her mental wellbeing. I shouldn't have been. She'd proven just how strong she was. Yet I couldn't stop the need to protect her in a much different way than I defend my teammates.

"Exfil one," I told her.

"Check." She wiped her hands on her jeans, smearing Trey's blood down her thighs. In a smooth draw, she unholstered her weapon, keeping it low but ready nonetheless.

Yeah, I needn't have worried. Despite her lack of battlefield experience, Lieutenant McCoy was far from stupid.

I knelt down and Trey's battered face twisted in pain.

"You wanna shot of morphine before we move?"

"Fuck no."

"We got half a mile, brother, it's gonna—"

"I'd prefer not to lose my fucking leg, just move."

I got my arm under Trey's back, the other under his knee, and hefted him up. His scream was both agony and a blessing.

"Bravo-two, go."

Luke moaned in pain as Logan lifted him. "Primary blast injury," Logan clipped. "Chest retractions. Globe rupture."

Fucking shit. None of that good. High-order explosives cause a supersonic shockwave. The overpressurization can lead to lung, abdominal, ear, and eye damage. Most of that being internal all but the globe rupture, which would be very noticeable. Meaning, Luke's eyes were fucked.

Shit, motherfucking, goddamn.

Matt radioed in the new information as Liberty guided us down the street, ducking into an alleyway that took us off the main street, giving us a modicum of safety. I didn't have to look behind me to know Matt was multitasking—updating the medevac and covering our six.

"Got company up ahead," Liberty shouted but didn't stop.

Our extraction point was not ideal. The industrial area had warehouses and not just a few—a lot of them, but we couldn't have a helicopter land in the street filled with civilians, tall buildings, and city traffic. So this was the best we could do. Anything could be going on in those buildings including nefarious shit that men would protect. It was a calculated risk, but one we needed to take.

"Keep going. Do not engage unless—"

Automatic gunfire rang out before I could finish. I was on my knees shielding Trey the best I could as I watched in horror as Liberty advanced, returning fire. Matt was at her side, both of them providing cover fire for Logan and me.

I would've been impressed at how Liberty seamlessly worked with Matt if my gut wasn't in knots—call it delayed reaction—but the situation hit with a force. This was not the worst position we'd been in, not even close. And it wasn't Liberty's nonexistent experience on the battlefield that had my stomach twisting painfully.

It was her.

Directly in the line of fire.

Standing between me and the bullets raining down.

There was something so wrong about the role reversal. It should've been me standing in front of her.

"Out," Liberty shouted and I watched her quickly and efficiently drop her spent magazine and slam a new one in, immediately reengaging.

The steady hiss of shots fired rang out and unease wrapped around my thundering heart. This was all fucking wrong. My jaw clenched and I blinked away the sweat dripping into my eyes as I followed behind Liberty and Matt. They operated as one as they moved us toward cover. Their position damn near suicidal, the thought had me battling gnawing fear. Not something I was accustomed to feeling—I was at home in the field, at ease. I controlled the chaos, but not with Liberty in front of me and in danger.

We ducked behind the metal shipping container as bullets pelted the box. Silently, Logan and I deposited our wounded and prepared to jump in the fight.

"Gun," Trey grunted.

I patted his ankle, found his backup, and shoved it in his hand. I hauled ass to the corner of the metal box and fought the urge to tell Liberty to go watch over Trey and Luke.

"Go." I slapped Matt on the shoulder. He immediately stepped back and seconds later, red smoke filled the air to mark our location.

Green good.

Red bad.

The Medevac crew would know they were coming into an active situation.

"Conserve what ya' got," I reminded Liberty and she slowed her return fire. "We got at least five minutes until we hear blades. Then we gotta get ourselves to that medevac. Let them dump their ammo. Make yours count."

"How's Trey?"

"Pissed off."

"And Luke?"

"Bitchin'."

I left out the part about what he was bitching about. The last thing I heard was him telling Logan he couldn't see out of his left eye and his right was foggy.

"I should've—"

"Not now," I barked.

Then like some fucked-up movie, Liberty and I crouched next to each other picking off bad guys as they became available.

"Jesus, how many of them are there?" she muttered. "They just keep coming."

She wasn't exaggerating. Every time one went down another came from the warehouse. I couldn't see what was happening on the other side of the container but I heard Matt and Logan exchanging fire as well.

"We picked the wrong fuckin' extraction point," Logan radioed.

"No shit," Liberty returned, and even in the clusterfuck of a situation, I couldn't stop the smile.

"Sierra-tango-one, this is Angel one. We see your smoke. ETA two minutes. Coming in hot. Prepare," the medevac called in.

Thank Christ.

"Angel one, this is ST-one. Be advised we're under heavy fire."

"Copy."

In all the missions I'd been on, I'd never been so goddamn happy to hear rotor blades and heavy artillery coming from the medevac. I had two wounded men—not the first time and unfortunately it wouldn't be the last. But it was the first time my ass clenched and my chest tightened.

In a moment of weakness, I glanced at Liberty and the tightness in my chest intensified. Fucking spectacular. Cool, calm, collected. Sexy as shit brandishing her firearm. Sweat beaded on her forehead and that was sexy, too. She was a mini-sized badass. I bet there were a lot of men who underestimated Liberty McCoy—all of them foolish.

"Hang tight, we're almost out of here."

Thank fuck, the whooshing of the rotor blades filled the air right before the medevac touched down.

I tapped Liberty on the shoulder. She looked at me with wide amber eyes. I jerked my chin, pointed to the helicopter, and even though it was doubtful she could hear, I still said, "Get us the fuck outta here."

Liberty took point and started to jog to medevac —weapon up, head swiveling, watching for anyone stupid enough to pop out of the nearby warehouses. Logan jogged behind Liberty with Luke, Matt behind him with Trey, and I brought up the rear.

There's something to be said about a confident woman. Never again did I want to be on the battlefield with Liberty. But that had nothing to do with her competence and everything to do with my heart unable to withstand the gut-clenching, crippling fear of losing her.

21

My hand shook as I picked up Trey's. The medics worked on him at a frantic pace. A few feet to my left, they'd ripped Luke's shirt and vest off and assessed him as well. I couldn't even look at him. Not with the trauma to his eyes. The membrane so swollen his pupil was barely visible. Not that seeing a piece of twisted metal in Trey's thigh was better, nor were the hundreds of tiny pockmarks on his face.

But his eyes were clear.

And they were locked onto mine, full of hate and anger, and fucking shit if I didn't deserve that look. I should've warned them earlier. I should've known Lore would make that play. I knew he was an extremist. His endgame would always be suicide.

Dying by his beloved explosives.

silent and broody—but he never left my side. Some part of him kept touching me, therefore I didn't miss the stiffness.

ONCE WE TOUCHED DOWN, everything happened in a flurry of commotion. Medical personnel swarmed, Luke and Trey were pulled from the Blackhawk and whisked away, Matt and Logan following close behind.

Much to my surprise, Drake stayed behind with me.

Which, considering Wick's fury, it was a good thing. We'd been escorted to the TOC where Wick had been holed up during the operation, undoubtedly watching in real-time as our body cameras transmitted to the large, wall-mounted screen that incidentally was now off.

"Trey and Luke?" Wick inquired.

Drake gave the general a list of their injuries. The manner in which he gave his report was a little scary—veiled, disguised, cloaked. He gave not a single emotion away. Not anger, not sorrow, not fear, nothing—blank.

Devoid.

Ice.

Wick's gaze came to me but his eyes didn't settle on my face. He did a sweep of my body while he asked, "And you?"

"I'm fine."

And I was. Other than the scrapes on the palms of my hands from Logan taking me down, I was uninjured.

"How'd you know?" Wick continued.

"That Lore was going to commit suicide?"

"No. Considering what we know about him, that was a given. How'd you know about the Mazda?"

I hadn't known—not until it was too late. Wasn't that the problem?

"The way he was racing to it. He saw us, me and Logan. If he wanted to escape, he would've hailed a cab. The street was busy, there were plenty to be had. But he was on a mission. Then when he spotted Luke and Trey, he didn't stop, he kept going even though that meant he was going in their direction."

"Why not a suicide vest?"

How the hell should I know?

"Maximum damage?"

Wick contemplated my answer before he nodded. "That's my thought as well."

"The R and S team?" Drake queried.

Holy hell. In the bedlam that had ensued, I'd forgotten about the art gallery.

"Insertion was a no-go." Wick's face twisted. "Can't say this isn't fucked, but it's true. That car bomb going off meant there was a mass exodus from the area."

"So, Liberty was correct. The gallery was set?"

Wick picked up the remote, turned the wall-mounted screen on, and after a minute of fiddling with his tablet, the monitor came to life.

"Drone footage," he clipped.

I watched in rapt horror as the Mazda exploded. Thankfully, a plume of smoke hid Trey and Luke being thrown several yards away. Wick hastily fast-forwarded the footage, the timestamp displayed twenty minutes had passed. We would've been on the helicopter and in the air by then. Seconds later, the gallery exploded, taking with it the restaurant, music hall, and most of the pier.

"Fuck," Drake growled. His eyes came to mine, filled with a concern I didn't understand.

"Casualties?" I asked.

Wick didn't answer but his brow lifted which was an answer but Drake would've missed this because his gaze hadn't left mine.

"Anyone from our team?"

been stabilized and it was urgent Trey was taken to Germany so they weren't delaying.

"Can I say goodbye?" I asked.

Logan's eyes shifted to mine and he gave me a small shake of his head. "Sorry, darlin'. No one's allowed back there, not even us."

"Right."

That killed, too.

"Tell them..."

Shit, what did I want Logan to tell them? Good luck? Hope you're not blind. Don't let the doctor amputate your leg? Sorry I wasn't up for a ball massage?

I didn't know what to say so I settled on, "Tell them I said thanks for saving my ass."

"We'll do." Logan smiled.

"And um, thanks to you, too. All of you. I appreciate you guys coming out to get me. And well, taking me back in. Appreciate the lessons."

"Anytime, ma'am."

"Seriously?" I wrinkled my nose. *We're back to this ma'am shit?*

Logan winked and pointed to the camera.

"Be well. Maybe I'll see you around sometime."

I turned to leave, sensing the three men needed

privacy to discuss whatever it was they discussed after a mission went sideways.

Reality was a bitch. But the truth was, as close as I felt to them, I wasn't one of them. I wasn't a teammate.

I was a tagalong.

"I'm sure we'll be seeing you," Logan called out.

Not wanting to turn around, I lifted my hand and gave them a wave over my shoulder.

22

When I finally saw Trey and Luke, I understood why Logan had lied to Liberty.

He was shielding her from seeing just how fucked-up they were. They'd removed the glass from Trey's face but now he looked like he had a hundred beestings. Luke's pretty much looked the same with the exception of his left eye. The membrane had swelled so badly you couldn't see the globe of his eye.

The sight was so difficult to look at, I was glad Liberty was gone even if we denied her saying her goodbyes.

She didn't need to see this.

Long after the C-17 was airborne, I stood on the tarmac staring into the inky black sky. It was fitting there was no moon, no light shining down, no glow, no ray of hope.

Nothing.

How the hell had everything turned to shit?

My hands went to my face. The pungent smell of ash and blood filled my nostrils, reminding me I needed to clean up and talk to Wick.

The faster the better.

Like a Band-Aid—swift and painless.

Who in the fuck am I kidding? There was nothing painless about leaving Liberty.

Fucking shit.

I stalked in the direction of the showers, every step heavy, taking me to the final moments I'd have with her.

Never should've touched her.

Never should've allowed myself time with her.

Never should've even looked at her.

Fuck.

The door slammed behind me as I entered the shower hut. The overwhelming smell of pine-scented cleaning agent did nothing to mask the must and mildew. Water ran in one stall, leaving four others available, and I quickly removed my boots and pulled off my shirt.

A moan filled the room and I reconsidered my

rinse-off. *Fucking perfect—some idiot having a combat-jack was not what I wanted to hear.* I decided I'd wait until after my debrief—blood, grit, and grime were better than listening to some fool whack his pud. I bent to pick up my boots when I heard it again, this time a whimper. Not one of pleasure—tortuous and painful. A sound that had my chest burning. I knew that whimper. I'd heard it before. I'd felt it seep into my soul as I held Liberty after a nightmare.

What the fuck?

Before I could think better of it, I stood half-naked in front of the shower curtain debating my next move. My hands shook with the need to console her. My heart conflicted—a burning desire to hold her but self-preservation told me to leave her be. Turn around, leave, and pretend I hadn't heard the woman who had captured my heart moaning in pain.

A sob tore from her and my decision was made. No way in hell could I walk away. I ripped open the flimsy, white plastic. Liberty turned, eyes red-rimmed and in shock.

"What—"

I didn't let her finish. I yanked the curtain closed, tagged her around the waist, and pulled her to my chest.

I closed my eyes and inhaled through my nose, trying my best to ignore her bare breasts against my chest, the soft curve of her hip under my palm, her wet hair tangling in my hand as I held her to me. All of it a full assault to my senses.

All of it bad and really goddamn great at the same time, especially when her thumbs pushed into the waistband of my cargos and she held on—pulling me to her. Not letting me go. Not fighting to push away.

Moments passed and Liberty relaxed in my arms.

Soft. Sweet. Sad.

Christ, the woman had me undone.

"What are you doing in here?" she whispered.

"What are *you* doing in the men's shower hut?" I returned.

"What?"

"The men's shower hut? Why are you in here?"

Her body jerked and I fought a groan. Overlooking our state of half-dressed and undressed was becoming increasingly difficult chest-to-chest with nothing between us there. But when she moved and her nipples brushed my bare skin, it wasn't difficult, it was goddamn torture.

"I didn't know."

"Babe, it's clearly marked on the door."

"I wasn't paying attention," she admitted.

"Right. Now you wanna tell me why you're in here crying?"

Liberty shook her head and I wanted to demand she stay still—every movement obliterated my good intentions. Shredded my decency. The need to touch her, run my hands over her slippery wet body, finally touch and taste every inch of her, grew at a rapid rate.

Her thumbs came out of my cargos, slid up my spine. Then her palms were flat on my back and on the move.

Christ.

Feather-light and unsure, her hands roamed my back. The feel of her touch woke every nerve ending. It wasn't an ache, it was a deep, intense hunger to take her—make her mine.

"I don't want to talk." Her soft voice barely heard over the pelting water.

Then her lips were on my chest, and much like her hands on my back, her kiss was timid and soft.

"Babe, that's not a good idea," I warned.

Liberty didn't heed my caution. Her confidence grew, her mouth moved, and this time the kiss over my heart was open-mouthed. She engaged her tongue and swirled it against my skin.

Fucking hell.

"We need to get out of the shower and get you dried off and dressed."

"No, we don't. We need to get these pants off of you."

"Not gonna happen, Liberty."

"Why not?"

"Because two seconds after my pants come off, I'm fucking you against the wall."

Her body shivered and my dick jumped.

Fuck.

"Works for me," she muttered, and to punctuate her response, her mouth found my nipple.

Another swirl of her tongue followed by a nip and my hips instinctively pressed deeper. Her moans that followed would be my undoing. My control was fast slipping, and the only hope I had of walking away was if I did it now. One more kiss, sound, or touch, and I'd snap.

"You don't want that—"

Liberty shoved away before I could stop her and took a step back, leaving every inch of her naked body visible. And being as I was undone, my eyes hungrily took their fill. Faint bruises still marred her otherwise flawless skin. Toned, lean muscle, full breasts, hips that were made for my hands to grip when she was on her knees in front of me.

All of her perfect for me.

A work of art.

"Don't tell me what I want." Her eyes flashed with anger and her shoulders snapped back. The change in her posture should've served as a warning. However, all it did was showcase her perky tits and tight nipples.

"Liberty—"

"Don't. Don't say my fucking name. Don't tell me how I feel, what I want, what I don't want. As a matter of fact, don't talk at all. Just fucking trust me. I don't say shit I don't mean."

Her chest heaved, her hands balled into fists, and her eyes narrowed. I should've walked away. But I couldn't, not from her. Not when all of her was on display, and not just her body. Every emotion played across her pretty face. Anger, hurt, desperation.

And that's when I knew I'd give Liberty McCoy anything she wanted. And if I'd thought that before, when I was holding her in my arms after a nightmare, I'd been wrong. It was there in the shower, water cascading over her face, her blinking it away, hair stringy and matted, naked, exposed, and asking me to trust her.

"What is it you want, baby?" I asked, not the least bit embarrassed my voice was thick with the desire I felt.

"I want your pants off."

Fuck.

Without thinking and overwhelmed, my heart slamming into my chest, my dick begging for freedom, I invited her. "Then take what you want, Liberty."

She didn't delay in taking what she wanted—and that was not only my pants off but her mouth on mine. Liberty's body collided with mine, my back hit the tiled wall behind me, her hands worked the snap and zipper of my cargos, and I swear to God, I heard every snick of the metal opening. Each hook and hollow that separated was one step closer to burying myself inside her warm body.

Her hand wrapped around my cock, her mouth pulled away from mine, and she moaned as she pumped my dick.

"Serious as fuck, baby, right here, right now, need you to tell me exactly what it is you want."

"You."

Through gritted teeth, I inhaled the best I could,

trying to keep what little semblance of control I had left and told her, "Need more than that."

Every muscle in my body burned with the effort it took to keep myself in check when all I wanted to do was dominate. I was damn near lightheaded as my cock throbbed in her hand.

"You. All of you."

"You have no idea what you're asking for."

"Then show me." Liberty's hand tightened around my cock, her eyes went soft, and reasonable thoughts fled.

My hands went under Liberty's ass and her hand fell away. I hoisted her up before I turned and pressed her back against the wall. One hand held her in place, the other glided between her ass cheeks, and finally slipped between her legs, finding her wet with more than water.

"Say no," I demanded, needing to give her a chance to stop this.

My fingers continued to tease her opening, Liberty's ragged breath came in choppy pants, my dick begged for release.

"I don't want to."

I could barely swallow past the lump in my throat but managed to ask one last time.

"Say no, baby." My finger dipped into her warm,

wet pussy and I lost sight of her because my eyes closed. Her low, guttural moan was the last straw. Deep, dark desire took hold.

"Too late," I growled, and with an urgency I'd never known, I pulled my hand away, took my cock in hand, lined myself up, and slammed home.

Then I found heaven in the form of Liberty's tight, wet pussy clutching my cock.

Her head was tipped to the side, eyes closed, back arched, arms around my neck, legs locked tight around my hips, and I was frozen. All that was her was wrapped around me, and fucking hell, it was beyond compare. Every part of me was hyper-aware of her.

"Mouth," I grunted. Liberty righted her head and opened her eyes in question. Fucking cute as hell. "I want your mouth when I fuck you, baby," I explained.

When her lips curved up into a smile, I swear to all things holy, I heard angels sing and sunshine warm my skin.

"Anything you want, Drake."

Oh, yeah, fuck yeah.

With our eyes locked, I didn't take her mouth. Instead, I unwrapped her arms from around my neck, lifted them above her head, and pinned them to the wall.

Once her pretty amber eyes sparked, I lowered my lips to her nipple and sucked it into my mouth. Her pussy pulsed, and I moved to the other side once she gave me more of the same. I lifted my head, then I took her mouth.

Hot, wet, and deep. There wasn't one thing sweet about our bruising kiss. And when I pulled my hips back and drove home, I didn't give her soft and tender. My pounding thrusts contradicted everything I felt inside. My body demanded raw and rough but my soul craved something different. The clashing emotions built higher, words I had no business saying simmered close to the surface. Requests I had no right to ask threatened to break free.

So I remained silent and took what Liberty offered—her body. I did it knowing this was goodbye. Not the last of many I wished it would be, but *the* last. There would be no "see you soon" when we finished. And the knowledge of that hit me with a force that would've brought me to my knees if Liberty's inner muscles weren't fluttering around my cock, and her tongue wasn't dueling with mine.

Liberty tore her lips from mine but didn't move far therefore when she panted, "Harder." I felt her demand fan across my lips, burn down my chest, and that heat didn't stop until it gathered low in my gut. With that blistering heat, I fucked her harder. Drive after drive, I listened to the sounds she made—the grunts and moans, the gasps for air as I pounded deep. So fucking sexy, I couldn't take much more.

The end drew near.

My hand went between us, I zeroed in on her clit, and I knew I found the right rhythm when her hips tipped and her moans turned into throaty groans pleading for more.

Fuck yeah.

From there, we raced to completion. Liberty's pussy tightened and pulsated around my cock, and in a rush of exquisite pain, my climax hit at the same time she fell over. The feel of our combined orgasm was too much. I slammed home, planted deep, and savored every last second of her pussy sucking me dry.

My head fell forward and I shoved my face into her neck, needing a few more minutes with her before the inevitable. More of her soft skin on my lips. More of her scent surrounding me. More of everything that would never actually be mine—no matter how badly I wanted her.

Liberty's hands twisted and I released them,

keeping mine braced on the wall above her head. Her hands fell over my shoulders. Her nails dug in and her breath hitched with a sound that was not sexy but final.

It might've made me a dick, but part of me was thrilled as fuck she felt it, too. The connection that was real and deep but any second would be severed.

The longer we stood skin-to-skin, so close I felt her heart pounding and I was sure she felt mine breaking, the harder it was to swallow those words. Plead for more time.

And I knew, fucking *knew*, when Liberty's lips found my forehead and in a gentle press, she gave me one last kiss. And with that kiss, she muttered the words, "I'll never forget you."

I knew what heartbreak felt like.

I knew I'd never recover.

And I knew I never wanted to.

There would never be another Liberty McCoy.

23

One would think that thirty days' leave would be welcomed—energizing even. After everything I'd been through, maybe even necessary.

However, ten days into my mandatory thirty-day leave, I was fed the fuck up. I was overcome with guilt. I was pissed off at everyone and everything. Which meant I felt like an ungrateful cow.

I loved my family. Loved my mom and dad, aunts, uncles, cousins, all the way down to the newest additions.

But if one more person asked me if I was all right, if I wanted to talk about it, or that I needed to get it out, I was going to lose my mind and commit hari-kari.

I was heartbroken, guilt ridden, and angry.

No, I wasn't all right. But that didn't mean I wanted to talk about it. And the more people pressured me to, the more I locked it away.

The way I was treating my dad made me a bitch. But the way I was shutting my mom out made me the worst kind of human. Every time my mom approached, apprehension shone clear as day on her face and I'd done that to her. I'd made our once-tight relationship distant. But I didn't have it in me to tell her what was going on.

It would kill her.

And my dad wasn't an option because he'd go ballistic. Which meant my uncles were off-limits because if I talked to them and not my dad, he'd be crushed.

So I was fucked. I had so much weighing heavy on me I could no longer carry it. And the only person I wanted was lost to me.

I'd felt the connection snap back in Golan Heights, with my back against the shower wall, his dick still inside of me, and cold water spraying my face.

I'd kissed his forehead and he broke the last piece of me left.

His response, unmistakable.

Now my parents' house was full of family and I

wanted to shrink away. I wanted to be invisible. I wanted to be anywhere but there. I'd even settle being back in the hands of a madman hellbent on revenge if it meant my loved ones stopped looking at me with sad eyes and frowns.

"Hey." My cousin Delaney stopped next to me and bumped her hip into mine. "You need to talk to Carter."

Without my permission, my heartrate spiked and my stomach clenched.

"About?" I asked, deciding my best option was to play dumb.

"Everything."

"Laney—"

"Nope. Nah-uh, I've seen you five times in ten days. There's something very wrong and each time I see you it's worse than the last. I'm not going to insult you and say that I understand because we both know I damn well don't. But he does. He knows what you're going through. You need to talk to him."

"Not insult me?" I huffed. "Right, and telling me I look like shit isn't insulting?"

"You know that's not what I said. And by you twisting my words, you've made my point. My cousin, my friend, my Liberty, doesn't purposefully *twist* words so she can be offended," Delaney hissed.

"Talk to him. If not for you, then for him. He's torn up inside watching you go through this and not reaching out."

"I see. This isn't about me, it's about your husband and making him feel better."

What the hell am I doing?

"You know that's not right," she whispered. Every word full of hurt.

"No, Delaney. What I know is, everyone needs to mind their own goddamned business."

Pain slashed through my cousin's features. Pain that I put there and I did it on purpose so she'd leave me alone.

What the hell is wrong with me?

Before I could turn and flee, a strong hand gripped my elbow. Reflexes took over and my fist swung. I connected with nothing but air, then I was wrapped in my cousin Jason's arms. His mouth at my ear, he growled, "Outside."

"Let me go."

"No fucking way. Outside."

"I can't believe you," I grunted.

"Either you walk outside, Moira, or I drag you out. How do you think your mom's gonna feel, she sees me hauling you out?"

She'd die a thousand more deaths.

"Fine. But seriously, this shit is jacked. Everyone needs to—"

"Out. Side," he grunted.

Jason's arms loosened and I ripped free, then I noticed all eyes were on me. My dad's full of hurt. My mom's, agony. My uncles', angry. My aunts', pity.

I stalked across the room, ignoring the stares. By the time I'd made it to the sliding glass door, I'd made my decision —after this, Jason was done with his macho bullshit and I was leaving.

Oh, and one more fucked-up thing that'd happened in the long line of fucked-up that was my life. The Army in all their infinite wisdom had transferred me from Washington state to a post in Savannah. Meaning I couldn't even escape back across the country since I was now stationed close.

I mean, what in the actual hell was that about? I needed thousands of miles between me and the people who I was hurting. It wasn't fair to them, I didn't want them witnessing my downward spiral. I needed time to pull my shit together.

Warm, fresh air hit my face. I took ten paces— yes, I counted—and whirled to give Jason a piece of my mind.

But I didn't find Jason.

Suddenly, I couldn't swallow. I couldn't breathe.

Dad, Lenox, Clark, and Jasper.

Nick, Jason, Carter, Ethan, and Jackson.

Nine men.

All of them towered over me. All of them wore alarmingly menacing scowls. All of them loved me to the depths of their souls.

Because I knew they loved me, I lashed out.

"This is bullshit."

"You're fucking up, baby cousin," Nick started. "Ten days we played it soft waiting to see if you'd come around. You're not. Time's up. You need a reminder."

"How big of all of you to give me *ten* days." Then because I was feeling especially vicious I went for the kill. "Funny, not too long ago another group of men treated me to ten days as well. What happens now? Are you guys gonna strap me down, too, try to drown me? Maybe you'd prefer to start with the electrocution. I'm assuming because y'all are my family you won't strip me down to my skivvies. But I have to say, the technique is oddly effective."

My gaze sliced through the men. Not one flinch, not even a blink.

"Feel better?" Jason asked.

"Better?" I laughed. "Yeah, I feel great."

I highly doubted they missed my sarcasm though again there was no reaction.

Movement in the house caught my attention. Brice had the front door open and was ushering my aunts, cousins, and the kids out of the house.

What the fuck?

My eyes went to my dad and I asked, "Where's everyone going?"

Dad didn't answer but Jason continued, "You should've known we weren't gonna leave you to hide."

"That's fucking rich coming from you. The man who locked himself away in the very house his wife died in and shut all of us out when we reached out. Including me, *Cousin.* You told me to mind my own business. Return the favor and butt out of mine."

That was so low, so fucking wrong my stomach roiled and bile creeped up my throat.

Please God, forgive me.

"Yep. I sure did. One of my biggest regrets. Turned my back on everyone I loved and wallowed in self-pity until I was drowning in it. Pushed everyone away and in the process of doing that, *hurt* everyone I loved," Jason growled, and to make his point, his arm swept the area indicating our family.

That was a sock to the gut.

My eyes landed on Ethan. I don't know what I expected to find but it wasn't his green eyes hard with anger. He was one year older than me. Out of all my male cousins, I was probably closest to him, he'd been my protector growing up. Not that all of us cousins hadn't stuck together, but Ethan and I shared a bond. I was the first to know that his daughter Carson was on the way. He'd trusted me with that. At sixteen, when he was scared as hell, he'd turned to me and told me that he'd knocked up his girlfriend and no matter what, he was keeping the baby. And damn if he didn't step up.

All of my cousins were big strong men, but it was Ethan I admired the most. It was he who was the most selfless. And right then, Ethan staring at me in disgust shattered my heart.

No, he wasn't going to protect me, he wasn't going to help me out of this bullshit. And that hurt me more than Jason dragging me out to the porch. It hurt worse than my uncles looking at me like I was a disappointment.

"You don't understand." I was looking directly at Ethan but I meant those words for everyone in attendance.

"You're right, I don't. Because you won't let me," Ethan returned.

"I don't want you to," I seethed. "I don't want you to know what a failure I am."

"Mimi, the last thing you are is a failure." That name had me taking a step back and wrapping my arms around my middle. When Carson was a toddler, she couldn't say Moira, so she called me Aunt Mimi.

I loved that name, it was special. Nick and Meadow's kids called me Mimi. Soon, Hudson and baby Emma would be talking and I wanted them to call me Aunt Mimi, too.

"Why can't everyone just leave it alone? Let me work things out in my head myself."

"That's not the way it works," Carter told me and the hair on the back of my neck stood up.

There were so many reasons why I'd been avoiding Carter. The biggest were Drake, Trey, and Luke. All three of them he served with, was close to, and considered brothers. Two of whom were seriously injured when I failed. One I was more than halfway in love with.

The other reason, I knew he knew what it was like to be captured and tortured. He knew and he'd want to talk about it.

I didn't.

I wanted to shut down, be left alone, and forget.

"Liberty, look at me," Carter demanded.

My gaze went to him, and as always, it amazed me how much he looked like his father. Carter Lenox Sr. and Carter Lenox Jr. were damn near identical. Only now, my Uncle Lenox has salt-and-pepper hair instead of Carter's dark. Same build, same eyes, same posture, same everything.

"You know, I understand. You know I've been where you were and I've been where you are now. This is not something you keep inside, lock down deep, and file away for another day. If you don't unpack it now, you'll be stuck. Your head will keep going back there. Those nightmares you're having, they'll get worse."

My jaw started to ache as I clenched my teeth. I couldn't believe my dad had shared I was having nightmares. I knew he'd heard them—I was staying in his house, he'd come in a couple of times to wake me. But I'd refused to talk about them.

Traitor.

"I was fucking scared as hell," Carter told me. "Scared when the gun was pointed at my head. Scared when I was alone in a cell after a beating. Fuck, Liberty, there wasn't a moment I wasn't scared. I knew how close I was to dying. I knew all the shit I'd left unsaid at home. I knew that if I died, my team was worse off. All I could do was fucking take it. No control, my hands zip tied, my ankles chained, no way to fight back—and for a man like me to have to suck it the fuck up and be at the mercy of animals, it fucked with my head. I know what that shit does to your head. I'm telling you, you need to get it out."

"It's not that easy," I muttered.

"It damn well is."

"Maybe for you, but not for me."

"Why? Why not for you?"

"It's just not. It's complicated."

"Fuck complicated, Liberty. Jesus Christ, spit it the fuck out and stop acting like there are not five of us standing here who know what you've been through. You're damn lucky, you know that. You have people close, people who love you, people who would do anything for you who have been in your shoes. Exactly in them. We've all been there and—"

"No, you haven't!" I shouted. "You haven't been in my shoes because what happened to you—to them," I pointed at my dad and uncles, "that was an act of war. What happened to me was fucking personal. It's their fault." I jabbed in my dad's direction. "And you, Cousin, should be thanking me, because I took a beating that was meant for you. You were the first choice. You were the one they wanted, but when they couldn't get to you, they took me instead. The sins of the father. They took something from him, so he was taking something precious from them.

"So, don't tell me you fucking understand because you've never taken a beating for this family. You've never looked into a man's eyes while he pinned you down, his hands around your throat, strangling you—choking the life out of you while he told you you were too dirty to fuck because you were a McCoy. Never has a man left you for dead because your father killed his. But you see, Cousin, I have. I took that—his anger, his revenge—and I took it for your dad and for you. I had those hands around my throat. So, no, you don't get to tell me you know what it's like."

I was so lost in my head I missed the change. I missed the nine men go from pissed and hurt to off-the-charts furious. I missed my dad's swift intake of oxygen. I missed my Uncle Lenox's eyes flash in pain. I missed all of this because I realized that I wasn't the worst daughter. I wasn't even the worst human, I was simply a fucking bitch, because there it was—I blamed my dad and uncles.

I blamed them for every second of torment I endured, for every punch, every drop of water, every zap of voltage that seared through me, for five men dying, and for my fear.

I blamed them because I needed to.

I needed to do something.

Anything.

Because I had nothing.

24

"What the fuck?" my dad rumbled.

I said nothing.

"Walk me through the part about me being the first choice." Carter's voice had gone hard, his face had blanked, and damn if it didn't remind me of Drake. How easy it was for him to slip into his role as a SEAL.

"Classified."

"Call Drake," Lenox barked.

"He won't tell you, either."

"The fuck he won't."

"He won't and you know it."

I prayed I was right. Besides, Drake had enough to worry about with Trey and Luke being injured. He didn't need Carter in his face.

Carter was studying me in a way I didn't like. He was smart, too smart, and I watched as he worked through something. When he nodded I knew I wasn't going to like his conclusion.

"Dad, dig through her last mission. Where she was, what the objective was, who she was with. If this was personal, that ambush was a setup."

"Did that. Dead end. Reports are bullshit," Lenox answered.

Carter's eyes narrowed on me. "Why the cover-up?"

"There's no cover-up. It's classified."

"What units are at Hunter?"

No, no, *no,* Carter was getting too close.

Clark rattled off the different battalions who called Hunter Army Airfield home while my uncle listed the different tents from Airmen, Marines, Coast Guardsmen, to the soldiers. I had to admit, it was a little scary he knew them off the top of his head. But what was scarier was the way Carter scrutinized the information so quickly.

"Un-fucking-believable," Carter seethed.

"Don't," I pleaded, knowing he was putting everything together. "Leave it alone."

"What unit, Liberty?"

I remained silent—there was no correct answer.

My dad and uncles had worked under the veil of secrecy when they were in the Army. Their unit was classified as a logistical unit, when it was anything but. Being former members of the combat application group, they'd know. Carter being a former SEAL, he'd figured it out.

"Fuck this!" I shouted. "Leave it, Carter. I don't need this shit on top of everything else. You might not think so, but I'm dealing. I've left it behind me. I'm fine. Or I was until all of you thought that interrogating me was your best option. Now, you've pissed me off."

"You're not dealing with it," Carter pushed. "You've—"

"Stop telling me what I'm doing. I'm so sick and tired of people telling me what I am and what I'm not doing. First Drake, then Logan, Dad, Mom, you, fucking hell. Leave me alone."

"Not gonna happen." My Uncle Jasper entered the conversation. His tone took me by surprise. I'd never heard him angry.

"What do you want from me?"

"The truth."

"The truth? You want it, fine." I welcomed the pain my nails caused digging into my palms. I needed to feel something other than all the ugly shit eating at me. I was not this person, I didn't lash out, I didn't hate my family, I didn't hurt people.

"I hate myself. I hate that I was weak. I hate that I was afraid. I hate that my team died because of me. I hate everything. Is that the truth you wanted? Or did you want to know all the ways I failed to protect my men? How I couldn't get out of my head fast enough when I was getting the shit beat out of me and I felt every fucking punch. I'm not strong, I couldn't do what you all taught me. Fuck!"

My dad broke away from the others and stalked toward me. I put my hand up to stop him, I had no words because I couldn't breathe.

Weak. Why was I so weak?

"Moira, I need you to listen to me." Suddenly my dad sounded oddly defeated. His words so pained, knowing I did that to him, I wanted to crumble. I wanted to beg for forgiveness. "There's not one weak thing about you. Everything you're feeling is normal."

"You call this normal, Dad? I want to crawl out of my skin."

"I know you do."

"Why can't I make it stop?"

"Because you're avoiding it. The flashbacks, the nightmares, the guilt—they don't just go away. And the more you try to push them away and pretend you're not feeling those things, the worse it gets. It's not healthy, sweetheart. You have to unload it. And if you can't trust us to take it, then we'll find someone for you to talk to. But, Moira, you have to talk about it. All of it. Even the uncomfortable shit."

I bit my cheek until I tasted blood. This was too much. The bile I'd been swallowing rushed up and I turned just in time to empty my stomach on my parents' lawn. Once that started, the seal was broken and I couldn't stop the sob that ripped through me.

A strong arm went around my stomach and a hand gathered my hair away from my face. Warm, familiar arms that had held me thousands of times.

"So proud of you, Moira. So damn proud. Me and your mom couldn't have asked for a better daughter," my dad cooed as I continued to heave. "But more than that, couldn't be any more proud of the woman you became. So strong, my girl."

"Weak," I said and spit the saliva that pooled in my mouth. "I killed them."

"You didn't kill anyone."

"They died because of me. Same thing."

"Not even close."

My dad shuffled, then pressed a paper towel in my hand. I wiped my face but remained bent forward, afraid there was more poison churning in my stomach.

"When'd you go through SF school?" Dad asked.

Yeah, once Carter had started down that line, there was no hiding it.

"Last year," I admitted.

"How many missions?"

"Two."

Dad made a sound that was halfway between a growl and grunt that had every muscle in my body tightening. Deciding I was not going to throw up again—but more than that, not wanting to be in my father's arms while he was vibrating with anger—I stood and pushed away.

Carter was staring at his dad in silent communication.

Then just like I wasn't standing there, the men took over.

"Bait or traitor?" Carter weirdly asked.

"Depends on the target. If they needed him disposed of off the books—she was bait. If he's low-level priority, then someone sold her out," Lenox returned.

"Pull up our ops," my dad instructed. "Family, friends, anyone who would hold a grudge."

"SF's tight. Their chain is going to be limited," Clark added.

"True. But flights have to be arranged, gear moved, that's not kept in-house. A clerk could've seen her name on a manifest and easily given it up," Jasper said.

"I want satellite—"

"Stop!" I cut my dad off. "This is exactly why Wick wanted you guys to stay out of it."

Wrong thing to say—way wrong.

"Come again?" Dad grunted.

"This is Army business. You need to stand down. If not for Mom, then for me. You poke your nose in this, he'll know I ran off at the mouth and said too much. I could face a court martial."

"Nothing will touch you or your mom."

"You say that, but it will when the four of you dig and find you don't like the information you've found. Then when you go off on a mission of destruction and get your ass in a sling, it will be me, Mom, Aunt Lily, Aunt Reagan, and Aunt Emily who will be swinging in the wind. And if you pull Carter into this, then Delaney and Emma are out there. Not to mention Drake, Trey, Matt, Logan, and Luke. Wick will never believe they didn't take Carter's back. And right now, with Trey and Luke and what happened to them, I think they've had enough of my shit to last a lifetime. They don't need to get fucked again because of me."

"You were in Beirut with them?" Carter asked.

Well, fuck me running, now I was spewing out information.

"Carter—"

"Serious as shit right now, Liberty, spill."

That's when I spilled. And I did it because Carter was worried about his friends. I did it because he was looking at me with his green eyes imploring, and after all the screwed-up, mean stuff I'd said, I felt obligated to tell him about his brothers.

When I was done running down what I felt comfortable telling them, without breaking operational security—too much, Carter was staring at me. Then he smiled, and when he did, his face lit and he shook his head.

"Christ. I'm not sure if I'm thoroughly impressed my baby cousin's a badass Special Forces soldier or if I'm furious you were sent out with them a week after you'd been captured and tortured. But what I am sure of is, I'm proud as fuck."

"What? Did you miss the part where I told you I warned them too late?"

Carter's smile died and his eyes went hard. "No,

I heard everything you said. Including the part where you warned them and they didn't beat feet. I know Trey, he wouldn't have ignored your warning unless he thought he had time to take the shot. He miscalculated and that's on him. Not you. And what you did, helping him probably saved his leg."

"Logan would've had it covered if I wasn't there."

"No doubt he would've. But he didn't, you did." Carter's posture softened before he continued. "Pissed you didn't tell me this sooner. Pissed Drake didn't call me to tell me what happened. I understand, but I'm still not happy Trey and Luke are hurt and that was kept from me."

"I'm—"

"Don't want you to apologize—as I said, I get it. I understand all of it, including why you were taken and what happened. But you're flat-out wrong."

"I don't know how to talk about it," I admitted.

"Open your eyes," Jason said and my gaze sliced to him. He'd been so quiet I'd forgotten he was there.

"What?"

"That's what you told me when I was sitting in the cold, dark, lonely house beatin' myself up. Holding on to guilt like a security blanket. Blaming myself for everything that happened with Kayla.

When you tried to talk to me and I shut you down, you told me to open my eyes and look around. That there were people who loved me and wanted to help. Then you told me to look in the mirror because I looked like shit." His lips twitched and he smiled. "I think the day you stopped by I hadn't showered in something like five days. I did look like shit. Bet I stunk, too, but you kindly kept that to yourself."

"When I came to you bawling my eyes out—literally crying like a baby," Ethan started, "you told me I didn't have anything to worry about. That after Mom and Dad kicked my ass for knocking up Chrissy, they'd see me through. Then you told me you had my back no matter what and you'd help me raise my kid. But it was you reminding me that our family always sticks together and no one would let me fall, that's what gave me the courage to tell Mom and Dad."

"Did she tell you to do that at my housewarming party, or was that your bright idea?" Nick chuckled.

Ethan gave him the middle finger but didn't take his eyes off me. "Now, the first time in your life you need me and you don't trust me enough to take your back. That's jacked."

"You've had my back more times than I can count," Jackson said. "To this day, you're the only one who knows I was thinking of dropping out of the academy. I failed a time trial, my knee was fucked, and I was worried about failing another and I was close to quitting."

"Seriously?" my Uncle Clark asked. "You never talked to me about that."

"Didn't need to, Dad. Liberty sorted my shit. She told me to suck it up. Then she told me to man-up and stop acting like a baby. Failing one timed run didn't mean shit. After she was done calling me names she reminded me that Clarks, Walkers, Lenoxes, and McCoys never quit. Never, no matter what. We push through. And if there ever comes a time we can't walk over that finish line, someone will carry you. Of course, she was right. That time, she carried me. But, Cousin, now you're not letting me carry you."

"You got a lotta people who love you." Lenox's deep, rough voice hit me and an ache in my chest started to grow.

"I know," I whispered.

"A lotta people who have your back."

"I know."

"No, Liberty, you don't know. If you did, first thing you would've done was call us all together and unpacked the weight you've been carrying around."

"I didn't want you to know."

"Know what? That you're seriously tough? Girl, we know that. Know that while you were in the hands of a terrorist you were hit, shocked, tortured, starved, bled, slept in the dirt, cuffed, kicked? Girl, we know that, too. Me, your dad, Jasper, Clark, Carter, we've *been* there. That's the part you're forgetting. Because we've been there, we know what happened to you, so we know down to our souls that you aren't just tough, you're *goddamn* tough. You've entered into a club that no one wants to be in. But fuck, girl, you survived and you did so with honor. So, darlin', what didn't you want us to know?"

"I didn't want my dad to live with that knowledge," I whispered. "Didn't want Mom to have nightmares about it. Didn't want any of you to look at me differently."

I heard Dad's audible intake of air and I glanced from Uncle Lenox to him to see tears in his eyes.

Tears.

"Moira." My dad's voice hit my ears, thick with anguish. One word and I was gutted. "Since the day you told me you were enlisting, I've lived with the knowledge that my daughter had grown into an exceptional woman, one who answered the call, one who would willingly lay down her life for God and country. That knowledge was hammered home when I was told you'd been taken. As your uncle already told you, I don't need details to know. As far as your mom's concerned, other than you, she's the strongest, most capable woman I know. And that's saying a lot because your aunts are mighty strong. But your mother spent years in the field, she doesn't need you to tell her what happened to know her daughter's in pain. All she needs is for you to let her be your mother.

"Somethin' else." Dad stopped and swiped a tear from his face, cleared his throat, then pinned me in place with his eyes. "Wish I could've seen you through SF school. Not so I could tell you how proud I was of you—because you already know I am. Not so I could tell you how much I love you—because you know I do down to my soul. But, so I could've told you that every day you inspire me to be a better man."

I took in the men around me, and the reality of my situation slammed into my chest and stole my breath. Red, hot, searing shame burned me to my core.

Nine men.

Dad, Lenox, Clark, and Jasper.

Nick, Jason, Carter, Ethan, and Jackson.

The best men I knew.

"I'm sorry. So sorry. I shouldn't have... I didn't mean.... God. I'm broken. I can't. Please, I need help. I can't—"

Before I could say another word, I was in my dad's arms. Not in an embrace, but cradled in his arms like a child. Like he'd done so many times. His lips pressed against my forehead.

"Swear to you, Moira, we'll get you all the help you need."

After a few minutes, I was pulled from my dad and found myself in my Uncle Lenox's strong arms. From there I was passed around. Each man offering me strength, but more than that they were telling me without words how much they loved me.

When they were done I caught my Uncle Jasper's gaze. His smile was small but approving, he tipped his chin and winked.

They had faith in me, even if I couldn't find it myself.

They'd see me through.

They always did.

25

I listened to the hum of the tattoo machine and relaxed into the incessant sting of the needle dragging against my back as the artist finished the fine lines and detail work. The bite of discomfort doing nothing to push the never-ending pain of losing Liberty out of my head.

Nothing is working.

WITH EACH POUNDING STRIDE, my muscles burned, my chest expanded with each breath, my ears throbbed from the blaring death metal I had cranked up to full volume.

Liberty. Just a fleeting thought.

I ran harder, faster, keeping a brutal pace and trying to erase her from my memory.

Nothing is working.

With the high fence and barbwire noting I'd reached the far end of the annex in sight, I slowed to a stop and turned to the surf. The sun was beginning to rise, the sky painted with an orange hue, the beauty of it only pissing me off more.

My hand automatically went over my heart to soothe the excruciating agony the mere thought of her invoked.

Christ.

My head tipped back, my eyes closed, salty air filled my lungs, and visions of Liberty against the tile wall, moaning in pleasure crowded my mind.

Two weeks since I'd last seen her, yet I could still see, smell, taste, and feel her.

Heartbreak.

"Fuck!"

My shouted curse was met with silence.

I turned back to the compound and while my muscles protested the punishing sprint, I welcomed the pain.

"HAYES!" Command Master Chief Brenner called my name when I passed his office.

I stopped and leaned back so I could peer into the room.

"What's up?"

"Need a minute. Come in and close the door."

Brenner remained seated behind his cluttered desk when I entered. His face was devoid of expression, but his fists resting on the papers in front of him gave away his agitation. Not that I could guess what his tension stemmed from, unless something had happened with Trey or Luke.

"What's going on? Trey and Luke okay?"

"Have a seat." Not liking his tone but wanting to get this talk over with so I could head to the gym, one of the many strenuous ways I tried to occupy my time, I sat.

The silence stretched to uncomfortable. Brenner's icy stare remained vacant, body taut, jaw clenched.

Something was seriously fucked.

"Spit it out," I demanded.

"I don't even know how to start."

"Start what?"

Brenner shuffled some papers around then

handed me a Manila envelope. I took it, opened the flap, and pulled out the contents.

I turned the papers over and my lungs seized.

"What the fuck?" An eight-by-ten image of me hugging Liberty. We were standing next to five flag-draped boxes. I flipped to the next picture and I was kissing the top of her head. "What the fuck are these?"

"There's a recording as well."

"Come again?" I asked and looked at the next picture. My hand was on Liberty's lower back as I helped her into my hut.

"A...um...recording."

"You said that already. A recording of what? And who the fuck took these?"

"Anonymously reported."

"Reported?"

"Fraternization."

That one word sliced through me like a hot blade and my vision blurred as fury rose.

"Are you fucking kidding me?"

"'Fraid not."

"And the recording?"

"It's bad, brother." Brenner shifted in his chair and averted his gaze.

What the fuck? Had we said something on the radio that could be misconstrued as misconduct?

"I wanna hear it."

"You really don't."

"Yeah, Brenner, I do. You got it, fire it up."

"You need to trust me, Hayes. Nothing good will come from you hearing it. We need to figure this out and start damage control. The troop commander—"

"Right now, I don't give a flying fuck about damage control. I want to hear the recording."

"You need to care. This could end your career and Lieutenant McCoy's."

Red hot rage bubbled to the surface and I shot to my feet.

Fuck my career. Nothing was going to touch Liberty.

"Play. It."

With an irritated sigh, Brenner turned to his laptop.

A moment later my world stopped.

"I want your pants off." Liberty's voice filled the room.

No, fuck, no.

"Then take what you want, Liberty." There was a pause before I heard my gruff, lust-fueled demand over the sound of the shower. "Serious as fuck, baby, right here, right now, need you to tell me exactly what it is you want."

"You."

"Need more than that."

"You, all of you."

Christ, hearing Liberty tell me she wanted all of me was a dagger to the heart. Too bad she hadn't meant those words. Just hearing them again made the heartbreak intensify.

"You have no idea what you're asking for."

"Then show me."

"Say no."

My heart pounded against my ribs and I was choking for oxygen. This couldn't be fucking happening.

"I don't want to."

"Say no, baby. Too late. Mouth, I want your mouth when I fuck you, baby."

"Anything you want, Drake."

"Enough!" I shouted and my hands went to my hair yanking handfuls until my scalp tingled. "Who the fuck recorded that?"

"Told you, it was sent anonymously to the troop commander."

"Did anyone trace that shit?"

"Sure did, came from an unsecure computer in

the exchange. No way to track who used the computer."

Fucking shit.

Anger rolled through, my mind still muddled with Liberty's cries of pleasure. Someone had taken the single best moment of my life and turned it into an X-rated shit show for my commanding officers to hear. Moans and private words, meant for just the two of us had been shared and exploited.

"What do I need to do to keep Liberty clear of this?"

"Not sure you can."

Wrong answer.

"So, what, this shit was just emailed over? No demand, no explanation? Nothing?"

"Nothing. Lennard is recommending we handle this in-house. A summarized article 15, fourteen days duty, and leave it at that."

In other words, sweep it under the rug, saving me from an article 135, a possible dismissal, forfeiture of monies owed, and the possibility of two years in the brig.

"And Liberty?"

"The *lieutenant's* not Lennard's concern. Saving your ass is the only thing he's worried about." The censure in Brenner's tone wasn't lost on me because he didn't want me to miss how pissed-off he was.

That makes two of us, buddy.

My throat clogged as I looked around Brenner's office. Awards. Team flag. A hand-carved trident proudly displayed.

Brotherhood.

Honor.

Was I willing to walk away? Damn near twenty years of my life had been dedicated to the cause.

"You ever been in love?" I asked Brenner.

"You know damn well I'm married."

"I'll assume that's a yes."

"You'd assume right."

"You ever known me to fuck up?"

"Not sure where you're going with this, but as they say, there's a first time for everything and I'm feeling like this might be the first time I witness Drake Hayes make a monumental fuckin' mistake."

I didn't make mistakes, especially not monumental ones.

Except one—allowing Liberty McCoy to walk out of my life.

And right here, right now, I was going to rectify that.

"I'll take the full hit, but I want Liberty cleared. However Lennard needs to do that."

"You cannot be fucking serious."

"Deadly."

"You take this hit, it could lead to a dishonorable discharge."

"I'd prefer honorable, considering I've given a lot of years to this country. Not to mention, the amount of blood I've spilled means I've earned it. I'll even take an other than honorable if necessary. But the bottom line is, I don't give the first fuck what my DD-214 reads as long as Lieutenant Liberty McCoy is shielded. However that happens, I don't care."

"Brother, that's—"

"Tell me—you love your wife, would you let her ass swing in the wind?"

Brenner didn't answer, he didn't need to. I knew he would never cover his own ass and leave his wife unprotected.

"You're gonna throw everything away for this woman."

"Same as you would for your wife," I answered.

"She's my wife," Brenner argued.

"Don't need a piece of paper binding me to her for me to know, I'd fight and die for her. Don't need her to wear my ring or take my name to know that I'd give up everything for her. And I mean everything, Brenner. This shit doesn't touch her. She's a damn good soldier. She's earned her commission and then some.

"And when you take this back to Lennard, remind him that less than a week after she'd been held hostage, beaten, tortured, yet she still went out with us on an op. One that went to shit, yet she still had the wherewithal to get us clear of it. Then you remind him that during her time in captivity, where she was fucking tortured, she didn't break. She took it. She endured the fiery pit of hell and gave up nothing.

"With all of that, you tell me, does that sound like a woman, a soldier, worth saving? Because to me, Liberty McCoy is the very definition of a United States military officer."

"Fuck," Brenner clipped. "We can do this another way, without you taking the hit."

Peace settled over me when I looked at the command master chief. A man who I'd served with for years. Good. Solid. Honorable.

I tried again. "You know damn well, the higher ups are gonna want someone's ass for this. I'm asking for them to bury this, protect Lieutenant McCoy, and make it go away. I will gladly take the hit if this never touches her."

Brenner let out a low whistle and shook his head. "I don't know if—"

"Tell Lennard to get in touch with General Wick. Between the two of them, they can entomb this shit and it will never be found. And I'd suggest someone go to Golan Heights and find the mother-fucker who recorded me and my woman."

Brenner continued to stare at me in silence. I wasn't sure what he was looking for but I was done.

"Anything else?"

Brenner shook his head and looked to the ceiling. "Christ, Hayes."

When he said no more I offered, "You need my badge?"

"Fucking. Christ." His eyes came to mine, regret clear.

That was a yes.

I reached into my pocket, shuffled Liberty's dog tags to the side, and fished my plastic ID badge out and held it out to Brenner. Once I handed it over, I would no longer have access to the compound.

Surprisingly, the pain of that knowledge didn't begin to touch the constant ache in my chest.

"You'll be on mandatory leave pending an investigation," Brenner told me. "Pay restriction will start immediately."

"Understood."

"Last chance to change your mind."

"Not gonna happen."

Brenner finally took my credentials and I swallowed the lump in my throat. Carter's words came to me in a rush, *when you're in you're the best, when you're out you're a pest.* That was what he'd said to me the day he separated from the teams.

Fucking hell.

I'd no longer be welcomed in the house I'd bled for.

"Hate this," Brenner muttered.

"Me, too. But I see no other way."

"I know you don't. That's why I'm gonna work my ass off to protect her."

Brenner would. He was a good man.

"Much appreciated."

Without sparing him another glance, I went for the door. I didn't take a full breath until I made my way through the building and hit the parking lot.

Fucking shit.

Gone.

In the span of twenty minutes I'd lost everything.

That wasn't true. I'd lost it fourteen days ago.

26

"How are you?" I asked into the phone.

"Fucking miserable," Trey grouched.

He totally sounded it.

"When are you being discharged?"

"Today. After I piss in a cup, they poke me fifty-two more times, and Nurse Ratched watches me give myself a sponge bath and I don't fall over."

"She can't be that bad." I laughed.

Or at least I hope Trey had exaggerated when he spent fifteen minutes bitching about the nurse. She sounded awful, but in her defense, I doubted Trey was a very good patient.

"There are no words to describe how horrible she is," he returned.

"Well, then, it's good you're blowing that popsicle stand. How's Luke making out?"

"Oh, Luke's peachy, he's got some leggy blonde over at his place nursing his ass back to health."

My heart constricted at the reminder that women fall all over themselves to get to SEALs. It had been three weeks since I'd seen or heard from Drake and every night when I went to bed, my body craved his. Then as I drifted to sleep, in the space between awake and when the nightmares started, I would dream of him. And in the morning, sleep deprived and desolate, I wondered if he had someone lying next to him, easing the loneliness.

I'm sure he did.

"Is that jealousy I detect?" I teased.

"Fuck yeah, it is."

I couldn't stop my burst of laughter. "Hopefully, you can find your own leggy blonde to nurse you back to health tomorrow."

"Don't like blondes. In my experience, blondes aren't more fun, they're more drama. I prefer my women no-maintenance and drama-free."

"Good luck with that, friend. You're searching for a unicorn."

"No shit. There's a reason I'm wild and free."

There was a beat of silence and when I heard Trey sigh, I braced. "Have you talked to Drake?"

Hell to the no, we aren't going there.

"No, and I'm gonna do you a solid and be no-drama and no-maintenance and tell you straight out, I don't want to talk about Drake."

"Then why did you call?"

"To check on you," I huffed.

"Right, so now you know my ass is sitting in a hospital bed in Bethesda, with new hardware including a rod, two nails, and a few screws. It hurts like fuck. And the muscle relaxer they're giving me makes my dick tingle, so I refuse to take it. So, let's talk about you."

I bit back my retort about not needing to hear about his dick tingling, because frankly I didn't want to say the word dick to Trey.

Instead I told him, "Nothing to talk about. Told you already I PCS'd to Savannah and my leave was extended another week."

"Cut the shit, Liberty, and tell me how you're doing."

Since Trey wasn't going to give up, I decided to give him something.

"I'm seeing someone," I admitted.

"Come again?" Trey's growl took me by surprise.

My back snapped straight and I was happy Trey couldn't see me because I was seriously hurt. It had taken me a few visits with Dr. Barlow to understand I had nothing to be ashamed of.

"Who is he?" Trey asked and I frowned.

"He? What are you talking about?"

"You said you were seeing someone. Who is he? Old boyfriend or you'd—"

"Seriously?" I spat. "I'm seeing a therapist."

"Fuck, Liberty. I'm sorry, I assumed—"

"I know what you assumed." Trey'd automatically lumped me in with every other Frog Hog who nailed SEALs just to say they did. *Fuck him.* "Glad you're doing okay. I should go."

"Don't go. I said I was sorry. I wanna hear about it. Is it helping, you talking to someone?"

I blew out a breath and reined my temper in. Something that Dr. Barlow was helping me with. These days I had a short fuse, but the more I talked with her the longer it became. I was nowhere near back to my old self but I did feel marginally better.

"The nightmares are worse on the days I see her. That part sucks."

"Yeah. You're dredging up shit. Night's always the worst."

"Do they go away?" I asked.

That was one of the burning questions I had, yet I was too afraid to ask my dad or uncles about it.

"They do. But you have to put in the work and dig all that bad shit out."

God, he sounds like Drake.

"So I've been told. The guilt still eats at me."

There was a long stretch of silence and I was ready to call Trey's name when he spoke.

"Funny thing about guilt, it's the easiest to pile on and hardest to let go of. Word of advice, don't fight it."

"Fight what?"

"When you feel the guilt start to lift. Don't fight to hold on to it. It does you no good. And, Liberty, trust me on this, it's easy as hell to cling to it, especially when it starts to slip away." I heard Trey's growl of annoyance before he said, "Sorry to cut this short, she's back and smiling. That doesn't mean good things for me."

"Maybe she wants to be friends," I joked.

"The only thing she wants to be friends with is my dick."

"Trey!" I snapped. "I doubt that's true."

That was a lie, I bet he was right. Trey was seriously hot.

"When I woke up and took a look in the mirror and saw how fucked-up my face was, you wanna know what I thought?"

Oh, shit. Trey sounded sad and resigned and I wasn't sure I wanted to know what made him sound that way.

"What'd you think?" I asked on a whisper then held my breath.

"That my whole life, I've attracted a certain type of woman—the wrong kind. And maybe, just maybe, with all these fuckin' scars on my face I'd finally have a chance with a woman who had something in her other than shallow intentions. I'm sick to death of women who want to fall on my dick because they think they like what they see, when really they couldn't care less about the man I am. So, honey, when I tell you Nurse Ratched wants to be friends with my dick, unfortunately I know what I'm talking about."

Damn. I didn't know what to say to that. I could see that happening, all of it. Trey was that good-looking that women would fall over themselves to get to him without caring who he was on the inside, which incidentally happened to be a really good guy.

"Well, Trey Durum, I see you. The man you are, that is. And it's an honor to call you my friend, and that has nothing to do with your face or your dick and everything to do with the badass warfighter I know you are."

"Badass warfighter." He laughed and I smiled, happy my joke broke some of his sadness. "Girl, you're too much. I'll check in soon."

"Sounds good. Hang in there."

"Later." I heard Trey disconnect and I tossed my phone on the counter.

Then I jumped and spun around when I heard Carter ask, "Why're you talking about Durum's dick?"

I took one look at Carter's scandalized expression and I couldn't stop the giggle that bubbled up. The harder I tried to hold it back, the worse it got, then I started making these ridiculous noises with my lips pressed together like those girls on Instagram who think it's sexy to make duck lips or duck face or whatever the hell it's called. I was proud to say I wasn't hip on social media lingo and didn't know that all the cool kids called Instagram The Gram until very recently. So once the duck lip noises started, there was no stopping the laughter.

Bust-a-gut.

Real.

Tears-to-your-eyes laughter that felt so damn

good once it started I couldn't stop. Unfortunately, my cousin didn't think this was funny. Not even a little bit because he didn't laugh. Not even a smile cracked his hard face so I bent double, lost sight of his frown, and worried I was going to pee my pants.

I shook with it and made no effort to stop because finally I was feeling something other than heartbreak and despair.

"Liberty!" Carter snapped.

"Wh-what?"

"Trey's dick?"

"Oh, God." I laughed harder. "Don't...don't ever say that to me again. Gross."

This time before Carter spoke he waited for me to finish chuckling. "Well?" he prompted.

I explained why I'd called Trey and finished with what he'd said about women and his looks. Carter's eyes darkened and he looked over my shoulder before his gaze came back to mine and settled.

"I've watched it happen. The guy can't go anywhere without women coming up to him. Sounds lame, cause most men would love that shit. But not him. It gets old. There's nothing that Trey hates more than an aggressive woman. Except maybe an aggressive one that won't take no for an answer."

I hated that for Trey. The woman who finally saw past his looks to the heart of him would have herself gold.

"I can see how that would get old."

"What about Drake?"

My muscles tensed and the more I tried to play it cool, the more Carter's eyes narrowed.

"What about him?" I squeaked.

Shit. What the hell is wrong with my voice?

"Did Trey mention how he, Matt, or Logan were making out?"

Phew. I relaxed a bit and fidgeted with my cell, unable to make eye contact, which was a mistake and I knew it. But, Carter was like a mind reader, going all the way back to middle school and my first kiss. Carter'd taken one look at me and knew. Then he blabbed and I got The Talk from my mom.

"Nope, he didn't say anything."

"You wanna tell me why you're not looking at me and suddenly you're nervous?"

"Nope."

"So you're admitting you're nervous?"

"Nope."

"Liberty?"

Goddammit. I tried to think up a lie, something

believable, but standing there under Carter's watchful gaze, I was coming up empty.

"Something happen between you and Drake?"

Yes, I fell in love with him. Had sex with him. Then he broke my heart.

"Nothing worth talking about. Why are you here? Dad's at work," I told him something he should know considering he worked at Triple Canopy with my dad.

"Know that. Just left there." He paused for a moment. "I came by to check on you. You had an appointment with Dr. Barlow this morning, right?"

It was getting easier to talk about my therapy sessions, at least it was with my mom. She and I had talked a lot about what happened and what I talked to Dr. Barlow about. After the night on the patio, when I had my breakdown, Dad had spent a few hours with me. During which time I gave him every dirty detail. When I was done, he held me while I cried. Then I asked him to go over the mission with me—from a tactical standpoint. He did, and his insight was helpful, however he gently reminded me that hindsight was twenty-twenty.

This was true, it was but it also helped me understand what I'd missed and what I didn't miss because the signs weren't there, which was another way he helped me.

I wasn't so comfortable with my sessions that I wanted to talk about them with everyone. However, talking about anything other than Drake sounded good.

"She's helping," I admitted. "Today we talked a lot about me blaming my dad and the uncles about what happened." I sucked in a lungful of oxygen and when I let it out I continued. "I'm sorry for the way I acted. I knew it was wrong when I was saying all those nasty things. But I couldn't stop them. It felt like I had all this nasty stuff fighting to get out and the harder I tried to stop it, the more power I gave it until I had no control over it. I was totally wrong and out of line."

"'Preciate that, Liberty. But you know we don't hold any animosity. It needed to come out, and however that happened, we were prepared. Blaming them is a natural response, but I hope you get that it's not their fault."

"I do know. I knew all along, I just hurt so bad I wanted the world to hurt with me. I said some fucked-up stuff to you." I gulped down the lump gathering in my throat and pushed through. "I'd never wanted it to be you and not me, I hope *you* know that. I never wished it was you Roman took. I'd made my peace and I was ready to die that day."

Carter wasn't saying anything—his eyes stayed glued to mine, but his posture shifted and his breath came in tight gasps. Something had changed. Something big.

"What's wrong?" I asked.

"Nothing."

"Don't bullshit me, Cousin."

After a long stretch of silence, he whispered, "Roman?"

Oh, fucking hell.

What have I done?

"You can't tell them," I begged. "Please, Carter."

"They know. Or at least Roman Bolick's son is on the short list of people who'd want revenge. That is, after they found out he had a son."

This is bad. Beyond bad. Super fucking bad.

My palms started to sweat and my legs shook.

Oh, no.

"You have to stop them."

"Stop them?" My cousin's face screwed into an ugly snarl. "Why the fuck would I stop them? Roman targeted you and—"

"I know what he did," I cut him off, not needing the reminder—it was forever burned into my brain. I'd never forget a second of it, even if by a miracle the doctor could help me stop having horrible nightmares, I'd never, ever forget. "If you think what I'm going through is bad, I'd never be able to live with myself if something happened to them."

"Nothing's gonna happen to them."

"I just lived through *two* fucked-up operations that say otherwise. Anything can happen out there and you know it."

"Listen to me. Nothing is going to happen." Carter's hardened features, the way he enunciated his words, told me nothing I said was going to change his mind.

He was on their side, he would help my dad and uncles exact revenge, uncaring of the repercussions.

"I guess it doesn't matter what *I* want. All of you are hellbent on payback. Just remember, Cousin, that blade—it cuts both ways, and sometimes when that knife sinks in, you feel it worse." I grabbed my phone off the counter and started to walk out of the kitchen. "You can let yourself out."

Five minutes later, I was lying in my childhood bedroom hugging my pillow tight, wishing Drake was there. He'd be able to talk some sense into my family. He would remind them how bad it is out there and all of the reasons why they should allow the military to handle Roman.

Exhaustion started to pull me under, and no matter how hard I tried to blink the sleep away, it was pulling me under. Bad dreams would follow.

Then I'd wake up alone and cold.

And Drake would still be gone.

27

"This is motherfucking bullshit," Logan scoffed. "Who the fuck took the pictures?"

My hand in my pocket rolled Liberty's dog tags through my fingers, the weight of them not doing a damn thing to calm me. Each day that passed, I felt her slip further away. Her leave would be up soon, she'd go back to Washington to her post, and eventually rotate out and deploy.

I couldn't stop wondering if she was sleeping. If she was still having nightmares, and if she was, who was waking her up and holding her.

The thought of her being alone ate at me. Not even knowing that she was tight with her family pacified the throbbing in my chest.

"Don't know who took the pictures. And to be honest, I don't really care as long as Lennard and Wick make them disappear."

"You don't care?" Logan's torso jerked. "Well, I do."

"Some prick walking around snapping pictures with his phone is the least of my concerns. I just want Liberty protected."

"And you think by taking a dishonorable discharge that's gonna what, magically shield her?"

I knew Logan would give me a hard time about this. But he needed to hear it from me. Not as the squad leader but as a friend. I remembered how hard it was after Carter left the team. It's a hit on a personal and professional level.

"What I think is, the lieutenant commander is going to need to cover his ass. If someone should ever come poking around he can truthfully say he took disciplinary action. And Liberty stays free and clear of charges."

"Brother, I know how you feel about her. I watched the two of you. I get it—she's a cool chick, tough, smart. I admit, she impressed the hell out of me out there. But you're throwing everything away for her. Not just your naval career. You take a dishonorable discharge, where in the fuck do you think you're gonna find a civilian job?"

I stared at Logan and knew he wouldn't understand. The man's childhood was fucked, yet he'd beat the odds and never turned to the dark side like his old man. Still took care of his mom and three sisters. But something he'd taken away from his younger years was the belief there was no such thing as love. Straight out, he thought the emotion was bullshit. He thought there were varying degrees of caring. He thought there was lust, want, and sex. He thought there was attraction. But love was not something real.

So I knew he'd never get it.

"You're wrong, you don't know how I feel about her. What you saw, the temptation of her, the lure, the fascination—that's nothing. That's the outward draw of her. What you cannot see, is the recognition, the way my body responds when she's near, the way deep down, in the darkest parts of my soul, Liberty's mere presence sheds light. You can't understand, no more than I can explain it, but from the moment my mouth covered hers to breathe life back into her, a raw, pure, overwhelming, primitive need came over me. It was immediate. I knew in those first moments

I would lay down my life for her. So, if I'd die for her, giving up my profession seems to pale."

"Christ. First Carter, now you with this voodoo love shit." Logan shook his head but the smile stretched across his face belied his sarcastic response.

"Look on the bright side, friend, you've been on my dick about sliding in the squad leader position for years. Now it's yours."

"Shit. They only gave it to you so you didn't embarrass yourself and cry like a girl."

"Right." I chuckled.

"So, you're done?"

"Considering I got no way to get back on the compound, I'd say I'm done. Lennard called me direct to tell me he was calling Wick. He also conveyed he wanted this shit done soon. No one wants a shit stain."

"I don't know what to say." Logan's shrug was nonchalant but his deep frown was full of disappointment. "Fucking jacked, all of it. Nothing changes between you and me."

That was cool he said that, but we both knew everything had changed. Just like with Carter. Sure, we kept in touch when we could, I'd still drop everything to take his back, but there was a level of closeness that was gone, because we no longer had the teams in common.

The same thing would happen with me and the guys. The thought made my stomach recoil.

"Nothing," I confirmed.

I WAS NUMB.

When Lennard had told me he wanted this situation off his desk and away from his command, he hadn't lied. There were many differences between the teams and the regular Navy. We, or *they* as it were, had more latitude. Most of the rules and regulations regular sailors had to follow, team guys did not. It seemed everything moved faster in naval special warfare.

I tossed my separation papers on my coffee table and glared down at them and fought the urge to rub my sternum as pain radiated.

I loved Liberty McCoy with every breath I took and I'd protect her until my last, but fuck if this wasn't killing me.

Everything was gone.

It had taken me years to get to the height of my career and days for Lennard to chapter me out.

DISHONERABLE.

The word taunted me.

There wasn't a goddamn thing dishonorable about the way I served my country. Not a fucking thing dishonorable about loving Liberty. Yet there it was, line six, character of separation: dishonorable.

Fuck!

There was a knock on my door and I ignored it.

I couldn't face my former teammates.

Not yet.

I didn't want their words of consolation or encouragement.

I couldn't look at the men who I'd gone out on countless missions with knowing I was no longer one of them. I'd never go into battle with them again. And fucking shit, I couldn't stop the jealousy from invading my thoughts.

Another knock came, this time pounding. I scrubbed my face and dug the heels of my palms against my eyes in an effort to ward off the headache that had been threatening since I was escorted through the very compound I'd called home for years. A motherfucking escort—in my own home.

If that wasn't a kick to the gut, signing some shitty piece of paper that negated my good service was.

A third knock came and I gave up the hope they'd go away.

Wooden feet took me to my front door, my clammy hand turned the knob, and when I opened the door prepared to tell my former friends to beat feet and leave me the fuck alone, I was shocked to find a man I'd never seen standing there.

"Can I help you?" I inquired as I studied him.

About my height, older with some graying around his temples, he was fit in a way that suggested there was a time he was built. But it was the man's eyes. They were hauntingly familiar. Hazel, but unusual, flecks of gold and yellow that made them look like cat eyes.

"Are you Drake Hayes?"

What the hell?

"And you are?"

"Levi McCoy."

My torso jerked and fear rolled through me.

"Is Liberty okay?"

"No." Every muscle tightened and my fists clenched at his words. "But she's slowly getting there. May I come in?"

I stepped aside, allowing Liberty's father to enter.

"What do you mean she's slowly getting there? Is

she still having nightmares? Did you get her to talk to someone?"

Levi frowned and narrowed his intelligent eyes, his gaze searching, penetrating, and I didn't give the first fuck what he'd find. I needed to know what was going on with Liberty like I needed my next breath.

"She told me you're the one who saved her life."

I remained silent. I didn't want to talk about her rescue or CPR or missions. I needed to know what was so wrong with Liberty her father would come up to Virginia Beach from Georgia to meet with me, a total stranger to him.

"She's talking to someone. It took a few weeks, and a confrontation I'd rather forget but never will, because watching my daughter break down is something that's tattooed on my soul."

"Break down?" I growled, unable to keep my emotions in check. "What the fuck does that mean?"

I was already mentally checking off shit I'd need to pack a bag and get in my truck to go to her, so I missed the change in Levi. But when I refocused on the man, he stood taller, shoulders stiff, eyes no longer narrowed but wide in shock.

"So, it's true. Something happened out there between you and my daughter."

"Levi, I mean no disrespect, but you have two minutes to explain why you're here and what's going on with Liberty before you find yourself alone in my apartment because I'll be in my truck heading south."

The man had the balls to smile at me. What he didn't do was start talking. *Fuck this.* I needed to get to my woman. Levi wouldn't come all this way unless there was a serious problem.

I turned to head to my bedroom when his words stopped me.

"For ten days I watched my girl struggle. She'd wound herself up so tight, it was a wonder she could breathe. Her uncles and I talked and agreed some tough love was in order."

A surge of anger took over thinking about Liberty being pushed to talk about what had happened to her. There was no doubt she needed to get it out, but my heart slammed into my ribs thinking about how scared she must've been. I'd witnessed the devastation firsthand. First when I found her, then when she'd dreamt about it.

"So you forced her," I snarled.

"Yes, and it was ugly."

Fucking shit.

"I have to go."

Ugly.

Breakdown.

Jesus Christ.

I stalked into my bedroom with the singular mission of getting to my woman. Haphazardly tossed shit into a bag, not caring what it was, I'd buy whatever I needed when I got to her. Two minutes later with my backpack over my shoulder, I walked back into my living room and found Levi studying a stack of papers in his hand.

Even though I didn't mean to, I glanced at my coffee table now clean of the documents I'd thrown there.

"What's this?" Levi held the papers out for me to see and I bit the inside of my cheek until I tasted blood.

The man didn't need me to answer, it was clear what they were.

"Dishonorable. The Navy burn you?"

Why did that feel so good? His first question hadn't been, what had I done to earn the characterization—instead he'd assumed I was wronged by my command.

"Doesn't matter. As of today, I'm out."

He looked back at the memorandum attached to

the notice of separation and his brows pinched together.

"You declined a trial by court-martial. No persons to speak on your behalf. Ineligible for VA benefits. Nineteen years, six months into your service, paygrade E-9, six months from hittin' your twenty and you decline a trial?"

"Know what it says, McCoy. What I don't understand is why you're interested."

"I'm interested because this shit doesn't jive with the man my nephew's told me about. So, tell me, why the fuck you'd let them railroad you like this? And was the rest of your team treated to this bullshit?"

I crossed my arms over my chest and stared.

"Right. Either you can explain this to me, then I can explain why I'm here. Or, you can get in your truck, drive to Georgia, and I'll get my team started on digging through your life until they find it—so by the time you get down there, I'll know just how bad this shit stinks and *then* we can have the discussion we should be having now. But instead of six hours. Your choice."

Goddamn, hearing Levi speak put a whole new spin on my friendship with Carter.

"Anyone ever tell you, Carter's just like you?"

"As much of a compliment as that is, Carter is a

spitting image of his father. Now, we gonna talk now or in six hours?"

No bullshit. No nonsense.

My kind of man.

"What I'm going to tell you stays between us."

"Won't make that promise to you. If I feel like Lenox, Jasper, Clark, or Carter needs to know, then they know. We don't keep secrets in our family."

"All right. Then I'll amend. This doesn't get back to Liberty. That's a promise you'll make or you can dig all you want, but the only thing you're gonna find is a bunch of falsified documents. And I'll give you this, I know the documents and charges are false, because I made sure they were. It was the only way I'd agree to a DD."

"Will this information hurt my daughter?" he asked through gritted teeth.

"Yes, it would hurt her. But it will not harm her or her career. I made goddamned sure of that."

"Fuck. Tell me." Levi's agitation was clear as day, therefore, I didn't make him wait.

It took me twenty minutes to run down the situation, and that was only because before I told the man that basically a sex tape had been made of his daughter and me, he needed to know how I felt about her. She was not a quick, adrenaline-fueled fuck against the shower room wall. I was in love with her.

Throughout my explanation, Levi McCoy's hand tore through his hair, his face paled, and at one point I was afraid my new eighty-inch TV was going to be thrown across the room. He was not a man who was angry—he was a father who was beyond livid.

Liberty had been through enough. She didn't need this shit piled on top of an already high shit sandwich.

When I was done, Levi stopped pacing, turned to face me, and stared at me like he was looking at me for the first time.

"You lookin' for a job?"

"Come again?"

"Seein' as of today, you're officially unemployed, no retirement, no insurance, no paycheck, are you looking for work?"

"Retirement, insurance, and a paycheck aren't on my radar. However, getting to Liberty is. I told you what you needed to know, now it's your turn."

Levi started talking and it was my turn to pace, shove my hands through my hair, and ball my fists as he explained what tough love entailed and Liberty's breakdown. Then he further enlightened me about Triple Canopy's investigation into their past targets, and finally what they'd concluded and Liberty had inadvertently confirmed.

They knew about Roman Kushnir.

"I hope you understand why Wick didn't want you in the know," I told him even though I knew a man like Levi would never understand.

"Not even a little bit, but that's a conversation between me and Stew."

"Right. So I'm sure in all your intel gathering, you found that Roman was supplying the bomb maker known as Lore with materials."

"Indeed. Also know the bastard blew himself up and almost took two of your guys with him."

Regret and pain swirled in my gut thinking about Trey and Luke. Both had a long road ahead of them, especially Luke. His vision in his left eye was bad enough that if it didn't start healing, he'd be facing a med board. Something that would kill him.

"Why'd you come all this way to tell me that? You could've called."

"I needed to see for myself if my wife was right."

Levi's odd response took me off-guard. "Right about what?"

"That my daughter's heartbroken and it has nothing to do with her being captured and tortured by the fucker. I didn't see it. Then my wife, Blake, brought it up. Carter added his suspicions so I decided to come up here, and see for myself."

"Heartbroken?"

A flicker of hope sparked and adrenaline surged like a shot of dope in my veins.

Does Liberty miss me as much as I miss her?

Fuck, I hope so.

"A long time ago when I was young and stupid, full of anger and pride, I made the biggest mistake of my life and walked away from Blake. I did it knowing she was the only woman I'd ever love. That mistake cost me twelve years. My wife took one look at her daughter and knew there was more in play. She told me that looking at Liberty was like looking in the mirror. Because you see, while I knew Blake was the only woman for me, she knew that I was the man that was meant to be hers and she knew it so deeply that for twelve fucking years my woman lived in pain. Pain that I caused. So when Blake says she knows my daughter's heart is broken and it's because the man she knows was meant to be hers walked away, you better believe I listened."

"I didn't walk away," I defended.

"Then why aren't you at my house fixing my daughter?"

"Because I was trying to prevent *that* shit," I

jabbed at my separation papers now back on the table, "from happening to her. As a commissioned officer, she doesn't get reduction in rank, she doesn't get restriction, she gets stripped of her commission and a fucking dismissal. I don't need to tell you how hard she's worked to earn her place. If Ranger school wasn't hard enough, SF school put it to her. But she saw herself through. I was not going to let that be taken from her.

"She doesn't need even a hint of a blemish on her record, most especially a whisper of a sexual allegation with an NCO. I don't need to tell you what that would do to her reputation, and as fucked as that is, Levi, you know it's true. So while you may see it as walking away, I saw it as protecting her. And when shit came down the pike, I made damn sure I took the hit and not her. And lastly, if you think I can fix your daughter, then you don't know Lieutenant McCoy. Because that woman is so fucking strong, she'll fix herself. But what I will do is stand beside her and watch."

When I was done with my outburst, my woman's father was staring at me smiling. Again, I didn't see one fucking thing to smile about. I wanted this over so I could get in my truck and get to Liberty.

"Heard she walked across that tarmac."

He was talking about after her rescue.

"You heard right. Most beautiful thing I'd ever witnessed. Lieutenant McCoy, injured, bruised, and fucked-up, walking on battered feet with her chin high. She walked into battle and goddamn but she was determined to walk out. Proudest moment of my life walking beside her."

"Fuck." Levi's strangled curse sounded painful. "I've watched it happen twice now. Seen the look in a man's eyes when realization dawns his daughter's a woman and she's found the man that will replace you. I gotta say, Hayes, thought it'd be harder than this. Thought I'd fight this feeling until the bitter end then I'd resent it. But if you're the man I'm walking my daughter to, then I got nothing but joy and appreciation."

"You'll be walking her to me," I confirmed.

"Then you better get your ass to Georgia. And while you're there, you better find yourself at Triple Canopy. HR will need you to fill out some paperwork."

"Don't need a job, Levi. Haven't you heard, my future wife's a Special Forces soldier and a lieutenant in the United States Army. I've heard they make a whack on hazardous duty pay."

Liberty's dad made a choking sound to cover his

laugh. "Right. Former SEAL turned dependapota-mus. Now I've seen it all."

Former SEAL.

Christ, that hurt. But knowing I was headed straight to Liberty lessened the agony to a dull, roaring ache.

28

"Can I ask you something?" Delaney asked.

She and my mom bookended me on my parents' couch while Quinn sat on the floor with the twins and I cuddled Emma on my lap. I'd just apologized profusely to Delaney and she'd graciously accepted. Then she told me about losing Carter's baby and the toll it had taken on her, and how she'd pulled away and lashed out. She also shared something everyone already knew—that their relationship had been going on for years. She and Carter had thought they were sneaky.

I gave her a no-shit-sherlock shake of my head and she busted out laughing.

Now she and Carter were blissfully happy and their daughter Emma was icing on their cake.

"Sure," I answered, but I didn't take my eyes off Emma.

Her chubby feet were on my thighs, her tiny hands in mine, and she was bouncing herself silly.

"What's going on with you and Drake Hayes?"

"Wh-what?" I stammered and set Emma's tush on my knees before I dropped her.

"I heard Carter talking to my dad about him," she semi-explained.

"And?"

My mom giggled next to me and I turned to look at her. "What's funny?"

"Oh, nothing." She smiled.

"Seriously, why are you smiling?"

"I'm smiling because my girl's home on leave and this is the longest stretch of time I've spent with her in years."

Blake McCoy was a trained liar. She was good at it, the CIA had made sure of it. But right then, my mom was doing it badly.

"I don't believe you," I told her.

"You callin' your mama a liar?" she teased.

"Yes."

"I know you're in love with Drake Hayes." Her singsong voice hit me like a ton of bricks.

Impossible.

I hadn't told anyone, not even Dr. Barlow.

"Why would you think something like that?"

My heartrate picked up and my palms were starting to sweat. Something that happened a lot these days. I fought the need to squirm, knowing my mom wouldn't miss it. Not only had The Agency trained her to lie, they'd also taught her how to read people. Which, as a teenager, sucked big time. I got away with nothing. If my mom missed it, Dad hadn't.

"It's in the way you talk about him."

"I don't talk about Drake any sort of way. I've hardly said two words about him."

My mom laughed and looked from me to Delaney. Then her gaze took in Quinn, and finally went to the twins, Hadley and Adalynn.

"It's funny how all you girls forget," my mom said.

"Forget what, Aunt Blake?" Quinn asked.

"That we were young once. That there was a time me, Reagan, Emily, and Lily were falling in love. And part of that is when we first met our husbands."

"Um, Aunt Blake? Hadley, Addy, Quinn, and I haven't forgotten. Mom tells us all the time how hot Dad was when they met. It's gross and I think she drones on and on about how her and Aunt Lily watched them workin' shirtless in the backyard because she knows it's like nails on a chalkboard."

My mom smiled huge. Delaney wasn't lying, that story had been told so many times over the years we knew it by heart.

"Right. No doubt they were and are still all good-looking men, what I'm talking about is how we felt. The butterflies, the anticipation, the need."

"Mom!" I snapped and my cousins groaned. "That's worse than you telling us about our dads' abs. Just an FYI."

"You're twenty-seven years old, and while your father is still under the self-imposed illusion his daughter has never and will never have sex, I, sweet girl, am not."

Hadley barked out a laugh and I cut her a you-are-a-traitor glare that did nothing to make her stop giggling.

"You think she had sex with Drake?" Laney whispered.

"I think she's madly in love with him and doesn't know what to do with herself because she thinks he's lost to her."

"I'm sitting right here," I unnecessarily reminded them.

Though I had to admit, I was happy my mom

didn't answer the sex question and instead trudged on about love.

"Tell us about him," Addy said, her pretty green eyes sparkling with fairytales and rainbows.

Quinn liked to say that the twins were full of drama, but she was wrong. Addy was a dreamer, a homebody, quiet unless her twin and older siblings wouldn't let her get a word in, then she could be loud.

Hadley was drama. Which was funny because she had a degree in library science and for as long as I could remember, she was a bookworm who always wanted to be a librarian. Yet there was nothing shy and calm about the girl—she was so far from the stereotype it wasn't even funny.

So I wasn't surprised at the way Addy was staring at me. Hadley and Quinn would ask about sex. Delaney would want to talk about feelings. But Addy would want the romance.

"There's nothing to tell."

Lie.

There was so much to tell but I couldn't. It still hurt too bad.

"Moira, need I remind you that I know what love looks like, but more than that, I know what a broken heart looks like. Been there, done that. I have the t-shirt, the plaque, and the ribbon. I know the look because for years I saw it every time I caught a glimpse of myself. But what I don't get is why you haven't reached out to him since you've been home."

Moira. She'd pulled out the big guns.

Using my real name told me that now that the topic had been broached, there would be no putting a lid on it.

"He saved my life," I told my mom.

"I know that."

"He carried me to safety, he dressed me, he wouldn't let me pull into myself, then he carried me the rest of the way to LZ. He stayed by my side when I needed him. He held me when my nightmares gripped me and wouldn't let me go. But more than that, he trusted me, he treated me like an equal, not like I was broken."

"Then what's the problem, honey?" my mom asked softly. "All of that sounds really good."

Emma started fussing in my lap. After a kiss to her baby-soft, black hair, I set her down on the floor wherein she promptly took off crawling in the direction of her Aunt Quinn. Suddenly my throat constricted. I'd never thought about having kids and I knew I was far away from wanting but I couldn't stop myself from picturing a gaggle of little Drakes running around.

"He made it clear he didn't want anything to do with me when we came Stateside," I confessed.

"He said that?" Quinn huffed.

Her disbelief almost made me smile.

"He didn't have to say the words for me to know."

The room fell quiet and I swallowed back the painful memories of Drake setting me on my feet after we were done. The gentle yet distant look in his eyes. The way he brushed his lips across my forehead. Not a word was spoken as he turned off the water, dried me off, and helped me dress. It wasn't until we were exiting the building, him in soaking-wet ACU pants, holding his boots, did he finally speak and that was to tell me he'd see me at the TOC for debriefing.

Cold, detached, reserved.

He gave nothing away.

And the debriefing was worse. He called me ma'am and referred to me as the lieutenant. Intellectually, I knew he was showing me respect in front of Wick and the battle captain, but damn if it didn't hurt.

And I didn't even want to think about our

painful goodbye at the airfield when he shook my hand and wished me well.

Gah! I mean, we'd had sex—rough, dirty sex against a wall—and he shook my hand. If that wasn't a brush-off I didn't know what was.

"Is there a possibility you misread the situation?"

"No, Mom. Trust me. It was loud and clear."

"Honey, I think you should—"

"No, Mom, please trust me." I scooted over so I could look at her. I really needed her to understand how serious I was about this. Then I picked up her hand and held it in both of mine. "It hurts too bad. I feel like my heart's been ripped from my chest. From the second I opened my eyes and saw him staring down at me. It wasn't like some TV romance, it was actually painful like I'd been hit in the chest with a sledgehammer. I brushed it off as hero worship since he saved my life, but it was just a lie I was telling myself because I knew who he was. I felt this tether or something that kept drawing me to him. I miss him so much I can't breathe. I know I love him, and in his own way I know he cares about me, but believe me, that connection was severed and he was the one who cut it."

My mom's eyes were full of unshed tears and she

finally got it. Why I wasn't going to call Drake. I wasn't in a place where I could handle rejection.

"You need to tell him how you feel." I heard the hitch in Delaney's voice but I didn't take my eyes off my mom.

"Laney's right, Liberty."

Three words and my world shifted.

Chills raced up my spine. My heart pounded in a crazy rhythm that made it hard for me to breathe.

I told myself he wasn't really there. It was an impossibility—I must've finally snapped and my mind had conjured him up. Those were my thoughts as I slowly turned from my mom's now shocked expression. When my eyes landed on him, all the oxygen seemed to disappear.

There he was.

Drake Hayes.

In my parents' living room that was not small by any means, but with him standing there looking like sex on a stick next to my dad, the room suddenly felt like a shoebox. An overcrowded, suffocating, shoebox.

"What are you doing here?" I wheezed. Then I was on my feet because there was only one thing that I could think of that would make him come down to

Georgia. "Are Trey and Luke okay? Did something happen?"

"Yeah, Liberty, something happened," he returned, and now my heart was racing for a different reason.

I hadn't spoken to Trey in a few days but he'd been discharged and was back in Virginia Beach. Luke had another appointment scheduled to recheck his eyes but that wasn't for a few days.

"Tell me," I demanded and braced for the worst.

"I realized that I was all the way up in Virginia and you were down here in Georgia," he told me and I blinked at his bizarre response. "And the more I thought on that, the less I liked it. More like I fuckin' hated it."

"What?"

"Maybe we can go somewhere and talk?" he asked, and his gaze swept the room, reminding me we had an audience.

I glanced back at my mom who was smiling at me so wide it was splitting her face. Delaney's expression was soft and thoughtful though she was smiling at Drake. Quinn, Hadley, and Adalynn were all looking at Drake, too, but they weren't smiling— they were staring up at him with varying degrees of shock.

After I was done taking in the women, my eyes locked with my dad's. He was standing to Drake's side but set back—watchful, alert. Pleased.

What in the world is going on?

"Babe?" Drake called and Adalynn's dreamy sigh drew my attention to her.

When she caught me staring, my crazy cousin widened her eyes, then started jerking her head toward Drake. When I kept looking at the weird faces she was making, she added hand gestures, pointing her thumb at Drake and smiling.

Crazy girl.

"Yeah. Um. Sure," I stammered, sounding like a total idiot.

When I didn't move, mostly because my legs felt like jelly and I was still finding it hard to breathe and, yes, I was a little scared to find out what Drake wanted to talk about, he obviously lost patience. I knew this when suddenly his jeans-incased legs took him across the room. My mind was stuck on the fact that was the first time I'd seen him in something other than his uniform or cargos. My eyes landed on his feet and I was contemplating his footwear when I felt the glide of his fingers on my neck. That glide stopped under my chin and he forced me to look up at him.

I'd missed him. Missed everything about him. But as I stared into his beautiful brown eyes, I realized just how much.

"Baby," he whispered, and I felt wetness gather in my eyes and I prayed it wouldn't fall.

My prayers went unanswered. Drake's hand moved from my chin. His thumb brushed away the tears, then his hand slid into my hair and he pulled me to him. I did a very unladylike face plant onto his chest. And even though I was still having trouble with my breathing, I still had the good sense to take in Drake's fresh, crisp scent. I missed that, too. Even in the field, he'd smelled good—strong, manly, virile.

Drake's arms wrapped around me and for the first time since I'd been home, I felt like I was *home*. Safe, like nothing could touch me—not even my nightmares—as long as Drake was close.

I heard someone clear their throat and I knew it was my dad when he said, "You should go."

Tension coiled low in my belly when Drake nodded his agreement. I didn't want him to go. Not yet.

"Liberty," he called softly but I didn't move. "Baby, come on, we're gonna go someplace where we can talk."

He didn't wait for my response, which was good,

because my throat was clogged, and I was fighting back a full-blown sob-fest in front of my family.

And without another word, he led me outside. The big, shiny, black pickup that was parked in my parents' driveway was so Drake, I couldn't stop my smile.

"Pure Drake Hayes," I mumbled.

"What, baby?"

"I was just thinking that your truck fits your personality."

"You think so?"

"Well, I couldn't picture you trying to fold into a Prius."

Drake opened the door and helped me inside and waited until I was settled before he looked up at me and smiled.

"Right."

The twitch of his lips drew my attention there and the memory of how those lips felt on my neck sliced through the shock.

I watched as he rounded the hood then climbed in and buckled up.

Once he'd backed out and was driving, the panic started.

He still hadn't told me why he was in Georgia other than his cryptic remark that I was there. And I was thinking maybe I'd misread the meaning of that and was getting my hopes up only to have them crushed.

"Why are you here?" I asked when I could no longer contain the question.

"Give me ten minutes then I'll answer that."

I wasn't sure I'd last ten more seconds.

"Where are we going?"

"To my hotel."

A prickle of heat surged between my legs. Alone in a hotel room with Drake—yes, please. But I tamped down my racing thoughts by reminding myself he'd made it clear the night we left Golan Heights that whatever we'd shared was over.

"How's Trey making out at home?" I asked for no other reason than to get myself distracted.

"Fine." I jerked at Drake's clipped response.

"Fine, as in he's making out okay? Or fine as in you don't want to tell me something?"

"There a reason why you keep asking about Trey?"

What the hell?

"Well, let's see, Drake. I saw a piece of shrapnel sticking out of his bloodied thigh, after I failed to warn him and Luke in time that Lore was going to commit suicide. I know Luke's at home being taken care of by a leggy blonde, as Trey describes her. But as far as I know, Trey's home alone and I'm worried about a friend. Is that a good enough reason for you?"

"Damn, Liberty, I'm sorry." Drake blew out a breath. "Yeah, he's fine. Logan and Matt are taking turns going over there during the day to check on him and Matt's been staying the night."

"And you?"

"And me what?"

"You said, Matt and Logan. What about you? Have you checked on him?"

I swore I saw him flinch with guilt but I couldn't be sure.

"I've seen him. But I've been caught up in meetings and briefs so I haven't been over as much as they have."

There was an edge to his answer. My mom would call it a deceptive misdirection—or a lie without lying. I couldn't understand what there was to hide, but swore I heard tension in his tone.

What was that about?

29

I was screwing this up—big time. Liberty was standing ten feet away from me in my hotel room with her arms wrapped around her middle, unsure and nervous. From the moment I'd led her into the room, she'd put distance between us.

There was a lot that needed to be said, explanations given, feelings aired. I just didn't know where to start.

My body was at war with my mind.

My mind warring with my conscience.

And I seriously had to get my jealousy in check. What the hell was wrong with me, snapping at Liberty when she asked about Trey? I knew she wasn't interested in him as anything more than a friend, but her asking about him twice in thirty minutes had crawled under my skin. I was behaving like a jackass and I knew it. Not the best way to win my girl over.

"Drake? You wanna tell me why you're here?" she asked, and my gut clenched at the uncertainty in her voice.

"You wanna tell me why you're standing across the room looking freaked?" I volleyed.

Again, not the best way to start this particular conversation—an important one where I needed to convince her the connection we had was not severed. And I needed to do that in a way she couldn't twist in her head, because the rest of what I had to tell her was likely going to piss her off.

"Because I *am* freaked. I haven't seen or heard from you in weeks and you show up out of the blue— with my dad, which I don't understand how *that* happened. I asked you why you're in Georgia and you give me some strange non-answer. Then I ask you again and you tell me to wait. Now I'm standing in a hotel room with you and you're staring at me but still not talking."

My eyes moved lower, from her arms wrapped protectively around her middle, and caught sight of her bare legs. I'd never seen her in shorts, never seen her in flip-flops. The Liberty I knew wore ACUs, tactical vests, and even wearing jeans and my shirt in Beirut, had multiple weapons strapped to her body.

I quickly formulated a new plan—I needed to prove to her our connection was more than adrenaline, battlefields, and rescues. She needed to see me as a man—*her* man—not the Navy SEAL. Which was important, considering I was no longer an active one.

So I changed tactics and decided to lay it out for her.

"I'm out of the Navy," I told her.

Her arms didn't unwrap but her body jerked back and her eyes widened.

"What? Why? How?"

The lie was on the tip of my tongue. I could bullshit and tell her my enlistment was up, but that shit would inevitably come back to bite me. Not to mention, it was all kinds of wrong and as a habit, I didn't deceive people. But the truth was going to infuriate her, possibly worry her.

And worst case, scare her that there was a creepy psycho taking pictures of us.

As quickly as I could, I told her about the pictures someone sent my command. Her expression ran the gamut—shocked, angry, very angry, then slid to furious. When I was done explaining that I'd been discharged due to our fraternization, Liberty McCoy was well beyond infuriated and nearing thermonuclear.

"What?" she thundered.

I didn't feel her scathing response warranted an answer so I didn't give her one. Instead, I remained quiet and let her sort through what she needed to.

I'd find that was the wrong play. I should've reminded her what we shared. I should've led the conversation with how I felt about her and why I was there. But it was too late and I knew it when her already red face turned crimson.

The anger drained and hurt crept in.

"Liberty—" I started, but got no further because she'd stepped closer, unwrapped herself from the protective display, and cut me to the quick with her cold eyes.

"What have you done?" she whispered.

It didn't take a genius to know her quiet words were in contradiction to the battle that raged behind her stare.

Fucking shit.

"Let me—"

"I can't believe you did this to me," she hissed through gritted teeth.

To her?

"I didn't do anything to you, Liberty. I did it for you."

Disappointment. Pain. Hurt.

What the hell?

"I can't believe it." Her fists went up and drove into her eyes. Then her tear-filled gaze came to mine, the look so raw it gutted me. "I can't believe you'd do this. I thought you understood. I thought...I was wrong."

I was walking through a minefield, one I had no clue how to navigate, and one misstep and it was over. Worse yet, it felt like those mines were hidden on an iced-over pond, one that wasn't completely frozen, and it was cracking under my feet.

"Baby—"

"Don't, Drake. I can't even look at you right now." Her hands dropped to her sides and her fucked-up declaration sliced through me. But even though she'd said she couldn't look at me, her haunted eyes hadn't left mine. "I don't know why you came down here, but I do know whatever your reason is, I don't want to hear it. Don't know why you were with my dad, but that doesn't matter, either."

"I came down here because I missed you."

"Don't say that."

"Say what? The truth? That when your dad showed up at my apartment and told me that you were working through some stuff but there were things that were hurting you, things you hadn't shared, the tight leash I had on my control slipped? That hearing that you were hurting made it impossible to stay away? That I missed you and thought about you every day to distraction until I had to find physically taxing ways to exhaust myself so I could sleep? That I couldn't stop myself from thinking about you, even though every time I did, it hurt so goddamn bad I couldn't breathe?"

Liberty's lip curled in disgust. Her hand shot up and she jabbed a finger in my direction.

"Your *control*? Must be nice for you to have that. I wouldn't know what that's fucking like."

"What?"

"You said, the tight leash you had on your *control* slipped. Must be nice to have *control* over your own life. Must be nice to be allowed to make decisions pertaining to your own life. Must feel really good to know that you *control*—something." Liberty finished on a hiss, still stabbing her finger at me. "Sorry it slipped and you wasted your time coming down here."

I'd never thought I was a stupid man. However,

apparently I was a complete dumbfuck. In my haste to clear the topic so we could move to the next, I totally screwed up. No, screwed up was a far cry from what I'd done.

"Let me explain."

"No. I don't want an explanation."

"Liberty. I didn't mean to hurt you. I wanted to protect you."

Again, wrong thing to say. That knowledge was slammed home when Liberty started to shake. Not a small tremble, oh no. Her body convulsed, her hands balled into fists, and her face scrunched in agony.

"There's the problem, Drake," she snarled. "That's everyone's problem. I don't want to be protected, goddamn it. I want my fucking control back. I want everyone around me to stop. My family's going after Roman against my wishes, not caring that it's killing me. The Army, which means General Wick, gave the order to move my post to Savannah. My cousins are tiptoeing around me, at least the females are. The men are looking at me like I'm a child who needs to be coddled. No one is listening to me. I talk and they ignore me. But I get them doing it. To them I'm Moira. To my uncles, I'm their little niece. To my parents, I'm their only child and they're worried. But you? What you did, how you went behind my back, how you took away any say I had in my life, my career, stripped me of the control I've been fighting to get back. That doesn't kill me. Oh no, Drake, that rips my heart out. I thought you knew me. I thought you respected me. I thought you at least cared about me a little. But you don't."

"Baby, please, listen to me," I begged.

The gravity of my mistake hit full-force and a paralyzing fear gripped my chest. How had I mishandled the situation so badly?

"There's nothing you can say. You gave up your career, gave up something that was important to you, something that was vital, and good, and honorable. You did it. And you didn't even ask me if I wanted you to. So now, on top of everything else I'm dealing with, including you not being that man I thought you were, now I have to live with more guilt. And you did that, too. You piled that on my shoulders. And you've destroyed any chance of me one day completing the massive task of unfucking myself enough where I felt I was strong enough to seek you out, see if there was a chance what we'd shared was real, and build on it. You made it impossible because one day you'll resent me. One day you'll resent that *dishonorable* discharge. You'll remember the hit you took and you'll remember it's my fault. You lost everything because of me."

Before her words had stopped dicing me to shreds, she was on her way to the door. I moved to block her path and her hand shot up in a defensive measure that told me she didn't want me anywhere near her.

Too damn bad. I'd listened, no, I'd *felt* every word Liberty had to say, even agreed with most all of them. I hadn't seen what I'd done as taking away her control, or that by me giving up something that was indeed vital, honorable, and even if she hadn't said it, made me the man I was. And that was protective— apparently to a fault, if there could be such a thing.

But there was a lot she was not right about and I intended to make her understand I wouldn't give up on us or lose her because she was somewhat right, but also wrong.

"I did give up something important to me." Liberty tried to step around me but I sidestepped, impeding her advance. "Take a minute and think about that. Nineteen years I served. Nine-teen. I think you get my job meant something to me, more than just service to my country, more than a paycheck, more than a rank before my name or some letters after it. I didn't join the Navy because I had nothing better to do with my life. I didn't go to BUD/s to accomplish a goal. I didn't go through Green Team so I could be the baddest of the bad or brag about being a part of DEVGRU. I did that, all of it, because it's who I am. I was born this man. Born to protect.

"And faced with the fucked-up decision of choosing to protect you or my job, I didn't hesitate. I didn't need a day to contemplate, I didn't even need a minute. This is not me falling on a sword so you don't feel a moment of discomfort. This is not me taking away your choice, or not respecting you, or trusting you. This is me being the man I am, and taking the hit, so you don't."

Liberty started to protest but I talked over her muttered objections. "But you're right, I shouldn't have done it the way I did. I should've talked to you about it, told you what was going on. But, babe, straight up, it wouldn't have changed my mind. But you had a right to know. I was wrong for keeping it from you, because it does involve your life. Someone took pictures of us and I should've told you about them immediately. I'm not gonna make excuses for why I didn't, just know it wasn't done to be malicious.

"Now we're gonna talk about something else. Control, and why you think you don't have any."

"*Think* I don't? People are maneuvering around me, not giving me a say in what's going on."

"Right, like your family tracking Roman. Baby, that's not *you* losing your control. That's about them regaining *theirs*. Roman took something that means something to them. And if that wasn't bad enough, he violated it. You understand that *something* is you, right? Roman took you, held you prisoner, put his filthy hands on you, and he did those things to hurt your uncles. Put yourself in their place, and tell me how you'd feel if someone hurt them because of you.

"Something else we're gonna get untwisted. I didn't lose anything. And believe this, I'm man enough not to blame others for my choices. I made a decision, one I stand behind, and I did it knowingly. I did it because you mean more to me than anything. I did it because it was the right thing to do. And I will never regret it."

"We'll see," Liberty mumbled.

"Yeah, baby, we will. And the way we're gonna see it is years from now when all of this is behind us. You'll see I still don't regret it."

Her gaze snapped to mine and hostility radiated from every pore. I wasn't sure how to make this right, so I reverted to my original plan—the one I should've stuck with before I had a major lapse in judgement. I went about reminding her we not only had a connection, but it was strong and true and unbreakable.

"I missed you and I mean that down to my soul. When you were gone, nothing felt right. I couldn't escape the loss of you."

"Then why did you let me go?" Her voice was thick with emotion, so raw I felt her words abrade my skin like sandpaper.

"Because when you told me you'd never forget me, I thought I was doing the right thing giving you a clean break. I thought you were saying goodbye and I needed to have a mind to what you wanted even though I wanted to beg you to give us a chance. To figure out a way to make something work while we were both in the military until I could get out. I wanted to plead with you not to cut me out of your life. This is what you fail to understand. I respect you. I respect your hard work and dedication. I respect your commission, I respect you as a Ranger, as a Special Forces soldier. I respect all of that so much I would do anything to protect it. So I let you walk away."

Some of the hostility faded but none of the hurt. Liberty broke eye contact and looked at the floor, her lips pinched together in two thin white lines. I wasn't sure if that was good or bad—Liberty in her head thinking about what I said. She could've been regrouping for another round. What I did know was, I never wanted to be the source of her hurt.

"I would've taken responsibility, Drake."

"I know you would've. That's why I did what I did and didn't tell you."

Any inch of headway I'd made dissipated with my admission. "You took that from me."

"You're right, I did."

"And you're not sorry," she noted.

I was back to that minefield, and so far I had all my limbs intact, even if I was a little bruised. I'd be damned if I hit one now.

"I'm sorry I handled the situation poorly. But I am not sorry I took the discharge and you didn't lose your commission."

"Did it ever occur to you, that, had I been given the opportunity to protect you, I would've taken it? And I wouldn't have seen it as losing something? That I would've gladly taken the punishment if it meant you got to stay in."

I didn't answer, mainly because Liberty wasn't done. "You know, as disturbing as it is that someone took pictures of us, I'm not sorry. I'm not ashamed you were holding me after I said goodbye to my team. I'm not ashamed that you held me through my nightmares. The only part I care about is that some asshole took memories that meant something to me and shit all over them by sending them to your command. That person stole something special from me."

"From us," I cut in. "Those memories are special for both of us."

"If they were so special, then why'd you do this to me?"

A prickle of unease shifted over me.

"Babe, I told you why."

"Yeah, you told me some bullshit about how you felt the need to swoop in, protect me, take my choice away, and saddle me with the responsibility of you giving up your naval career."

"Fucking hell, Liberty," I bit out and clenched my jaw until my molars ached. "Would you listen to me?"

"I did listen. But you're not hearing me. Go home, Drake, I don't ever want to see or hear from you again."

While I was recovering from her kill shot, she made her way to the door. But before she could open it, I placed my hand on the metal and leaned my weight against it so she couldn't pull it open.

Her wounded eyes came to mine, a sight so painful I had to suck in a lungful of oxygen. The vision so unsettling, I was at a total loss how to make this right—how to make her understand that I'd give up anything to be with her.

Liberty's eyes closed. When they reopened, I braced when she whispered, "If there's any part of you that cares about me, you'll move out of my way."

Fast and hard, everything clicked into place.

With no other option but to give her the play, I pulled my hand away from the door.

Liberty flung open the door and rushed out.

Fucking hell.

30

Fuming mad and not paying attention because I was outrageously angry, I continued my fast-paced clip down the sidewalk.

My temples throbbed, my heart hurt so I almost missed him, but when my gaze scanned the lot, I saw Carter was standing next to his SUV waiting for me. Drake must've called him as soon as I walked out of the room.

He was also wearing a frown.

Great. Perfect. Another lecture.

I felt like I was stuck in a movie, being visited by ghosts of the past, present, and future. It was the yet-to-come that had my stomach in knots.

"You my ride?" I asked when I got near.

"You want one?"

"Well, it beats walking all the way back to my parents' house in flip-flops." I picked up my foot and clacked my sandal for emphasis. Or maybe I did it because I was nervous.

Carter, being the nice guy he was, smiled and nodded. "Get in."

I climbed into Carter's SUV. But when he pulled onto the road, he headed in the wrong direction.

"Where are we going?"

"To blow shit up." He smiled.

"Blow shit up?"

"Yep. You've got that look."

I couldn't stop myself from returning his smile. "What look?"

"Like you need to blow some shit up," he told me, but what it really sounded like was, *hello, dummy, aren't you listening?*

This was the Carter of my youth—funny, teasing, always smiling. All of us cousins had been close growing up and to my knowledge, they were all just as close now as adults. But not me. I was removed, and before Carter came home, so was he. It wasn't that we lacked a bond, but the physical distance had been hard.

In no time, Carter was pulling through the gates of Triple Canopy and my heart swelled. My dad and uncles had done well for themselves. They'd started and grown Triple Canopy into one of the most respected training facilities in the US. They also contracted with both the government and civilians for private protection.

He pulled around the back of the building and parked. After he killed the engine he reached into the back seat then dumped a bag on my lap.

"Laney's gym bag. Grab her tennis shoes, I'm not taking you to the range in flip-flops."

I couldn't stop the sigh as I rummaged through Laney's workout clothes. Gone was the lighthearted banter—Carter's tone had taken on an edge, one I didn't think I had the strength to deal with.

Maybe I should've walked home.

I could've used the time to clear my head and sort through what Drake had done.

No sooner had I gotten the laces tied on Laney's shoes, did Carter slide out of the SUV and move to the rear.

How has my life come to this?

Lonely. Uncomfortable. Despondent.

By the time I reached the open hatchback of the SUV, Carter already had one bag flung over his shoulder. He wasted no time pointing to the two hard plastic rifle cases in the back.

"Grab those."

Again with the clipped, gruff tone that I was getting used to everyone using with me. There was this tiny part of me, a sliver in the back of my mind, that wanted to lash out and remind them all that I was working through—survivors guilt and what my therapist called normal stress response PTSD.

And all of them being a bunch of assholes wasn't helping. But there was this voice that sounded a lot like my old self that said I was the one being an asshole, not them. That I was overreacting, cutting myself off from relationships.

From Drake.

Why did he have to ruin everything?

We spent the next thirty minutes setting up targets. Conversation was kept to a minimum and only consisted of where to set the containers of Carter's homemade blend of explosives. Once again, he'd slid back to the fun-loving cousin bragging about his new recipe and how I was going to be impressed.

My dad and uncles owned twenty acres behind the Triple Canopy offices. Part of the land had a handgun range. They'd also built a breech house and some rifle lanes. But Carter had taken us to the sniper course. In the years I'd been gone, they'd added and changed a lot.

"Dad and the uncles have done a good job," I noted as we walked back the quarter mile to the shooting platform.

"They have," he agreed. "We're lucky. They've built this for us."

I'd heard that a lot over the years, that one day when the guys retired, Triple Canopy would be left to the next generation. The very thought of them retiring had me grinding my teeth. Wasn't that my issue? Lenox, Jasper, Clark, and my dad had spent years serving our country. When they were done doing that, they'd spent years building the family a legacy. Something good and prosperous that we'd all benefit from.

And now they were risking it all for revenge.

They deserved to enjoy their retirement, not spend it in prison. Or worse yet—dead. All for what? To seek vengeance on a man who'd wronged me.

More guilt. More responsibility.

Why couldn't everyone see I didn't want to shoulder it? I wasn't strong enough. I would crumble under the weight of it and cease to live.

"I want to explain something to you," Carter started, and my stomach pitched and soured. "You're mixing up anger and worry. No one is mad at you about anything, we're scared. Not for your safety, but your mental health. I know you can't see it, but we all feel it. You've changed in a way that makes us all feel like we've lost you."

"What's that mean, that you've lost me?"

"Like you don't want to be part of the family. Like you've pulled away from all of us. And I have to tell you, Liberty, it hurts like a bitch."

I felt the sting of tears in my throat. I didn't want my family to hurt. I didn't want any of them to think I didn't want to be part of them.

"What's wrong with me?" I asked.

Carter stopped abruptly and faced me. "Not a damn thing is wrong with you."

"Then why am I doing this?"

"Because you're scared."

Am I scared?

I didn't think I was, not of Roman. I hadn't been scared when I'd gone back out into the field with Drake and his team. I didn't have any panicked reactions to gunfire. I hadn't been scared I'd be taken hostage again.

"So, you think I'm scared and weak and that's why I'm pulling away from everyone?"

"There's that word again," Carter growled. "It's a reoccurring theme with you. Why is that, Liberty? What's your hang-up? Has anyone ever made you feel inferior? Have I ever treated you like you're less than?"

"No."

"Then why do you keep calling yourself weak? And why in the hell do you keep accusing us of thinking you are?" Carter blew out a long breath but it did nothing to soften his expression. "What comes out of your mouth, your ears hear, what your ears hear you start to believe. The more you say you're weak, the more you believe it."

He was right. That was something our parents had told all the cousins over the years. Words that I lived by. I'd told myself over and over I was strong when I was going through Ranger school. That I was going to finish. I repeated that so many times until I believed it.

"I feel weak," I admitted.

"Then change it."

Right, change it. Like all I had to do was flip a switch and I'd go back to my old self.

"How?"

"For starters, never say that goddamn word again. Never, Moira. Erase it from your vocabulary. You're so stuck on this notion that you're weak that you can't see past it. But that's *you* thinking that, not us. I'm not blowing sunshine when I tell you, you're a strong and brave woman. I'm proud of you, Cousin. So damn proud I'm bursting with it. We're not giving you special treatment because you are some weak, broken woman. Fuck, I hate that you think that.

"After that, start talking, and not just with your doctor, with us, your family, the ones who love you. Trust us to be strong for you. You're a survivor, say *that* word. And then get out of the house and start living. You have a few weeks until you have to report back to work, come to Triple Canopy. Shoot, blow shit up, work out, climb the rappelling wall, go have lunch with the girls, go to the station to visit Jackson. Anything but sitting around thinking about shit that's fucking with your head."

Carter started walking again and I thought about what he said. He was right about one thing, I had to stop hiding in my parents' house.

"I'm not scared of Roman. I'm scared Dad and the uncles and you are going to do something reckless and get into trouble or dead. Neither I'd be able to live with."

"Then it's good we're the best at what we do."

"I'm being serious, Carter."

"And so am I. Think about this. After years of loving Laney from afar, not allowing myself to take what I knew was mine, that now after I finally pulled my head out of my ass and I have her, have my Emma, would I ever do a single thing to risk losing them?"

"No," I answered, because he wouldn't.

Carter had loved Delaney all his life and had forced himself to live in misery, denying them both for stupid reasons. He'd never do anything to lose them.

We silently made our way back to the shooting benches. Carter jerked his chin to the two rifles set up.

"Your choice. McMillian TAC-338 or the Savage AXIS."

My eyes hit the weapons, landing on the flat, dark-earth finish of the TAC-338 and I smiled. My heartrate ticked up and excitement started coursing through me.

"What kind of glass?" I asked Carter about the scopes he had mounted.

"The TAC-338 has a Steiner and the Savage has a NightForce."

"I'll take the Savage."

Carter smiled and shook his head. "You've always been a sucker for NightForce glass. But today, it's not gonna help you, baby cousin."

"Wager?" I teased.

"If you lose, you have to eat a handful of fried crickets."

My stomach revolted at the very thought of putting those nasty, crunchy insects in my mouth. Devil's food, that's what they were, and the problem was everyone in the family knew how much I hated them. Therefore, they were used in every bet.

"Fine. But if you lose, you have to eat three peanut butter sandwiches." I smirked.

Carter hated peanut butter so much the smell made him gag.

"One," he countered.

"Two, and that's final."

"Fine, but the handful of crickets are measured by my hand, not yours."

"Fine," I agreed, feeling confident I was going to win.

"There's ten targets out there. Good luck."

"Don't need luck, Cousin. I got mad skills. Hope you've found time to stay sharp between diaper changes and feedings."

"As a tack, Liberty."

"Right. I've noticed Laney's been feeding you well, too. Looks like you've gone a little soft to me."

Carter tossed his head back and laughed. He slid

behind the TAC-338, adjusting his ass on the bench so he could rest his shoulder on the stock.

"You're procrastinating. Sit your ass down so I can win. After you've eaten your crickets, you can call my wife and ask if I've gone soft."

"I think I'll pass asking that."

Carter chuckled again and gave me time to take my seat.

The second my hand glided over the anodized frame of the rifle, the smell of cleaning solvent filling my nostrils, and the cool, hardened plastic of the cheek rest pressed against my face, peace settled over me.

And in that moment, I felt normal.

Everything felt right.

Not so much because I had a weapon in my hand, but because it was familiar.

"You better not be cheating," I told him.

"How could I cheat?"

"Oh, I don't know, have me sighted in at three-hundred yards rather than five-hundred. And before you deny it, you knew I'd choose the NightForce."

"Would I do that?" Carter asked with humor lacing his tone.

"Yes."

"Guess we'll have to see. On three."

Carter counted us down and I was already peering down my scope, slowing my breathing, and readying myself for my first shot.

I flinched when Carter got the first shot off and the target exploded. After I'd mentally scolded myself for startling, I had to admit that Carter's exploding targets were awesome.

With one in my crosshairs, I slowly compressed the trigger and seconds later, a fireball shot up. I barely contained my whoop of celebration and moved to acquire another container.

Back and forth we went until Carter had five and I had four, both of us searching for the tenth target. At five-hundred yards, a paint can looked like a speck even through my high-powered scope. If they hadn't been painted silver they would've blended in and been damn near impossible to find.

I caught a glimpse of reflection from the sun and quickly sighted in. I had to take precious seconds to calm my excitement so I didn't blow my shot.

Finally I pressed the trigger and the resulting detonation was music to my ears.

No eating crickets.

"How do you like me now, sucker?" I hooted.

"You always were a sore winner," he returned.

"I didn't win, we tied."

"If I don't have to eat peanut butter I consider that a win."

Okay, that was true. I didn't have to eat those disgusting little crickets so indeed I had won.

Carter told me stories about baby Emma as we cleaned up our brass and put his guns away. The smile that appeared when he talked about his daughter would've been painful to see if I wasn't so damn happy for him.

Happy for Delaney after all the years she'd waited for him.

At some point in my life, I wanted that and thought I had all the time in the world to find it. But now, I wasn't sure I'd ever have it. I knew deep down I'd found the man I was meant to be with, the person who made my heart race, my skin tingle, my hands itch to touch. But he'd destroyed me.

"Did Drake tell you what he did?" I asked Carter and watched as he closed down and gave me a guarded, blank stare.

"He did."

"Have you talked to him since he told me?"

"Yes. He called to tell me you'd bolted and asked me to pick you up."

Well, that explained how Carter had found me. I

figured Drake had called my dad or Carter but I didn't know which one.

"And?"

"Not sure what you want me to say, Liberty."

"I'm asking for your opinion."

"Are you? Or are you hoping I agree with you so you can justify your behavior."

"What's that mean?"

Still not showing any emotion, something that Drake was awfully good at doing, too. Made me wonder if they taught SEALs that particular skill during BUD/s.

"It means that I wholeheartedly, one-hundred percent disagree with how you handled him."

"Handled him?"

"Yep. Drake's a good man. Great friend. He was a phenomenal operator. And how you reacted was messed up. Not only does he care about you, he's madly in love with you, and you handed him shit and you did it without even taking a minute to think about the situation he was put in and why he did it."

"He said it was to protect me."

"Yeah. And that pisses you off?"

Swear to God, I was going to have to make a dentist appointment soon, the way I'd been grinding my teeth recently.

"Hell, yes, it does. I don't need to be protected by all of you."

"You're so fucking stubborn. You always have been. Remember before I left for the academy, and Jenny whatever-her-name-was went around and was telling everyone that I had texted her some picture and she was showing it around?"

"Yeah."

"And what did you do?" He held his palm out. "Wait, don't answer that. I'll remind you. You committed a crime and broke into her locker, stole her phone. Then you went about proving I didn't send her a picture of my dick, some kid Pete, or whatever his name was, did. No one could talk you out of it. You were hellbent on protecting me, even if it was just my reputation. That's you. Always has been. You will do anything to protect us—your family."

"That's different."

"*Right,*" he bit out sarcastically, "You were protecting me. Drake was protecting you. One more thing. Drake was nineteen years in. He had six months until he rolled out of there. Do you think that maybe he also took into consideration that you're only what, six or seven years into your career? That maybe it was time he got out anyway?"

"With his retirement stripped."

"Fuck, Cousin, you're gonna find anything to be pissed about. You're fighting just to fight. Do you think that man cares about his retirement? Christ, he'll make more money. He fucking loves you. And he proved it by making it possible for you to go back out and do your job. He made sure that all of your hard work wasn't wasted. And something else that's gonna piss you off, but he did it in a way that you are free and clear without so much as a blemish on your record. And he'd do it again, even if it means he loses you, because he loves you that much. And it fucks me to admit this, pains me down to my soul, but he did something for you that I wasn't willing to do for Delaney until it was almost too late, and that was give up my place on the teams so I could be with her."

Fire scorched through me, so hot, travelling so fast, burning me from the inside out.

What am I doing?

Did I overreact? Was I wrong?

Everything came at me too fast and I couldn't push it out of my head fast enough. Too many emotions slammed around in my head.

"I'm so fucking scared this is the person I'm going to be for the rest of my life. I'm scared that Roman snapped something that I can't fix. I'm scared

I'm going to lose my dad. I'm scared I won't be able to fix myself and I'll lose Drake. I'm so, so scared that Roman will take more from me and I won't be able to stop him. I'm scared that I'll never forgive myself for my team dying. I'm so goddamn scared of everything."

Carter yanked me into his arms and squeezed me until I wheezed, "I hate this. I hate how one second I feel rational and sane, the next I feel like I'm spinning out of control. And I can't stop it. I just want to be normal."

"Honey, you are normal. You gotta keep getting it out, but you need to stop disconnecting."

Was that what I was doing, disconnecting?

"I don't think I am."

"You are. You're seeing your therapist, you've told us what happened, but, Liberty, when you did, you didn't tell a single one of us how you felt."

My cheeks flamed red and I was happy he couldn't see me.

"Because I'm embarrassed."

"Embarrassed? What the fuck for?"

"I was afraid. I cried—no, I broke down and sobbed when he was beating—"

"Fuck, Cousin. I can still taste the helplessness. I couldn't help myself. I couldn't help my team, I was completely useless. And I'll tell you a secret, the only other person who knows this is Trey.

"We were sitting in a cage. No lie, Liberty, it was a cage. In the distance, we could hear Drake taking a thrashing. It was so bad, we heard him crying out, something he hadn't done in the three days we'd been held. And I lost it. Tears running down my face, I didn't bother to try and hide them. I know Trey thought it was because I was scared—and yeah, part of it was that—but the real fear I felt was for everything I'd left unsaid. The way I was gonna leave this earth without Laney knowing, really, truly, know how much I loved her.

"Then we were rescued, and I couldn't stop the flight, fright, or freeze response. My mind kept me in a constant loop of what-ifs, so I stayed disconnected and did it until Laney lost our baby. Losing our child was the only thing that woke me up. So you want to talk about guilt, if I hadn't continued to push her away, she would've been living up in Virginia Beach with me, she wouldn't have been caught up in that shit with Mercy and Jason's case. She wouldn't have been kidnapped, beaten, and had to endure the loss of her baby. I live with that. That's what not dealing with my demons bought me."

Sweet Jesus. My heart hurt so bad for Carter.

And Laney, she was a wreck after she lost the baby, as anyone would be, but she'd kept it bottled up until she finally couldn't anymore and exploded with grief and anger.

Is that what I'm doing?

And Carter almost lost the love of his life. His sweet, baby girl wouldn't be here because he would've never admitted he loved Delaney and finally pulled his finger out and came home to marry her. All because fear was ruling his life.

Am I doing that, too? Letting fear rule me?

"I think I messed up with Drake," I whispered, and Carter's body started shaking.

"Yeah, Liberty, you did." There was humor in his tone and after what he'd told me, I was happy to hear it.

"I think I need your help."

"With Drake? No, you don't. He's sitting in a hotel room in misery. All you need to do is call him."

"I can't, not until you help me get some of this shit out of my head so I don't behave like a psycho again."

"A little crazy, yes. Psycho, no. And I have all the time in the world for you."

"I know you do. I'm sorry I keep forgetting. Thank you for not giving up on me."

"In this family, we never give up."

"I kinda forgot that, too."

And I had. I'd forgotten that together our family was strong. We could weather any storm if we stood together. I just hoped everyone had battened down the hatches because I had a feeling this storm was gonna be bad.

31

I knocked on the door when what I really wanted to do was pound on it. Or better yet, open it, walk right in unannounced, and snatch my woman up. The thought had crossed my mind, then I remembered who I was dealing with. Liberty would likely shoot an intruder and right now, that's what she'd consider me—an unwanted guest.

That was about to change.

After what seemed like a millennia the door opened. My skin prickled with the now-familiar awareness I felt anytime I was around Liberty. So close, yet so far away. That's how it felt. She was standing right in front of me wearing a tentative smile, looking nervous but no less beautiful. But, she might as well have been miles away.

"Hey," she said and stepped to the side. "Would you like to come in?"

Her invitation was tempting but we had someplace to be.

"Actually, I need you to come with me."

Real smooth, idiot.

That was not the intro I had planned, but seeing Liberty, wanting her so damn bad and not being able to touch her, had me sounding like a fool.

"Where?" she asked tensely and I couldn't blame her. Our last meeting hadn't gone well, and by my calculation this one wasn't going to, either.

"Do you trust me?"

The silence stretched, and as each second ticked, my body tightened and my irritation swelled. Not that it was her fault she hesitated—no, that was all on me.

"I do," she finally said. "But it's eight o'clock in the morning. Can this wait until after I've had coffee?"

It couldn't.

"I'll get you some on the way."

"Okay. Let me grab my purse."

Still tentative, shy, unsure. I hated what that said but she'd agreed. That was a step in the right direction, or at least I hoped it was.

Moments later, she returned with a big, slouchy, black bag slung over her shoulder. Something new to learn about Liberty McCoy, she carried a purse large enough to pack two days' worth of provisions and still have room for girly shit. There was a lot to learn about the woman I'd fallen in love with and a thread of excitement wound around my heart.

On that thought, I helped her into my truck and took a minute to appreciate the beauty that was her sitting her ass in my passenger seat—a place she belonged, a place I hoped she'd be a hundred-thousand more times. Then I started thinking about all the things I needed to tell her, some of which would likely piss her off. But I'd decided since she was already pissed, I was dumping the rest on her so we could talk about it and move past it all in one go.

But first I needed to get my woman coffee.

It wasn't until we were sitting in traffic that Liberty finally broke the silence.

"I was gonna call you today," she hesitantly admitted.

When she didn't continue, I prompted, "Yeah."

"Yeah. See, I um...had some time to think."

I knew she had. Carter had called me last night after he'd dropped Liberty off at her parents'. He hadn't gone into particulars, didn't break her confidence. What he did was interrogate me. I understood why, since Liberty was his cousin, but more than that, he cared deeply for her. So it wasn't unexpected but annoying nonetheless. Once he was done drilling me about my relationship with her, he offered his advice. That wasn't annoying, it was appreciated. I valued his opinion and his support.

And finally, he welcomed me to the Triple Canopy family and extended his gratitude that I'd taken Levi up on his offer. Carter had plans for the company. Plans that included adding more members to the team. His first choices were the brothers he served with but he hadn't thought that was an option. Now he had me and that was a start.

"Let's get you coffee, baby, then you can tell me what you had time to think about."

Liberty's easy concession would've made me worry if I hadn't known how much she liked her coffee. What I learned when she rattled off her order at the Java Shop drive-thru was that she liked her coffee complicated and sweet. Something I would never have guessed. Back in Golan Heights and in Beirut, she drank it black like I did. I found this new piece of information surprising and I filed it away for future use.

Once we were back on the road, with her warm

takeaway cup nestled between her hands, she turned sideways in her seat and I braced.

"I didn't handle yesterday well. And as much as I'd like to blame my behavior on the recent past events, I can't. Not fully, anyway. I've never reacted well to surprises or being blindsided. I was taken off-guard and with all the clutter in my head, I didn't know how to process it and I lost it. It was uncool and unwarranted. I'm sorry. I need you to know that. And I'd also like to talk about it further."

Her unexpected apology felt like a fist wrapped around my lungs, crushing the organ until all I could do was rasp in enough oxygen to not suffocate.

"I should've had a mind to you and what you're going through and found a better way to tell you. I fucked up," I admitted.

"Not sure there's a better way to tell me you gave up your life for me, Drake," she whispered.

And there was the problem. She saw what I'd done as giving up my life. When it was the opposite —I left my job, and now I could start my life. The one I wanted with her.

"Something else you need to know," I told her as I turned down the long stretch of road taking us to Triple Canopy. "Your dad came up to Virginia Beach to see me. And before you get pissed at him, his visit was a recon operation. He wanted to check me out before I showed up at his door looking for his daughter."

"Why would he think you'd show up?"

"I suspect it's because he knows his daughter, therefore he knows she's not gonna fall in love with some chump. So he knew it was only a matter of time before I came knocking."

"That's crazy, Drake. I didn't tell anyone about us. It hurt so much, I was doing everything humanly possible not to think about you."

Yeah, baby, I know the feeling.

"Only thing I can say about that is, neither of us was hiding that shit as well as we thought we were. My team knew what was going on before we got on the rescue copter. Trey called me out about it before our first debrief. Your dad said your mom saw it, recognized it, and knew what you were going through was more than just your capture. Not sure if she sent your dad to find me or if he did that on his own. What I can tell you is, he showed up, told me you were having a rough go of it and before he was done explaining exactly why he was in my living room, I was packing a bag to get to you.

"And that leads me to something else you need to know. Your dad showed on the day my separation went through and he saw my discharge papers. He knows what I did, he knows why, and he's offered me a job at Triple Canopy. I've accepted his offer."

The longer Liberty didn't respond, the harder my heart thudded in my chest. I didn't know if it was a good thing she was taking her time thinking about what I'd said or if she was plotting homicide and I was going to bite it as soon as her plan was complete.

"I'm glad you accepted my dad's offer."

Not the response I'd imagined. Liberty was full of surprises this morning.

"You understand that also means I'm moving down here."

She met that with another bout of silence.

"Good."

The front gates of Triple Canopy came into view and I knew I only had a few more minutes alone with her.

"Something else we need to discuss. I heard what you said to your mom yesterday." In my peripheral I caught Liberty fidgeting. The desire to reach over and touch her overwhelmed me, but I kept my hands on the wheel. I'd already made one grave error and I wouldn't be making another.

"We touched on this yesterday, but it bears clarification. I didn't sever our connection, and more than that, nothing can sever it. I told you what you mean to me, I heard what I mean to you, now I'm gonna set about proving it to you. Starting with my moving to Georgia, taking a job I'm looking forward to starting, and setting up a life that's absolutely going to include you. So, heads up, baby—you can fight me on this journey, but I'm dragging you along until you believe I gave up nothing, because I've gained everything."

Liberty sighed. "Yesterday, Carter told me I was disconnecting from my family because I was scared. At first I didn't get it, but then I did and I admitted all the things I'm scared of. Just so you know, you were on that list."

Fuck, that killed.

"You got no reason to be scared of me," I told her.

"I'm not scared *of* you. I'm scared I won't be good enough. I won't be all you think I am and then you'll realize you did indeed give up everything and you did it for nothing."

"That, Liberty, is impossible. I know who you are. I might not have known how you liked your coffee or that you carry the biggest fuckin' purse I've ever seen. I might not know the foods you hate, or the movies you like, or what books, if any, you like to read. But I know your strength, your determination, your loyalty. I admire your integrity, resolve, and independence. You're gorgeous, you've got great legs, you're the best kiss I've ever had. I know when I touch you, you go wild—even standing up in a dirty-assed shower stall. I love the way you are with my friends, the easy banter you have with them, even if I get jealous and make myself look like an ass. I love that they respect you, not only as a woman, but as a soldier, and they do because you earned that respect because you're bad ass. You're kind, empathetic, and strong. So damn strong. And I know that's only the beginning of all the things I love about you. There's more to discover and when I do, I'll love you more than I do now."

With that, I cut the ignition and turned to face her. What I saw took my breath. My Liberty was back. The one I'd held after nightmares who looked at me with her face relaxed, eyes soft. I don't know how I missed it when we were in the field, but I couldn't deny it now, that look wasn't lust and need—it was love. I knew she felt the same way about me as I felt about her, but I wasn't going to push for more now. We needed to find our way to those words and I was looking forward to taking us there.

"Before we go in, I want you to know I have your back," I declared and watched her shoulders tense.

"What does that mean?"

"It means whatever it needs to mean. No matter what happens in there, I'm on your side."

"Why are we here?"

"You want your control back. We're here so you can take it. However you need to do it, I'm at your side."

"Do they know I'm coming?"

"Nope."

"Are they going to be pissed?"

I'd venture to say that was a strong possibility. It was my first official day on the job and Liberty was with me like it was bring your woman to work day.

"Maybe."

"Maybe? This might not be a good idea."

"You told me you felt like no one was listening to you. That your family was making decisions that affected you and you were not being included in those conversations. You told me you wanted to be in control of your life. Do you still feel that way?"

"Considering I told you those things yesterday, Drake, and they didn't all suddenly change overnight, the answer is yes."

"Then pissed or not, this is what you need, so you're gonna get it."

"You're serious?"

"Absolutely."

A beautiful, heart-stopping smile appeared, and for a moment, that blinding smile stirred up vivid memories of the first time she looked at me. She had not been smiling, she was bloody, bruised, and beaten to hell. Pride swelled. The woman was extraordinary and she couldn't begin to understand all the ways she was. She could not see what I saw, what her family saw.

"Then let's get in there."

Moira Liberty McCoy had not broken. Roman Kushnir did his best and he'd failed. She was stronger than she'd ever been, and when she repaired the tiny cracks her capture had left, she'd be unstoppable.

32

My heart was slamming against my ribs for more reasons than one. I was almost grateful I was getting ready to face my dad, uncles, and Carter. Because the prospect of that was so frightening it took all of my energy. Therefore I didn't have it in me to freak out over what Drake had said to me.

That didn't mean I wasn't rolling his words over in my head like a crazy person. Especially the part about discovering more and when he does, he'll love me more than he does now. I wasn't sure what to do with that. I mean I did, I wanted to jump up and down and do a dance that would have him running for the hills because I'd look like a freak. But it also scared the pants off me.

And the part about him dragging me with him as he led us where he wanted us to go—sweet Jesus. That scared me for different reasons. In my current state of mind, was I ready for a relationship? I was a basket case and that was putting it mildly. I was having angry outbursts that I couldn't control.

"Baby?" Drake called.

"Huh?"

He jerked his chin and smiled toward the reception desk.

"Oh. Sorry. Hi, Lauren, sorry I spaced out for a second."

"Babe, Lauren's been talkin' to you for like three minutes."

My body froze and my back shot straight. "It wasn't three minutes, Drake," I snapped.

"Just joking with you," he muttered and kissed my head.

Lord, that felt good, almost as good as when he put his arm around my shoulders and tucked me close, which he did next.

"Good to see you, Liberty. You can go back, your dad's in the conference room."

"Thanks."

We started to walk out of the reception area

when something dawned on me. "Have you been here before?"

"Nope."

"Okay, so that's obviously reception. Lauren's been here a few years. She helped out with scheduling and stuff before Quinn started and took it over. Quinn's kind of a jack of all trades. She handles all of the finances, schedules, and contracts go through her before she sends them through to the uncles—"

"The uncles?" Drake chuckled.

"Yeah, that's what we all call them. Well, the cousins do. It's easier than calling them each by their names. So that's what Quinn does. She's hoping Hadley will come aboard and take over contracts. Hadley Walker is her sister, one of the twins. But Hadley's a librarian and is fighting the pull of Triple Canopy even though she makes jack shit at her current job and she has to deal with county politics, which she despises. Adalynn Walker, the other twin, is a physical therapist. She works with Triple Canopy when needed, but not exclusively. She has other clients.

"So, this hallway leads to the conference room, surveillance center, and gym. If we would've gone down the other hall to the right of Lauren's desk, that would've taken us to the offices. But you can get there from the end of this hall, too. It's like a big square with the surveillance room in the middle."

"Got it."

I slowed my pace and glanced up at Drake to find him grinning down at me.

"What?"

"Nothing, babe. I just like to hear you talk, especially when you're excited about something."

"Oh."

He used my momentary surprise to his advantage and leaned down to place a hard, closed-mouth kiss on my lips. When he pulled back, I blinked several times until he came into focus.

"What was that for?" I whispered.

"No reason." He shrugged then muttered, "Because I can. Because you're standing next to me looking pretty. Because it's been weeks and I couldn't stop myself."

Before I could respond or even pull myself from the trance I was in, I heard my dad's booming voice.

"Good, you're here. Let's get started."

Dad didn't wait for either of us to respond before he slipped into the conference room.

"Thought you said they didn't know I was coming?"

"Didn't tell a soul I was bringing you with me," he vowed. "You ready?"

"Yeah," I exhaled.

Then, before I was ready, we were at the door. Drake placed his hand on my lower back and he guided me into the room.

Jasper, Clark, Lenox, Carter, Brady, my dad, and my mom were all sitting. To say I was shocked to see my mom was the understatement of the century.

"Hi, sweetie," my mom cooed like she wasn't as surprised to see me as I was to see her.

"Uh, hi, Mom."

"Take a seat and we'll get started," my dad offered and I looked around the table noting there were two empty chairs. One that very obviously had been brought in because it didn't match the other eight nor the heavy oak table.

"What are we starting? And how'd you know I'd be here?"

"Figured this was how Drake would play it," Dad answered, then he breezed into introductions. "Drake, these are my partners, Jasper Walker, Nolan Clark, Carter Lenox." Dad pointed to my uncles as he said their names. "This is Brady Hewitt. He draws up our site security plans, installs systems, works the ranges and tac training with Carter, and he also heads the sniper course."

"Hewitt?" Drake asked in a tone full of wonderment. And when I glanced over at him, he was staring at Brady. "Were you with the 75th?"

"Yep," Brady clipped.

"Damn, brother, you have one of the longest kills confirmed. Twenty-five hundred meters, right?"

I looked at Brady to see him nod his confirmation.

"You still have that Accuracy International? Heard that was your personal piece. I'd love to go out with you sometime," Drake continued.

"Yeah, she's my personal build," Brady confirmed. "I'll take you out sometime."

"This is my wife," Dad cut in. "Blake McCoy. She's our head intel specialist but she only works high priority operations. We have two other tech guys in house, you'll meet them later."

"Good to meet everyone." Drake lifted his chin.

There was a chorus of "you, toos" and "welcomes." When that was over, Dad motioned to the seats and I took that as my cue to sit. Something about my father, he was stubborn, if he wanted Drake and me to sit before he explained what was going on, he'd wait us out, and he'd do it with patience like he had nothing better to do other than sit in silence.

Annoying.

The second my ass touched the seat, Carter slid two folders across the table. Drake reached out, grabbed them, and passed one to me.

"That's everything we dug up on Roman Kushnir," my mom started. "You'll also find a full workup on Roman Bolick, the man Lenox took out, as well as Annelise and her family. Take a look and tell us if I missed anything."

My gaze shot to my mother's. Her normal, easy smile was gone. She was all business sitting to my dad's right near the head of the table, about five seats away from me. This was new, I'd never seen my mom at work. Of course I knew she worked at Triple Canopy, she'd help start it. But at home, Blake McCoy was just Mom. This side of her, the no-nonsense, intel specialist was...different.

Different how, I couldn't explain, but a rush of excitement welled at the thought of working with my mom on a case.

"Fuck," Drake muttered from beside me.

"What?"

I hadn't opened my file yet so Drake slid a piece

of paper toward me and pointed at the bottom, tapping his finger angrily at the subsection.

"Either Wick purposefully withheld a lot of information or this wasn't in his packet on Roman's family history," Drake started. "When we were debriefed, Wick seemed genuinely surprised that the attack on the lieutenant's squad was personal, yet he came back rather quickly with Roman's name. Something at the time bothered me, but I didn't ask."

"What did he tell you about Roman?" Uncle Jasper asked.

I was too busy reading the document to answer so Drake did. "It was evident Roman Kushnir was on radar, or Wick wouldn't have had a half-assed report so quickly. Luke asked why Roman hadn't been taken out. Wick's response was Roman was connected, then he explained that connection was with Ukrainian organized crime. His grandfather was the Don of Nova, but Wick didn't get a chance to explain who'd assumed power as the Don after the grandfather's death. We switched topics to Lore and Roman's connection. They were both in Beirut and Roman was moving large quantities of citric acid, food-grade hydrogen peroxide, and hexamine fuel tabs."

"HMTD," my dad muttered.

"Right. That was Lore's signature," I interjected. "There were two attacks in Iraq, British supply convoys. It made no sense, because the area in which the armored troop carriers were ambushed had been cleared. In fact, the area had been marked friendly. Then suddenly, back-to-back attacks. My team was sent in to scout the AO. What we found was one of Lore's manufacturing sites. There was copper slag in the building. My thought was Lore was building precision copper EFPs. The armor plate troop carriers were demolished, and not by an amateur IED maker. Wick confirmed there was a shipment of copper going into Beirut. So, between the citric acid, peroxide, and hexamine, we had the copper, turning the loose connection into a solid one. Roman was one of Lore's suppliers."

Everyone in the room was staring at me. Well, that was, everyone except Drake, he was looking over the file.

"What?" I asked as my gaze swept the table.

"Babe?" Drake called before anyone could respond. "Take a look at the shipping manifest your mom found, page thirty-two."

Page thirty-two, good Lord, how fast could Drake read?

I shuffled through the papers until I found the

manifest and scanned the list of seemingly random and frankly strange items. "What am I looking for?"

"JB Weld. Methyl alcohol. Aluminum pipes. Silicone spray," Drake listed four of the items on the list. "What was Lore building with those supplies?"

"Um. JB Weld is two-part epoxy. To simplify, it bonds pieces of metal together. If he was cutting the pipes, he could use the JB to glue the caps on. He could've wetted the HMTD with methyl alcohol so the decomposition slowed. But I don't know what purpose the silicone spray would play. Beyond that, I don't know. Trey's an explosives expert, not me."

"Think, baby, you know Lore. You studied him, what would he be making?"

"Best guess, a detonator. HMTD is heat-sensitive, encapsulating it in an aluminum pipe would cause the off-gasses to heat. But, Drake, when the HMTD reached ignition temperature, the blast wouldn't be violent enough to cause damage. And if it was meant to be a detonator, again I don't think it would be powerful enough to ignite a secondary charge. Something like this wouldn't be a bang, it'd be more like a pop."

"TNT, RDX, and PENT have the lowest detonation velocities," Clark put in. "And ANFO if the nitrate pills were powdered."

The vibe in the room changed. It charged with something worrisome, scarier than my family going after Roman to seek vengeance, even more terrifying than the possibility of the men I loved most in this world putting themselves in harm's way to avenge me.

"What's happening?" I asked.

Drake slid another document in front of me, and as I scanned this one, I knew why the vibe had changed. I understood that the situation had shifted and it'd done so in a major way.

"How did Wick miss this?" I surged to my feet and Drake's hand shot out and grabbed mine, yanking me back down.

"He likely didn't," Jasper unhappily answered.

"Roman's uncle is in the envoy to the UN economic and Social council. How the hell is that possible?"

"Corruption," my dad responded.

"Marko Kushnir is the head of an organized crime syndicate. And from the intel Mom gathered, it's widely known. So, while I understand corruption, I don't understand how the UN allowed this to happen."

"Lots of ways for corruption to leak," Lenox noted.

Well, fucking hell. This puts a whole new spin on every-damn-thing.

"So I was bait. Likely Roman's ties to the infamous bomb maker Lore hit the radar, the government needed a way to take him out, which meant cutting off Lore's supply chain. And they needed to do this without it looking like an assassination, so we didn't piss off his uncle, the envoy and crime boss. If Roman was killed during a business deal, Marko would turn his sights on Lore, because that's who the government would point him to. Marko would take out Lore himself to avenge his nephew and everyone walked away smelling like roses. All they needed was a way to lure Roman out, and everyone knew he wouldn't pass a golden opportunity to take out a McCoy. Am I getting all of that right?"

The room remained quiet as my dad and uncles all exchanged looks.

"Yes, honey, you're correct," my mom finally spoke.

"So who leaked it? And was my team briefed we were walking into a trap of the Army's making? Did they know their objective was to kill Roman? And further, why the fuck wasn't I briefed?"

"All good questions, Cousin. Ones we'll get the answers to, but right now, our focus is on the UN economic meeting. Word is, Marko Kushnir and the Armenian envoy have serious bad blood."

"Page ninety-four," Drake told me.

"Jesus, are you a speed reader?" I asked.

"Read enough of these to know what I'm looking for and ignore the rest," Drake told me. "Your mom found chatter that Marko's fed up with the Armenian and he's using the meeting as his opportunity to take him out."

"With a bomb?" I inquired.

"Yeah, about that," Brady interjected. "Two flaws with the HMTD being used as a self-igniting detonator. You're forgetting it would need a heat source. Once it's dry, it no longer gasses. You're forgetting HMTD has to be dry to ignite, and it wouldn't if it was capped off. Second problem is, it's just too damn complicated. Simple and stupid, that's the key to any explosive device."

"Damn, you're right."

I felt my cheeks heat at my mistake. As the saying went, I knew just enough to be dangerous but not enough to be smart.

Drake's big hand landed on my thigh and he gave it a squeeze, then he shook his head.

"Analyze, evaluate, examine. You know we can't develop a course of action until all intel is studied.

Part of that is making assumptions then scrutinizing those theories. You're damn good at all of that and smart as hell. Your insight is valuable. Don't pull back and clam up."

How did he know that's what I was getting ready to do? The dark, ugly part of my brain that had recently developed was telling me I wasn't good enough to be sitting around the table with a group of seasoned professional warfighters. All of them had years of experience on me—not to mention they were all far more intelligent.

"Anyone mind if we call Trey Durum? He's our demo expert."

My heart clamped painfully at Drake's statement and I wondered if he realized what he said.

"If he's willing to give his opinion, we'd be obliged." My dad answered Drake but his gaze was set on me and his eyes were narrowing more and more by the millisecond.

Drake's hand left my thigh, and as he pulled his phone out of his pocket, I started thinking about all the possible ways Roman had found my squad.

"Was Wick able to get the commanding general of CID to agree to an investigation?" I asked as Drake held his phone to his ear.

"The lieutenant colonel in charge of your unit

refused. Though Wick expected that, and is trying a different route," Carter answered. "Standard denial. No one in your company wants CID poking their noses in a black ops unit. Wick knew it was a long shot."

"You're on speaker. McCoy, Clark, Walker, Lenox, Brady Hewitt, and Mrs. McCoy are present along with Church and Lieutenant McCoy."

"Ma'ams, gentlemen, Church, what can I help with?"

"Just curious, Razor, why'd you single me out?" Carter chuckled.

"Never known you to be a gentleman," Trey returned.

Carter shook his head and smiled at Drake. "You know there will be days you'll miss being on the teams, then there are days when you remember Razor's lame attempts at insults and you're glad not to have to listen to them anymore."

"You know you miss me," Trey returned.

"Like a case of vaginal warts... shit." Carter turned a bright shade of red and mumbled, "Sorry, Aunt Blake."

My mom smiled huge and started to laugh. Then one after another, my uncles joined my mom. But it wasn't until I heard my dad's deep, coarse rumble that I finally let the knot in my heart start to loosen.

Carter's face remained crimson and it reminded me of the way he used to look when Delaney would poke fun at him when we were teenagers. That was when I truly started to remember who we were— who our family was—and how we always stuck close.

33

I felt it, the instant Liberty's body relaxed next to mine. I didn't know what had caused it but I was happy for it.

"Is Carter a nice shade of his signature purple?" Trey asked through the phone.

"Gettin' there," I told him.

Church was easy to embarrass, or he was when we weren't on a mission. The slightest bit of impropriety had his face turning colors.

"We need your opinion on some materials on a shipping manifest," I cut to the chase.

"Hit me, I'm ready."

All the humor fled from Trey's tone as he morphed into operational mode.

I ran down the items and explained Liberty's

presumption on the HMTD and Brady's thoughts on why it was wrong.

When I was done Trey was silent for a spell. Then he asked, "You said cold packs and model rockets?"

"Correct," I confirmed.

"With those models, was there nitromethane?"

"Fuel for the models, again correct."

"First, in theory what the lieutenant—"

"Can you please stop calling me lieutenant and ma'am? Christ, Trey, you know my name," Liberty griped.

"Just trying to be polite. No need to get your panties twisted," Trey huffed then continued. "Liberty's theory was almost correct, but as Hewitt—and just as a side note, dude, I know who you are and I just have to say, that kill at twenty-five hundred meters was brilliant. Anyway, as Hewitt pointed out, you'd need a heat source. The pipe would have to be wrapped in a thermo blanket for the HMTD to ignite. He's also correct that setup is just too damn complicated. But the cold packs and nitro would make one hell of an explosive."

"How so?" Levi inquired.

"The cold pack has ammonium nitrate in it. Open the unbroken pack up, take that out, mix it with the nitro, bam—you have yourself an explosive."

"Detonator?"

"Shit, a straw, a pack of gum, a two-dollar cheap-ass Chinese timer, an electro match, and a pinch of HMTD. Does this have to do with Roman?"

"Just trying to piece this all together," Levi told him.

"Run me through what you have."

I barely suppressed my grin at Trey's audacity. Pure Trey, nosing his way into something that wasn't his business because there was a puzzle to be solved. Something he not only enjoyed but he was good at it.

"No offense, Durum, we appreciate your help but I think we've said enough over an unsecure line."

"Then send someone to the airport to pick my ass up. I'll be down in a few hours."

"What?" I laughed, not able to hold back.

Pushy bastard.

"I'm far from stupid. I'm also not gonna sit around on my ass in this goddamn apartment on med leave while Liberty's ass is still swinging. You got a thread of a lead, I want in. And if you'd give Matt, Luke, and Logan the opportunity, they'd be down there in a flash and you know it."

Fucking hell, I was seriously going to miss serving with Trey.

"Trey, you need to rest. You don't have to come down here," Liberty tried to dissuade him.

It wasn't going to work, but it was cute of her to try.

"I don't *have* to do anything, Liberty, but I'm still gonna come down there."

"Seriously—"

"Yeah, seriously. I owe you and I haven't forgotten. So far, my leg's still attached and that's because of you. The man who harmed you is still running around out there breathin' free. And that is unacceptable. So, until his ass is six-feet under, I'm at your service."

"Whatever you say, Trey. But fair warning, I don't give sponge baths and I don't have sympathy when someone's hurt, and if you don't believe me, ask Carter what happened when he broke his collarbone when he was ten. I'm telling you that so you don't think when you get here I'm gonna baby your ass even though you're injured."

"Noted." Trey chuckled. "Church, I'll text you with my flight info."

"Copy."

Trey disconnected and I looked around the room

noticing all eyes were on Liberty. I wasn't sure what they were seeing when they looked at her but I did know she'd be uncomfortable with the attention, therefore I broke the spell.

"Are you all comfortable with this? Carter and I can meet Trey at the airport and tell him to back off if you want us to," I offered.

Levi, Lenox, Clark, and Jasper exchanged looks and my gut tightened. The four men were a unit, a team—they didn't need words to communicate. A skillful art I'd shared with my guys as well. Something that gutted me to know I no longer had. I felt Carter's eyes on me and my gaze slid to him.

So much for not having it anymore, Carter knew exactly what I was thinking. Years of working with him meant he could read me whether I wanted him to or not.

He gave me a nod and tight smile. I reckoned that was his way of acknowledging my thoughts and telling me it would get easier.

"It'll be good to have Trey's input. Especially if we're dealing with explosives. Each of us can hold our own, but it's good to have someone with working knowledge. We'll take a break, Carter and Liberty can show you around. When you're done with that, Quinn has your employee contract ready. If you have any questions about it, come see me and we'll discuss it," Levi said and stood. "In the meantime, I'm taking my wife back to my office."

Liberty's face scrunched in the cutest grimace and she started to cough. "God, Dad, gross."

"Nothing gross about a man enjoying—"

"Don't finish that," Liberty demanded and stood. "Can you at least give Drake like a *day* to get to know you before you start talking about enjoying *things* in front of him?"

"I find it doubtful a man like Drake needs that time, Liberty," Lenox added. "Drake. It was a pleasure to finally meet you. When you have time stop by my office, I'd like a word."

"Will do. Heard a lot about you all over the years. Good to finally meet you as well."

With chin lifts, slaps on my shoulder accompanied by welcomes, the men filed out of the room leaving Carter, Liberty, and me.

"Well, well, well, who woulda thought," Carter drawled. "Drake and my baby cousin."

"Carter," I rumbled a warning before he said something that set Liberty off.

"I think this is where I'm supposed to grill my cousin's man. You know, put him through his paces, threaten him, maybe puff my chest out so he'll know

I'll kick his ass if he hurts her. But I'm fucked. Can't do any of that. You totally robbed me of the pleasure." Carter paused and looked between the two of us, then his gaze landed on Liberty even though his words were meant for me. "Couldn't have built a better man for her, brother."

Fucking hell, that felt good at the same time it burned. Carter's approval meant a lot, but I had a whole hell of a lot of work to do to make Liberty mine.

"Let's go give him a tour." That was directed to Liberty. "When we're done, we'll hit Brady up and see if he wants to go out to the range while we wait for Trey. Dad and the uncles won't want to meet again until he's here." Then Carter's gaze came back to mine. "Word of advice, don't ever make a bet with my sweet cousin. She's vicious and she hates to lose. It's a no-win situation—either you're following through with whatever fuckup wager you made, or she's pouting and bitching about all the ways it wasn't her fault she lost, complaining about having to do whatever the bet was."

"You're full of shit," Liberty huffed. "Your wife is the sore loser, not me. I never welch on a bet."

"Didn't say you welched, just that you bitched."

"Whatever." Liberty's eyes sliced to me and it

took me a moment to realize what I was seeing. No sadness. No grief. Just her pretty, unusual eyes. "Thought you said you'd have my back. But there you are all quiet."

"Baby, I don't know because we've never made a bet, but just to say when we were in Golan Heights and Luke mentioned playing poker, I saw the way your eyes lit up and I have to tell you it scared the hell out of me. It was excitement and vindictiveness all rolled into one. I'm not sorry we didn't get a chance to play."

"What?" she grouched. "I didn't look any sort of way."

"Babe, you totally did."

"Yeah, never let her sucker you into poker. She's a master and you'll be naked and running around the backyard with your junk swinging."

My body shook with all the effort it took to stop the laughter from bubbling out.

Liberty's eyes narrowed. "I only did that to you once. And only because you were out of money and still wanted to play."

"Whatever, that shit was a conspiracy. You, Delaney, and Quinn plotted that shit."

"Actually..." Liberty smiled. "It was all Ethan's idea."

"Little fucker," Carter mumbled and Liberty grinned so huge I couldn't stop myself from tagging her around the waist and pulling her to me.

"Vicious," I whispered into her hair and inhaled the fruity scent of her shampoo. A smell I planned to become intimately familiar with.

She melted against me and that felt so fucking fantastic I had to think about how stupid Carter must've looked running around with his junk swinging in the wind.

This was what I wanted. My girl smiling, her family exchanging light-hearted jabs, and the feel of her pressed against me.

That was it, that's all it would take to make me happy.

34

The last few hours had been the best I'd had since I'd been home.

Which made me wonder if it was because Drake was there. And I knew without thinking on it too hard or too long, the answer to that was yes.

And that scared me.

But I didn't have time to ponder why Drake being around made me both happy and scared because Trey didn't have Carter and Drake pick him up. He rented a car and drove himself to Triple Canopy. Something that worried me because I didn't think he should be driving. I'd voiced this concern and both Carter and Drake just shook their heads at me but didn't say anything.

Before Trey had arrived, I watched Brady,

Carter, and Drake take turns shooting Brady's prized Accuracy International rifle. I declined the invitation to shoot. I was enjoying watching them too much.

When the guys were done, we finished our tour. We left Drake with Quinn so she could go over the employment contract. Drake was only in there a few minutes when he left her office and prowled to my dad's. Carter pulled me away from the door so all I heard was Drake telling my dad that something was "too much" though I wasn't sure what that something was. Then I heard my dad rumble that it was "standard" but again I couldn't make out what was standard, and then Carter yanked me down the hall and told me to mind my own business.

Unfortunately, he didn't burst into flames no matter how hard I stared at him and wished it would happen. Though the truth was, I wasn't trying all that hard because I loved his wife and his baby daughter and figured they might not like him turning into a pile of ash.

When I told Carter how annoying he was, he burst into laughter, used one arm to put me in a headlock, and gave me a noogie. A bonafide noogie, like we were kids. My Uncle Lenox came around the corner just as he did and yelled at Carter to leave me alone. He released me and when I straightened, I burst into a fit of laughter.

So immature.

Totally childish.

But it was recognizable, well-known, familiar. Something that brought me back to my youth and the stupid ways we used to torture each other. The fact that Uncle Lenox broke up the shenanigans like he had hundreds of times made it better.

I hadn't felt like myself for so long, I'd forgotten how good it felt to just...be.

And yes, that had a lot to do with Drake being there.

So now we were all back in the conference room, an extra chair had been brought in, introductions made, and someone had kindly supplied Trey with a file with all the intel my mom had gathered.

We gave Trey a moment to scan the first couple of pages, and I found he, too, had acquired Drake's skill of speed reading. I needed to up my game if I was going to analyze a report that quickly.

Deep lines formed around Trey's eyes. The scowl highlighted the scars on the side of his face. They weren't as bad as they could've been, considering. But his once-perfect face was now flawed.

"I think Lore was teaching Roman how to build a bomb," Trey said.

"Why would you think that?" I asked.

"We know Roman was in Beirut. Actually, I think Roman was on the pier with you and Logan." I felt fear slither its way into my belly and coil. Drake had stiffened next to me which only ratcheted up my anxiety. "Never could figure out why the art gallery blew. It's so random, it makes no sense. Not a single terrorist organization claimed the bombing. Roman's a supply man, that's it. According to this intel, which I have to say, I believe, Roman's an errand boy for his uncle. He moves his uncle's contraband, he supplies the scum of the world what they need to spread their hate. But he only gets a cut of the money. He's a cog. He's not a boss. If he wants to move up, he'd need to prove something to his uncle."

Drake had gone from stiff to vibrating. "Roman's first move was to kill Liberty—a show of revenge to the *Don*. The next move would be to help his uncle take out the Armenian. Learn from the most sought-after bombmaker, and bring those skills back to Uncle Marko in hopes of moving up in the ranks."

"But why would killing me matter to Marko? Roman's dad wasn't his blood, hell, they weren't even related by marriage."

It was almost like an out-of-body experience talking about my near-death experience. I could remember the second I was certain I was going to die, yet I didn't. And I'd never forget the look in Roman's eyes as he strangled the life out of me, yet I couldn't remember what color they were. It was a strange juxtaposition of memories.

"No doubt for Roman it was personal, he was avenging his father's death. But this is about proving masculinity, loyalty to family, intelligence, and balls to carry out the kill."

I glanced at my dad. His face was devoid of emotion, once again reminding me he was a hardened warrior, even if it was something he'd kept mostly hidden from me.

"Mom, did you find any connection between my chain of command and Roman or Marko?"

"Not even a thread," she answered.

"Did you run Sergeant Jacobson?"

"No. Who is that?"

"The unit armorer. Jacobson's not part of the 8th. But he knows me, knew my team, he knew when we deployed. Not where. But he knew when we were called out."

It was a long shot for a variety of reasons. The first being Jacobson had no clue what part of the world we'd been deployed to, and as much as I hated to think it, the guy wasn't very smart. It would take a goodly amount of highly illegal hacking to find out the team's whereabouts and frankly Jacobson didn't have it in him. I didn't think he was smart enough to find someone who processed the skills needed, either.

I was missing something. There had to be a connection. It was impossible for Roman to stumble upon me. He had help. He knew exactly where we were going. Then there were those damn pictures, who the hell took those?

I hadn't spoken to anyone in Golan Heights other than a polite hello. So who the hell would want to take pictures of me and Drake?

There was a sudden nagging in my gut and the more I tried to piece everything together the worse it got.

"*Impossible.*"

"What?" Drake asked.

Shit. I hadn't meant to say that out loud. I hadn't put it all together yet.

"Dad, did Wick tell you if he got copies of those pictures?"

"Moira..."

"I don't care what he did with them, or who did

what to protect me. This is important. I need to know if Drake was the target, or if both of us were. If Wick didn't get copies and they were just sent to Drake's command, he was the target. But if Wick got them—"

"Wick received his copies the day before Drake's command got theirs."

I heard Drake emit a strangled growl and I knew this wasn't the easiest subject to discuss.

"Do either of you remember any Marines on the post in Golan Heights?" I asked Drake and Trey.

"Yeah, I saw a few, probably there for training," Trey answered.

"Goddammit," Drake muttered. "There was a Marine standing sentry before the ramp ceremony. I saw him when I approached you, but stopped paying attention to him when we started talking."

He was being nice by not saying he'd stopped paying attention to the Marine when I broke down standing in front of my team in their flag-covered boxes.

"Chief Warrant Officer Geoff Ball's brother-in-law's a Marine. When we were planning our op and Golan Heights was an egress consideration, he said he hoped he got to see him."

That's all I could get out, the rest was too painful to *think* about, so I couldn't bring myself to voice it.

"Picking up the vein," Drake stated, his voice tight, his tone deadly, "he shared that shit with his wife or his brother-in-law direct."

"Outstanding work," Clark declared. "You five explore that. Blake, get us more on Roman. What else and who else did he supply?"

"You thinking there's a connection to the Marine direct or the post in general and Roman?" my dad asked.

"Either would bring us a step closer. But I'm thinking the Marine direct."

"We can't forget Liberty's military affiliation is public record. If Roman was looking for her, he'd easily find she was in the Army, her post, and her battalion," Jasper added. "Same way he probably found out Carter was in the Navy."

"We have some calls to make," my dad announced then looked at me. His face gentled and for the first time since my life had turned to hell, he looked like my dad. The one who was easy-going and laidback. The one who was patient and worry-free. Not the man wrought with grief and hurt because his daughter was on the verge of losing her shit. "Smart as a tack, my daughter. Damn proud of everything you've accomplished."

Dad, Lenox, Jasper, and Clark stood, and without another word, left the room. Before my mom followed, she smiled at me then pinched her lips. "Good to have you back, my sweet girl." With a wink, she stood. "Thanks to you, I gotta long night ahead of me."

Am I back? I didn't think a few good hours meant I wasn't still a basket case, but I had to admit, it felt pretty damn awesome not to be in a constant state of upheaval. And it did feel like the chaos in my head had mostly cleared. I could definitely think better than I could yesterday.

"You know, he's gonna be on your ass to come work for us," Brady said.

"Yeah. I got years left on my contract and thanks to Drake, I have to fulfill them." I nudged Drake and grinned to make sure he knew I was teasing.

"Not you," Brady corrected. "Him," he said and pointed to Trey.

"Yeah? Not sure I'll be much of anything with my leg the way it is. At least that's what the med board's telling me."

Whoa. Trey hadn't mentioned that.

"Are you serious they're trying to board you out?" Drake asked.

"Not much good with a fucked-up leg."

"It's been like two goddamn minutes. You haven't even rehabbed. The command's got about a million dollars tied up in you, they're not gonna let you go," Carter insisted, but his face said otherwise.

"Not if I have nerve damage, or the fracture doesn't heal right."

"I told you, you shouldn't have come. You need to be in bed."

"Actually, I need to be up moving, it prevents *blood clots*." The anger in his tone couldn't be missed.

As a matter of fact, he sounded so angry I was dropping the subject altogether because I didn't want to be the source of his pain.

"Brady's right," Carter started. "The four of them want to retire but won't do it until we have a full management crew. Brady and I, and now Drake, can only handle so much and they built this company's reputation to what it is. They won't step down until they know it's in good hands. If you want it, you tell me and we'll bring you aboard. Until you say the word, I won't mention it again. But we'd be damn lucky to have you."

I agreed with Carter—hundred percent.

Actually, Triple Canopy would be damn lucky to have Matt, Logan, and Luke, too.

I glanced at Drake and saw he was thinking the same thing.

Oh, yeah, when we were alone later we'd be talking about how to bring his whole team into the Triple Canopy fold.

Alone?

That was damn presumptuous of me.

But damn if I didn't want some alone time with Drake.

35

It was well after closing by the time we left the office.

Carter and Brady had declined my invitation to dinner. Carter because he had a beautiful wife and daughter to get home to. And Brady said he already had plans, though the way he said it made me think he was full of shit but I didn't know the man well enough to call him out on it.

We said our goodbyes to Blake who barely looked away from the screens in front of her when she'd told Liberty Levi would get her dinner later and not to expect either of them home until late. To which I wanted to tell the lovely Mrs. McCoy not to expect her daughter home at all. However, I was cruising a ray of sunshine and I wasn't about to turn a good day into shit by opening my mouth.

Levi, Jasper, Clark, and Lenox were holed up in Lenox's office. Levi immediately took in his daughter while the other three looked at me.

"Apologize we didn't get that word, Lenox. Tomorrow?"

"Sounds good."

"I sent you our notes," Liberty told the men. "Drake, Trey, and I went over every detail of our stay in Golan Heights and our mission. We also went over the art gallery bombing. We sent Mom the list of guests and the confirmed dead. The more we went over it, the more I agree with Trey. Lore was teaching Roman how to build a bomb. The gallery was the final exam. Roman obviously passed."

"The UN economic meeting is happening in two days," Jasper began. "We've made some calls. They'll be on the lookout for Roman, and be extra careful."

"When's Trey going back up to Virginia?" Clark asked.

"Tomorrow night. He's got PT," I answered.

The men all nodded their acknowledgements and Levi smiled at Liberty. "See you tomorrow, sweetheart. Have a good night."

Tomorrow. Yeah, Levi wasn't a stupid man. He was also a father who knew exactly what this was and he'd made it clear I had his blessing in a multitude of ways, including giving me a job, a salary that was more than double what I made in the Navy, and after arguing that the amount was far too high, he shut me up by explaining I was the least paid member of management. After my six-month eval, that figure would be bumped up to put me on par with Brady. He further explained that my employment package included my stuff being moved to Georgia and the cost of a furnished executive apartment until I found a house.

I thought it was too much. Levi disagreed.

But right then, hearing him tell his daughter he'd see her tomorrow was more confirmation he knew what was going on between me and Liberty and he was good with it.

"'Night, Dad. 'Night, Uncles."

We said our goodbyes and found Trey waiting in the lobby, wearing a grimace and sitting with his bum leg stretched out. The man was in more pain than he'd admit. And there was more going on with his medical board than he was saying. But Trey was Trey. He doled out information as he saw necessary —not a minute sooner. I knew better than to prod him. Not only would he not open up, but he'd get pissed and shut down further.

"Ready?" he asked when he noticed us.

"Yeah, but there's been a change of plans," Liberty told him, which confused the hell out of me because we hadn't discussed changing anything. And if she thought she was blowing me off and I was taking her back to her parents' house, she was absolutely mistaken. "I hope you don't mind, I'm too tired to go out. We thought we'd all go back to the hotel, hole up there, order room service and chill."

Damn, she was smart. She'd seen Trey in pain and knew he'd never relent about going out so she switched it up, also knowing Trey would give her whatever she wanted.

"Fine by me. I'll stop and pick up a six-pack," Trey said and stood. His face carefully blank, no hint of pain, which totally fucking sucked he was hiding it from me.

"Actually, we'll stop. I want to browse the wine. You go get checked in and we'll meet you in your room."

Yeah, Liberty was brilliant.

We made our way out to the parking lot, the sun setting low in the sky, but not dark enough the outside lighting had come on. In other words, there was enough light for me to see the worry in Liberty's eyes as she watched Trey hobble to his rental. I didn't miss her wince when Trey stopped to pull the key fob from his pocket and had to adjust his balance so his bad leg didn't take his full weight.

I reached out, grabbed her hand wondering why I hadn't already been holding it, and brought her closer to me.

"He'll be okay," I whispered.

She didn't respond.

It had to be noted, Liberty didn't drink wine. When we got to the liquor store and I asked her what kind she wanted, she crinkled her cute-as-fuck nose and told me she hated wine. Then she realized why I was asking and she grinned.

Then I found she was a really good actress. After we consumed our dinner and the six-pack was gone, she yawned and stretched and apologized to Trey about how much of a party pooper—her words—she was, but she was exhausted and couldn't keep her eyes open. She made that play after she'd seen Trey eying a bottle of pain pills. He was being so fucking stubborn he wouldn't even take his meds in front of us even though his leg was seriously killing him.

Minutes later, we left Trey lounging on his bed. Something else Liberty had arranged—us going to his room instead of him having to walk to mine then back to his.

She was different.

Had been the whole day.

I'd fallen in love with her when she was beaten and broken down—when she'd had no choice but to be tough, strong, and resilient.

Now, I was falling in love again—with a different side of her.

A new side that was softer, kind, sweet.

She'd been none of those things in the field and I was just then understanding the distinctive difference between Lieutenant McCoy and Liberty. I hadn't seen it before, because I'd had nothing to compare it to. I had to admit, I liked discovering new things about her. I liked falling in love with her a second time, when I could enjoy it, savor it, not have to hide it.

The first time had been instant—raw and primal. A painful freefall I had no chance of stopping. This time I didn't feel like my lungs were being compressed.

We got to my room and she stepped to the side and waited.

"Wanna come in?" I joked.

Liberty didn't answer, not verbally, she just smiled which was her answer and I seriously loved what she was saying without saying a word.

I unlocked the door, pushed it open, and waited for her to enter. We walked in, I shut the door, threw the deadbolt, and turned to her.

"We need to talk."

"We need to talk."

We both chuckled. And once again simultaneously said, "Jinx."

That earned me one of her blinding smiles.

"You first," I told her. "But let's get out of the entryway first."

She walked farther into the room, and like an eager puppy, I followed. Unashamed, my eyes lowered to her ass, then down to her jeans-encased legs. I couldn't help my smile when I caught sight of the boots on her feet. She was the perfect mix of sexy tomboy and soft woman.

"Are you really okay with everything that's happened?" she started.

"What do you mean?"

"You leaving the teams."

My heart constricted and I wondered if that feeling would ever stop.

"I need to preface my answer with making sure you understand I don't regret my decision. And I mean that in a way that I will never regret it. But I'd be lying if I told you it didn't sting, knowing. Knowing I'll never go out with my team again. That the bonds and friendships with the guys, and not just Trey, Matt, Logan, and Luke, but the rest of my platoon, will drastically change. Not at first, but some of those friendships will fade as time goes on. They'll leave for work ups and deployments, there will be a lot going on in their lives they'll no longer be able to share with me and yeah, that sucks. I'm gonna miss them, that brotherhood.

"Will I miss being in the Navy? Of course I will. I've been in all of my adult life. It's all I know. But I have something new, something just as important, in my life now."

Liberty was studying me with a critical gaze. She was far from naïve, she understood why those friendships would fade. She also understood the transition from soldier to civilian was sometimes difficult. Not from personal experience, but she grew up in a military family.

"I have four years left on my contract," she stated.

"Okay."

"Four years, with no guarantee I'll stay in Georgia. I could be PCS'd at any time. You know how this works."

"Yeah, I know."

"I want to stay in." Liberty's chin jutted out stubbornly and that was cute as fuck, too.

"Babe, didn't think you were gonna go AWOL."

I wasn't sure where she was going with this, but I wasn't about to allow her to use her service as an excuse not to be with me. With me no longer in the military we were free of rules and regulations and I fully intended to take advantage of my new civilian status.

"I could be deployed."

"Yep."

"I will be sent out for training and missions."

"Yep."

"Why are you acting like this is no big deal?" she huffed, thoroughly annoyed I wasn't taking her bait and making this into an issue.

"Because I know all of this. And when the time comes, we'll deal. Something I've learned is when you're dealing with the military, you don't make plans, you roll with it. So, that's what we're gonna do. If you PCS, then we move. When you're deployed, we deal with it. When you're gone for training, we deal with it. The thing you need to remember is, I willingly and gladly left the Navy so you could remain in the Army—untouched. I never for one second thought or wanted you to get out. So I don't care if you finish your contract and separate or you reup for another four and stay in. Whatever you decide, we will *deal*."

"You make it sound easy."

"Baby, it is easy. There's nothing hard about supporting you, your career, your goals, and your accomplishments. You worked your ass off to get to where you are. Enjoy it. I'm just along for the ride. Wherever you go, I'm there."

Liberty grew silent and I knew she was mulling over something else. Her bringing up her concerns about staying in the military was actually the perfect segue into what I needed to talk to her about.

"I think you get I'm in love with you. So it can't be lost on you I took a job in Georgia and moved down here to be close to you. I think I also just told you, I'm all in. Wherever life takes us, I'm ready for that. But what I need you to understand is, we take this at *your* pace. I'm taking my cues from you and we'll go as slow as you need. But straight up, Liberty, I won't let you retreat. I get you have a lot you're working through and I'm all in with that, too. I'll help you sort through anything you still have lingering inside or I'll silently stand by you if that's what you need. What I won't let you do however, is bury it. We have to get it out of you so you can move on from it."

I watched as she swallowed, the movement slow. And in a direct contradiction of what I'd just told her, I wanted to rush her and demand she agree that we'd move forward together and she'd let me help her dig out the ugly shit I knew still plagued her mind.

"You make that sound easy," she whispered.

"There's nothing hard about loving you."

"You know I'm messed up. You got a taste of it yesterday when I served you up a big ol' pile of crap. Sometimes my thoughts are so loud, so chaotic, I can't hear what my mouth's saying. It's like I know I need to shut up because what's coming out is wrong, I just can't control it. This overreactive anger gets the best of me and I lash out—at everyone. I've yelled at Carter, my dad, I've brushed my mom off. I was a total bitch to Delaney. And I don't even want to tell you what I said to Jason and Nick when all they were doing was trying to help me. Today was good, Drake. But not every day is."

Without knowing what she was doing, Liberty

was unloading her burden. What she'd meant as a warning was the opposite. She was giving me exactly what I'd asked for—a chance to walk beside her in her pain.

I was done with the physical distance, and as much as it went against the grain of a man like me, I remained rooted and instead said, "Babe, come here."

Liberty's eyes held mine. I was elated to see desire flare but she didn't move.

"I'm scared to."

"Why?"

"Because I know once I go to you, there's no turning back."

She was wrong—turning back was no longer an option.

"Come here, baby."

"I'm scared tomorrow won't be a good day and you'll see the broken parts of me."

She wasn't broken—not even close.

"Baby. Come. Here."

"I'm scared you'll take it back."

"Take what back?"

"You."

"You're afraid I'll take *me* back?"

"Yes," she whispered and tucked her chin to her chest.

I lost sight of her eyes as she hung her head.

Fuck. That.

I closed the distance, placed my fist under Liberty's chin, and lifted it until her eyes met mine.

"Never, do you ever, hang your head. Not in shame, not in fear—not ever, Moira. And just to point out, you worrying about me leaving, or changing my mind about us, means that you think I'm an asshole."

"What?" Her eyes widened. "I don't think you're an asshole."

"You must if you think I'd change my mind because you have bad days. It is not lost on me what you went through. I have firsthand, up close and personal experience with all the ways a capture fucks with your head. You're not messed up, broken, or anything else. You're tough as hell, and fighting to get back what was taken from you. You've done the hardest part, admitting that something's going on in your head and you need help getting it out. You did it. The rest will just take time. So, give yourself a break and take the time you need."

"You think that?"

"Baby, I know *that*."

My gut clenched at the sudden shift in her features and I braced.

"I heard you that day, before I opened my eyes. I heard you telling me to fight, to breathe. Your voice was so far away but I knew I wanted to find you. And when I opened my eyes and I was in your arms, I knew who you were. I felt it, like it had been written you were mine. Then you kept talking to me, telling me to rest, and I knew I wanted to hear your voice for the rest of my life. But I thought I was crazy. I fought it because having you seemed impossible for so many reasons. But I knew I never wanted you to let me go."

Now my gut was tight for another reason.

My Moira.

My fate.

She was correct—it had been written and woven into the stars that she was mine. In return, I was hers.

Thank Christ she knew it.

"Not crazy, baby. Not impossible. And I'm never gonna let you go."

Liberty gave me a small smile, pink tinged her pretty cheeks, and all sorts of naughty thoughts started massing until I felt blood rushing in the wrong direction.

"I want to stay the night."

There was nothing I wanted more.

"Good. I wasn't planning on taking you back to

your parents'. Grab a tee out of my bag to sleep in. I'm gonna take a quick shower."

Her grin turned into a smug smile and my dick throbbed. It was debatable whether I'd be taking a cold shower, or rubbing one out to get rid of my hard-on.

"Babe," I warned and stepped back.

"You want company?"

I pulled in a deep breath and tried to fortify my control.

"Love company, but right now, I think it's best we not be naked together—especially alone in a hotel room."

"Why's that?" the little minx asked and stepped closer.

"I have a good memory, Liberty. I haven't forgotten a single sound you made, the way your wet, slippery skin felt against mine, the way you taste, the way your pussy hugged my dick, and I certainly haven't forgotten how great all of that was."

"If it was great, then I don't understand."

"Because the next time I have you, it will not be in a frantic dash to completion. I'll be taking my time enjoying all the parts of you I was denied. And right now, you're tired, stressed, and have had a long day. As much as it pains me, and trust me, baby, it fucking hurts to decline your sweet invitation to join me, I have to. You know damn well, I'm weak when it comes to you. So I'm asking you to have pity on me and give me this."

"You know, I know a great way to relieve the stress of my day," she pushed, and I groaned.

Christ, why couldn't I say no to this woman? Why did all of my good, smart intentions fly out the window with minimal coaxing from her?

"Strip and get on the bed. But just to warn you, my clothes are staying on and that's final."

"What fun is that?"

"Oh, honey, not sure how fun it will be with my mouth between your legs but I can tell you it will be satisfying. Now, you're wasting time." I watched in fascinated awe as her body trembled. "You want that, Liberty, my mouth on your pussy?" She nodded, remained silent, but that pink tinge on her cheeks came back in full-force. Hell yeah, she wanted it. "Then get on the bed so I can give my woman what she wants."

Liberty wasted no more time and neither did I. Once her clothes hit the floor and her ass hit the bed, my knees hit the cheap ass carpet. I yanked her legs apart and buried my face between her thighs.

I gave her a long, slow swipe of my tongue. The

resulting moan filled the room and fed my need. Her taste, the feel of her soft flesh under my palms, her soft mew, it all hit me at once. I took a moment to enjoy all of that, then I set about making sure Liberty knew I'd give her anything she wanted.

36

Something was tickling my inner thigh and pulling me from a peaceful sleep I wasn't ready to get pulled from. But the more I moved the more it tickled until I couldn't ignore it any longer.

"Baby, wake up."

My eyes snapped open so quickly my head jolted. After a few blinks a plane of bare skin came into view. Another blink and last night came rushing back. Drake performing a miracle between my legs, culminating in a mind-bending orgasm that left me wrung out. Drake tenderly dressing me and tucking me into bed before he'd gotten up to take a shower. And finally when he came to bed and pulled me close. It was a toss-up on which was best, my head on his chest, his arm around me resting his hand on my hip, or the orgasm.

The orgasm won out but just by a smidge. That's how good it felt to be in Drake's arms.

Then I'd fallen asleep. I didn't remember waking up with a single nightmare.

Now we were in the same position we were in when we'd fallen asleep and it was the hair on his thigh, tickling mine.

"I'm awake," I muttered and tried some deep-breathing techniques my therapist had taught me.

Not because I was going to lose my mind in a fit of madness. Because I was going to lose it for a different reason—I was in Drake's bed, in his arms, after he'd given me the second-best orgasm of my life. The first being against the wall in the shower.

"You good?"

He thought I woke up because I'd had a night-mare. My heart swelled to epic proportions and I breathed deep, held it, then released it.

"I wasn't having a bad dream, honey. I don't think I had any, did I?"

Drake's body went solid under mine and suddenly none of the stress management tools I'd learned were working. My anxiety level went through the roof—maybe I had a bad night and just couldn't remember. Maybe I'd kept Drake up all night and he was upset with me. Maybe I...

I didn't get to finish my thought because I was on my back and Drake was staring down at me. Hair mussed, brown eyes warm yet full of concern.

"Wherever you are right now in your head, stop. Look at me and relax."

Okay, he didn't sound upset, he sounded worried.

I inhaled slowly through my nose, relaxed my shoulders, exhaled through my mouth praying to God I didn't have dragon breath that would send Drake running for the Listerine. And slowly I came back to myself.

"Morning, baby." He smiled.

And there looming over me, Drake had never looked sexier.

"Morning."

"To answer your question, no, you didn't have any nightmares."

Weird. But good. That was good, right? Maybe I was getting better. Maybe the worst of them were over.

I waited for him to ask what had gotten me stirred up but he didn't. Instead, he leaned forward, kissed me on my forehead, and rolled off.

461

"You wanna order room service or stop some-where before we hit the office?"

"I need to stop by my parents' house and change."

"Figured as much. You wanna shower here or there?"

"If I say here, will you join me?" Drake's eyes narrowed and I couldn't stop the giggle from erupt-ing. "Jeez, relax. I was joking."

"Ha. Ha," he mocked, not finding my joke the least bit funny, which only made me laugh more. "You know what they say about payback."

"Looking forward to it, big guy."

"You say that now. And I'll remind you then—when you're begging me to finish you off but I leave you hanging."

"You wouldn't."

"Oh, I would and I will. With pleasure."

"That doesn't sound like payback, that sounds like torture."

Drake rolled off the bed, planted his feet on the floor, and raised a brow. My eyes hungrily ate up all that was Drake—perfect male beauty. Sculpted chest, washboard abs, and a very large erection tenting the athletic shorts he'd slept in.

"Oh." I chuckled and covered my mouth so I

wouldn't bust out laughing like an immature schoolgirl.

"No, babe, me bringing you to the edge then making you wait isn't torture. But you know what is?" He pointed to his crotch and shook his head. "That," he finished and turned toward the dresser with his open duffle bag on top of it.

My gaze landed on his back and the beautiful tattoo that covered its entirety. I didn't remember him having a tattoo and that back piece was something I'd remember not only because it was huge but it was also a true work of art.

Three cloaked women. The first was facing forward. The other two flanked her but were in profile. Golden thread strung from one of the women's bobbin and slashed across the vibrant blue cloak of the woman facing forward. It ended in the hand of the third woman who was also holding a dagger. It was magnificent. Then I looked lower and there was a finely detailed spinning wheel. All of it was beautiful both in color and design.

I crawled to the end of the bed for a closer look and my lungs started to burn. I came off the bed and Drake looked over his shoulder but I paid him no mind, I only had eyes for the woman on his back. Long brown hair that flowed wildly, delicate features. But it was the eyes—her eyes, my eyes, they were the same. Yellow-gold.

My eyes.

My hand moved and I traced one of the lines of thread.

Three women. Thread woven between them, draping, flowing. A bobbin, a spindle, a dagger.

The Moirai.

The Fates.

Then I looked higher near Drake's shoulder. In the wisps and flowing line work that surrounded the women, inked there into his flesh were the words, *Fate favors the fearless.* I continued to study the lines and found more, *My Moira.* I couldn't stop searching until I found another saying, *Fate will find a way.*

I sucked in a painful breath and held it until it scorched my insides.

"Liberty—"

"Don't turn around," I wheezed. "When did you get this?"

"I started it the day after I got back to Virginia Beach."

"Why?"

"Because you are my fate. My destiny. And if I couldn't physically have you, I was going to have you

464

inked on my skin. My Moira. My Clotho. My Lachesis."

His present and his future.

"You know it's Lachesis who measures the thread to decide one's destiny."

"Then I hope I measure up."

That was sweet so I smiled even though he couldn't see me.

"And Clotho is said to be the one who spins the thread, deciding when someone is born and when they die."

"Then I know my life is in good hands."

Drake started to turn but I wasn't ready to face him so I quickly pressed my cheek against his tattoo, wrapped my arms around his middle, and held on for dear life.

"I don't know what to say," I whispered.

"Nothing to say."

"It's beautiful. So beautiful it's a shame it's on your back and you can't see it every day."

"Don't need to see it. I know it's there. Tattooed not only on my skin but on my soul. Believe me, Liberty, you've been with me every moment even if you weren't there."

I felt the wet hit my eyes and didn't bother trying to stop the tears from leaking from the corner of my eyes. Drake needed to know what the tattoo—no—what *he* meant to me.

"Babe?"

My arms around him tightened, Drake's big hand covered my threaded fingers resting on his stomach, but he said no more.

He knew.

Drake was everything.

"You've been with me, too," I whispered.

Even though we needed to get to work, which meant we needed to get a move on, Drake didn't rush me. He let me take my time soaking in strength. Then he let me trace my name inked to his skin. After that I let him, but he didn't let me go far. One hand clamped on my hip, the other tangled in my hair, then his mouth hit mine and he took.

And took.

And took.

Until I was breathless from his kiss.

We made it to Triple Canopy on time, exactly on time, without a minute to spare. It was a minor miracle because from the time Drake had kissed me to the moment we'd pulled into the compound's parking lot, I'd taken every available opportunity to kiss Drake.

Some were playful. Some were sweet. Some were passionate. But however I'd started them, Drake had ended them and he'd ended them by taking over and making them deep, wet, and delicious. The man could kiss. I'd thought that the first time he'd put his mouth on mine, but what I'd learned since then was he could *seriously* kiss—like win awards for the magic he created with his tongue. That was true for all the places he used it. Though when he used it between my legs, that was gold medal worthy.

I was not surprised when we found Trey in the conference room with Brady. Drake had called him when we left the hotel and offered to take him to the office but Trey told him he was already there. That was surprising—it had been early, way too early to be at the office—but Drake said when Trey was on the hunt, he was rabid.

Apparently, Drake knew Trey well. There were papers and maps spread out all over the table and it looked like Trey had been at it for hours.

"Your mom texted me last night," Trey said conversationally, as if my mom texting him was commonplace. "She found something, and on a hunch, followed it. She hit pay dirt." There was admiration in Trey's tone. "Gotta say, I thought you got your grit from your dad, but now I'm thinking you got it from your mom. The woman is scary smart."

That she was. Not only was my mom smart, her intuition was spot-on. That's why my dad and uncles used her skills often. The men may've started the business, but my mom was the brains of the operation. They had another tech guy, but my mom could and did run circles around him. Considering Dylan Welsh worked for the NSA and did that straight out of college. Much like the way the CIA had approached my mom, recognizing she had talent—therefore the CIA wanted to exploit it—the NSA had done the same with Dylan. So with all of that, it was impressive my mom was better—and she totally was.

"She is scary smart," I returned. "But why didn't she text me?"

Trey tilted his head and stared at me like I was a few cards short of a full deck. Then the corner of his mouth curved up into a lopsided smile and I understood. Trey Durum was model good-looking but when he added the lopsided smile that turned into a playful smirk he was downright sinful.

Wowzer.

"Remember when we were in Bagram, we heard about the *Eight Hundred*?" Trey asked Drake, completely ignoring my question.

"Yeah, the go-to guy."

"Right. And when we were in Abu Ghraib, same thing. You wanted something, you asked the Eight Hundred."

"I remember. What's that got to do with anything?"

"Roman Kushnir is *the* Eight Hundred."

"Come again?" Drake muttered.

"Roman's the Eight Hundred," Trey repeated as if saying it again would somehow make sense the second time around.

"I don't know what or who an Eight Hundred is," I rejoined.

"The Eight Hundred is the man who can get military personnel anything they want. Booze, porn mags, cigarettes, dip, weed, street drugs, pharma, whatever you want, he'll get it for you," Trey explained.

"Why do they call him Eight Hundred?"

"Stupid name, but the only beer he smuggles is Olde English 800 forty-ouncers."

Yeah, that was a seriously stupid name. But then

again, I guess no one cared what they called the man who could get them what they wanted.

"No shit?" Drake moved to the table and started pushing papers around.

"No shit," Trey returned. "Don't know how Blake found it, like I said, she's scary smart. I've combed over everything she found and damn if she isn't right."

"Why the hell would a man who moves guns, ammo, and supplies every terrorist organization with whatever they need bother with booze and porn mags?" I asked.

Trey smiled like he had a really great secret. It was nice to see him happy and excited. Even if that excitement was about Roman. Though, I suspected it was more about being a step closer to finding and taking him out. Which in that case, I totally understood.

"Dear ol' Uncle Marko takes a huge cut of the guns and ammo. And when I say huge, I mean he pretty much takes it all and leaves Roman with shit."

"Earning his place," Drake announced. "Proving himself to the uncle, hoping to work his way to a larger cut. So in the meantime, Roman needs money, he's got the connections so he starts a side hustle of his own. Something the uncle can't take a cut of."

"Winner, winner, chicken dinner," Trey whooped.

"God, you're lame." I laughed.

Trey's gaze sliced to me, a panty-melting smile firmly in place and he proved me wrong. The lopsided smile wasn't what garnered him attention, it was *this* smile that did it. And I wondered if he understood that if a woman saw that, no matter if it wasn't directed at her, she'd approach. She'd take a chance even knowing she'd probably get shot down just to have him smile at her that way. It wasn't all about his looks—it was that playful, devil-may-care smile.

Then I remembered the pain in his voice when he told me no one saw *him*. He thought that, and maybe that was true a lot of the time, but I'd bet he'd become so jaded over the years he missed the ones who saw *that* smile and wanted their shot at getting to know him so they could bask in the warmth they'd feel if he'd turn that smile to them.

I felt sorry for him. He'd never feel what I felt for Drake if he didn't open himself up. And the way he'd spoken on the phone to me about women, he'd never do that. He was perfectly happy keeping himself locked away.

It's a crying shame.

"I could tell you about all the ass I tap—"

"Please don't. Drake bought me an awesome blueberry muffin and it's still digesting. I'd prefer it not to make a reappearance in the form of vomit. Which it will if you continue."

Drake was completely ignoring this banter, fully engrossed in looking at the intel my mom had given Trey.

"How'd Roman find Liberty?" Drake asked the million-dollar question.

"Still working on that. Lenox, senior that is, came by earlier. They got ahold of Wick and asked him to personally question the Marine."

"Wick's still in Golan Heights?" I inquired.

This surprised me. Wick didn't spend a lot of time OCONUS.

"No. The Marine unit is back in the States."

"And Wick agreed?"

"He was already at Twentynine Palms getting ready to sit down with Staff Sergeant Gannon."

"So, Wick put it together and didn't fuckin' call Levi?" Drake barked.

"Did you think he would? He was adamant none of Liberty's family knew. And just to say, Lenox said Wick was beyond pissed they were poking around."

"If this shit blows back on Liberty," Drake

growled, but luckily didn't finish what he was going to say because my dad and Uncle Lenox walked into the room.

One look at their stormy faces told me they weren't coming to the conference room to spread good cheer and salutations.

"Wick pulled that shitheel out of his rack and after some middle-of-the-night coercion, Gannon spilled," my dad cut right to it. "He took the pictures. He knew he couldn't touch Liberty when her *bodyguards* were around, so he did the only thing he could do—plotted to get her out of the Army. Drake, too, since he was protecting her."

"Bodyguards?" Trey asked.

"You and your team. He was pissed his brother-in-law was dead, blamed Liberty, and thought he'd teach her a lesson why women had no place in the special forces world. His first attempt was hindered when Drake showed up at the hangar. Every time after that, either Drake or all of you were with her so he couldn't get to her," Dad continued, his face getting redder and redder as he spoke.

That creeped me out. Not that Ball's brother-in-law blamed me—that I understood. But it freaked me out the guy had been stalking me and I hadn't noticed. And he was taking pictures.

Creepy as fuck.

"What about Roman? Does Gannon know him?"

I glanced at my dad, who looked like he was getting ready to blow. Not just a head gasket but a nuclear reactor getting ready to meltdown.

"Dad?" His eyes came to me and I flinched. There was so much raw hurt it was hard to look at. "Daddy, I'm fine. Whatever Gannon tried to do, Drake and the guys stopped it. I'm standing right here, safe and sound. There's no reason to get worked up—"

"Worked up? Darlin', worked up is a memory. My daughter was hunted. She was stalked, captured, and tortured because of something I did. And I'm not worked up. I'm murderous that some shit-for-fucking-brains staff sergeant made it easy for the man hunting her to find her because he told Roman your goddamn name. He broke every operational security rule set in place to keep our servicemembers safe for a motherfucking case of beer. If Wick didn't already have Gannon locked up where he's now untouchable to me, I would put his fucking ass six-feet under."

It was safe to say, the meltdown wasn't imminent. It hadn't just begun—that bitch was on fire.

"Dad, you know what happened to me is not your fault. And it's not the uncles' fault. You four had an objective and you carried it out. No one knew the Roman you took out had a son. Well, Wick apparently did, but none of you had the first clue."

"And there's the problem, Moira. We should've known. I should've known. How the hell can I protect you if I'm—"

"Stop!" I shouted.

There it was again—protect Moira. God, when would they all understand they had protected me?

"My whole life I was free to be me. We all were —me and the cousins all got to live carefree and some of them wild under the umbrella of your protection. You all made it safe for us to be what we wanted to be, grow up how we wanted, fall down, get back up, learn lessons, and thrive. All because you and the uncles made it so. You all protected us. You still protect us. You taught us to protect each other. But something you forget—most importantly you taught me to protect myself. You are not God. You are not all-knowing. There are things out of your control and this is one of many.

"I was so very wrong to blame you all. I was not right in the head. But I'm getting there, I'm getting back to me and I'm doing that because once again that umbrella is up and it is safe under there. It's so fucking safe, Dad, I can heal. But I'll never be able to do that if I know you blame yourself for something that was not your fault. I'll keep that guilt and I'll wrap myself up in it knowing the best man I know feels like shit for *something he didn't do.*"

My dad was still staring at me, but some of the hurt had crept out and warmth stole the icy shards.

"I'm sorry, Dad. I'm so sorry. I know I said horrible things. I knew—"

I got no further words out because my dad crushed me to his chest and wrapped his arms around me, making me safe in a different way. Wordlessly, he released me from the guilt. All was forgiven. God, my dad gave good hugs—always had.

Nowhere better than in his arms, except for Drake's. But that was only because Drake held me like I was his woman, precious, cherished, loved. Dad felt those same things but in a different way. To him I'd always be his little girl. His baby.

"You wanna run that by us again? Gannon told Roman Liberty's name?" Drake seethed, breaking the father-daughter moment.

"The idiot didn't know him ticking off the names of his brother-in-law's squad was akin to signing their death warrants, but he admitted to meeting with Roman, face-to-face. He was calling out names, ordering each member of the squad a fucking beer," Uncle Lenox fumed. "Gannon said Roman joked about a bitch being out on patrol with the men. At the time, Gannon didn't think anything about it—Roman knowing just by the last names one was a woman."

"Okay, so Roman knew she was in the region. But finding her would be like finding a needle in a haystack," Trey put in.

"Not if word got to the men in charge that Roman was asking around about a female soldier. Not if the female was a McCoy and someone thought they'd found their ticket for an assassination without it being an assassination, because a man dying in combat is just that. And no one thought Roman had the firepower he had. No one anticipated that leaking Liberty's whereabouts would lead to casualties and her capture."

There was so much anger bouncing around the room my breath became unsteady. Not because I was fucking ticked way the hell off that we'd been right all along. Because I was bait. I'd been used and my men died because of it. The confirmation burned like lava down my throat.

A new fear rippled through me. How would I ever trust my chain of command after this?

"Are you motherfucking kidding me?" Drake roared.

"Wish I were," Lenox returned.

"And Wick approved this shit?" Trey raged.

"Said, he knew nothing about it. Not until after she was captured, then he started putting pieces together and asking questions. No one gave him straight answers but the man's not stupid. Once Drake confirmed the man who took Liberty was an American, Wick knew he'd been right."

Without another word, Drake turned on his boot and stomped out of the room. And that stomp was so heavy I was amazed the floor under his feet didn't buckle.

My eyes went to Trey's. His green eyes glittered with malice and deadly intent.

"Trey?"

"Give him a minute. He'll be back," he said, misreading my query.

I wasn't worried about Drake, I knew he'd be back. He'd never leave my side for long. But I was worried about what I saw on Trey's face.

"Don't—"

"Liberty, I say this with respect for you, for your man, for your father, but do not say shit to me right now."

Oh, boy, he was in meltdown mode, too, and I didn't know how to defuse the situation. So I decided to keep my mouth shut. I might not have been as experienced as the men in the room, they may've tried and failed more times than I'd even started, but even I knew the strongest warrior didn't always know how they were going to win. They just knew they weren't gonna lose.

And I wouldn't lose—not to Roman, not to Gannon.

So I'd keep quiet and find a way to make Roman pay.

Then I'd figure out how I was going to continue to do my job after being betrayed in the worst kind of way.

37

"Brother, you look like you're ready to come undone," Carter said as he joined me behind the main office building.

I was taking in my surroundings, but not paying attention because I couldn't stop thinking about how there was someone responsible for what happened to Liberty. Someone who put her in danger—on purpose. Men had died, she'd endured hell, and we'd never know who that someone was. Not even Blake with all her skills could dig deep enough to find the bastard hiding behind layers and layers of protection.

"Have you been briefed?" I asked.

"Yeah."

"What's your take? You think Roman and Gannon meeting was a coincidence?"

"I've never been big on those," Carter admitted. "But in this case, it looks like it was sheer dumb luck Roman stumbled upon a stupid fuck whose only intention was to order a case and flex in front of his brother-in-law."

"You sure about that?"

My stomach twisted in that painful way that told me something wasn't right. Something was coming.

I knew it.

I felt it.

I tasted it.

The feeling so heavy, my boots were sinking into the grassy patch I'd wandered out to.

Something's coming.

"The way you asked that I'm not sure, I'm not so sure about anything now. What's on your mind?"

"Feel it, Carter, that sharp pain in my gut, the prick on the back of my neck. Something's not right. I can't put my finger on it. Don't know if we're missing something. If the unease is coming from something that's *gonna* happen. Or if it's only a matter of time my woman will be back in the field under the command of the person or persons who thought it was a brilliant idea to leak intel to a lunatic who wanted to kill her. Not taking into consideration that as well-trained as Liberty is—and she is, brother.

She's good, but she was still too inexperienced to be put in that position—unprepared for what was going to happen. At the very least, the squad should've been briefed and a secondary team put in place as overwatch. What happened to her is so fucked I can't wrap my head around it. But whatever it is, this shit is not right, I feel it."

"I agree with you. We'll be hyper-vigilant."

That didn't make the poison in the pit of my stomach disappear.

"Can't be with her when she goes back out. We have a week until she reports and you know as well as I do, they'll have her on recall and she can be called up and be sent out. A week, brother, to find and take out Roman before he'll get another opportunity to snatch my woman."

"Then we better get our asses in there and get to work."

"Can't lose her, Carter. I lived without her for weeks and felt like I was dying inside, and that was when I knew she was in Georgia with her family. She goes back out before that asshole's in the ground, it will eat me alive. If he gets his hands on her again, you know, you fucking *know*, there won't be anything to bring home but a pine box."

There was a small pang of regret saying something like that to Carter knowing that he loved her. She was his family, but hammering home that this was not something they could fuck around with, won out.

"Know that," Carter clipped.

"Yeah, I know you do. So I think you'll understand when I tell you if this shit's not done before she checks in with her new battalion, I'm going out to track this fucker and I'll need you to have my back with that."

"You're gonna go out and not tell her?"

"Fuck, no. Learned my lesson with that shit. But she won't be happy I'm goin'. That's where you come in. Seems you can be a voice of reason when it comes to her."

"That's because I'm highly intelligent and articulate."

"Yeah, you keep telling yourself that."

With a pound on my shoulder, Carter turned to leave. "Whatever you need, you know that."

And I damn well did. Carter was a good friend. But more than that, he was loyal to his friends and his family.

"How ya doin'?" I asked Liberty when the room cleared.

The guys were breaking for lunch and my woman looked like she'd been put through the wringer.

"I'm pissed."

I bet she was. Someone did her dirty and I was right—Blake dug and found nothing. She even had her counterpart Dylan look and he hit just as many dead-ends as she did. Levi had called Wick. He didn't know, and he'd looked far and wide and deep. Whoever had come up with the plan to use Liberty wasn't going to be found.

That was a hard pill to swallow, but priority one was finding Roman.

Lenox had been in contact with local law enforcement in DC. He'd been assured the UN meeting due to take place tomorrow would have extra security. And they'd be on the lookout for Roman.

With any luck, Roman would be there with his uncle and he'd be taken out.

The problem was I didn't believe in luck.

"I know you are. Your mom seems pretty pissed, too."

I'd learned something today, Blake McCoy was

not shy and arresting—she looked like she would be. The woman had class written all over her. But Blake was not to be underestimated, she was downright frightening, especially when her daughter's life had been threatened.

I'd also learned Blake had a mouth on her that rivaled the men I'd served with. She'd spouted so many cuss words, most of them sounded like she was making them up on the fly, and some didn't make sense. But when she was mad, watch out—her mouth got the better of her and she let it fly.

"You know everyone talks about how protective the men are in this family. But honestly, they got nothing on my mom and aunts. Those women are fiercely protective over the family. They're quieter about it, but each of them is loyal and strong and damn tough. All you need to do is look at my dad and the uncles to know there's no way they'd choose weak women."

I loved how close she was with her family.

Liberty looked around the room. Then her gaze settled back on mine and she asked, "Wanna get out of here?"

"Sure. What do you want for lunch?"

"No. I mean, get out for the day."

The rational part of me wanted to tell her we had

a case to work, we couldn't just leave. But then I looked into her hopeful eyes and realized she needed a break.

"Where to?" I asked.

"I wanna show you something."

Her face lit and I knew I'd made the right decision.

After I sent a text to Carter who was with Trey, and one to her dad, we headed out.

Both texted me back their own versions of "Thank God." They knew it, they saw Liberty needed time to clear her head after all this new information had been piled on her, and they were all for her leaving the office for a while.

"Where to, baby?"

"My cousin Jackson's house. It's a huge mansion called The Manor."

"Thought Jackson was a firefighter?" I asked.

A first responder's salary and a mansion didn't jibe.

"Hang a right at the next light," Liberty told me, then turned in her seat and tucked her foot behind the back of her other knee and smiled. "Let me tell you the story of Jackson and Tuesday..."

Over the next twenty minutes as she intermittently gave me directions, she told me how her cousin had fallen in love with a supermodel, how Tuesday had been terrorized by a stalker, and finally how they came to live in a beautiful mansion called The Manor.

And when we pulled down a long tree-lined drive and the very large house came into view she was wrong. It wasn't beautiful, it was over-the-top stunning. But it had nothing to do with the house and everything to do with the love that had been created in that home.

38

We were walking through Tuesday's orchard, a warm breeze blowing through the pear and apple trees, beauty everywhere. I was thinking about how lucky Tuesday was to have this. She could, and did, walk the path that Jackson kept expertly manicured for her anytime she wanted.

"This is where I told my dad I was going to Ranger school," I told Drake.

"Really?"

"I came home on leave for Jackson's wedding. It was a surprise no one but me knew. I'd just found out I was going so I thought it was the perfect time to tell him."

"Bet he was happy for you."

"He was nervous for me. He'd been through

Ranger school. He knew it would be difficult for me. First thing he asked was if I was sure. The second thing was if I'd been training, then he lectured me on proper foot care."

"Yeah, you gotta take care of your feet. If you don't, you're fucked." Humor laced his words but I ignored the teasing tone and thought back to Drake carrying me all the way to the exfil site because my feet were torn to shreds.

He'd carried me.

How could I not love this man?

We stopped in front of Carter and Delaney's cherry tree. Most of the pink blossoms had already dropped, painting the grass around the sturdy trunk with blush-colored flowers.

"Do you want kids?" I asked.

Drake startled at my change of topic.

"Yeah. You?"

"I never really thought about having kids until I was sitting in my mom's living room watching little Emma crawl on Quinn. Then I started thinking about what it would be like to have a bunch of little Drakes running around."

I heard his sharp inhale and pinched my lips together in an effort to stop myself from saying anything else.

"Baby?" he called.

"Yeah?"

"Look at me."

My eyes moved from the tree to Drake and he was smiling huge. "How many do you want?"

"More than one."

"I agree. Like you, I'm an only child. I always wished I had a brother."

"Sometimes I wished I had a sibling. Not because I was lonely—because I always had the cousins around—but because when we got into fights it was always uneven. Delaney and Quinn always stuck together. I wished I'd had someone who would always side with me even if I was wrong. But then they'd get into epic fights, too. And when those happened I praised Jesus I didn't have a sister who stole my clothes and would give me the silent treatment over a curling iron."

"I grew up in Texas. My parents still live there. My mom's family was in California. Dad's was in Maine so it was just us. They're good parents, they had friends that had kids and they entertained a lot so there were people around but no family. Love that about your setup. You grew up with lots of family and you're all still close. I want that and I want to give it to my kids."

My heart started to beat a little faster, my breathing coming in rapid pants.

"My family's awesome but a little in-your-face."

"Only because they care."

"This is true. Thick and thin, they're always there." I went back to staring at the tree. "Tuesday planted this tree for Carter and Delaney. Well, for the baby they lost. It was my Aunt Reagan's idea. She has a tree planted in her backyard for each of us and she didn't want the baby Laney and Carter lost to be left out. Tuesday loved the idea and planted this one."

"What?" Drake's voice had dropped to a painful whisper.

"You didn't know?" I surmised.

"No. Fucking hell. I know everything there is to know about Church, except for anything that pertains to Delaney. He kept her hidden away."

"She lost the baby a year before he got out."

"I never understood why he kept her a secret. I get it now. I only had weeks away from you and it felt like I was walking around dead on my feet, searching for anything that would dull the pain, something to take the edge off so I could just sleep. If Carter felt even half of that for all those years, Christ, I understand why he never told us."

Walking around dead on my feet.

If Carter even felt half of that.

God, I was so totally in love with this man I couldn't find the words to tell him how much.

"I'm scared to go back out in the field."

Another change of subject, another flash of confusion before he processed what I'd said.

"Know you are. But you're gonna be fine."

He was putting on a brave face for me, pretending he didn't have the same worries I had.

"Would you think I was weak if I didn't go back? I mean, if I took med leave from the field."

"Weak—fuck, no. Would it be a shame to waste all of your talent? Yes. But I'd never think you were weak for needing time after what happened and how that came to be."

"And if I wanted out of the Army?"

"Baby, just this morning I told you I would stand by you and follow you anywhere. If you cannot trust your leadership and you feel unsafe and want out, I will support that. If you want to go on profile and not go out for a while, I will support that. If you want to go back full Winchester and kick ass, I will support that, too. Whatever you want."

The ball of unease started to loosen. I didn't need to make a decision right now.

After we'd finished our walk around the orchard, Drake and I decided to go back to the office so we could spend some time with Trey before he headed home. And I'm glad we did. It was nice to see Trey back to looking relaxed. Even if I knew it was a façade, it made me feel better that he was no longer shooting fire from his eyes.

My dad and the uncles were all holed up in some secret meeting, leaving Brady, Carter, and Trey going over next week's sniper class that Brady would be teaching.

Drake had immediately jumped into the conversation and I had to admit, the normalcy was good. There was no talk about Roman, or a crazy man taking pictures of me, or a possible assassination attempt on an Albanian that Marko had a beef with.

The guys invited me to go with them out to the range but I declined. I wanted to remind them that Trey should not be out walking the mile it would take to get there but I didn't think Trey would appreciate my concern, and anyway, Brady said he was grabbing the keys to the Gator so they wouldn't be walking.

Drake gave me a hot but too-short kiss before he

left. This was met with Trey smiling, Carter smirking, and Brady looking extremely disinterested.

Once they were gone, I went in search of my mom and found her in the surveillance center where she had a workstation set up.

"Hey, Mama," I said and plopped down in a chair I'd wheeled over.

"Hey there, toots." She looked up from her computer screen, demonstrating what I already knew—she always had time for me. "Everything okay?"

"Am I crazy?"

"Narrow that down for me," she teased. "Crazy about what?"

"Drake."

"You certainly seem crazy *about* him."

"I am. Is that crazy? I mean, I fell in love with him before I even opened my eyes and saw him."

Mom shrugged and shook her head. "I fell in love with your dad in the parking lot of a Tastee-Freez. I can still remember what he was wearing."

"You cannot. That was like forty years ago."

"Not quite forty. And I sure can. He was in jeans, a button-up flannel, and he had boots on. It was a Friday night and earlier that night he'd made the winning touchdown."

"Thought Dad played quarterback?"

"He did. But there was three yards to go, no open receivers, so he went for it." I was looking right at my mom so I didn't miss it when her gaze turned soft and wistful. She really did remember the exact moment she fell in love with my dad. "So to answer your question, no, I don't think you're crazy. I think you're in love. And I have to tell you, I like him."

"There's a lot to like about Drake."

"I'm sure you're right. But I specifically like the way he is with you. He's good with you."

"Gee, Mom, good with me, like I'm an animal?"

My mom rolled her eyes at me, something she did frequently when I was being a drama queen.

"Yes, good with you. He's protective but in a way that works for you. He knew you needed to be involved in the investigation into Roman and didn't hesitate to bring you in—without discussing it with anyone. Likely because he didn't care what anyone else had to say about it and not in a nasty, disrespectful way. But he was prepared to give you what you needed and that's what he did—gave you a voice."

"I did need it and I didn't know I did until we got here."

"Sign of a good man, Liberty, knowing what you

need before you have to ask. It means he's paying attention. I like that about him, too. He's sharp."

"I'm going to ask him to move in with me," I announced and held my breath.

"Why are you turnin' red, girl? You're twenty-seven, not twelve."

"Do you think Dad will be upset?"

"Honey," my mom started and smiled. "Your dad is far from stupid. He drove to Virginia and knew within five minutes of meeting Drake that not only had I been right, you were in love with him, but that Drake was also in love with you. Five minutes after that, your dad came to the realization he was standing in front of the man he'd walk his daughter to. Trust this—Drake wouldn't be here in Georgia if your dad wasn't very sure he was the man he wanted for his only child."

"Thanks, Mama. You're the best."

"I know I am, toots."

And with that, I burst out laughing.

That was my mom—humble.

39

It was official—Liberty McCoy would be the death of me, or at least the cause of permanent damage to my dick.

Last night after we'd said goodbye to Trey, we went to dinner then came back to my hotel, whereupon Liberty initiated a sneak attack, and before I could stop her, she'd jumped me. Really and truly jumped into my arms, wrapped her legs around me, arms around my neck, mouth on mine. I stumbled back as her body hit mine, and she used it to her advantage, throwing herself forward until my legs hit the bed and my ass landed on the mattress.

All of this happened within seconds. And as it was par for the course, when Liberty's mouth and hands were on me, I lost my mind. She'd taken me to the brink and it was by the last thread of my control that I got creative and shut down her quest to get me undressed. To accomplish this I used my mouth and fingers.

This time, I got her naked before I got my mouth between her legs and it took a good amount of tasting, sucking, and biting. And as I lay there in bed, with Liberty's still-naked form pressed against me, my hand cupping her ass, I still thought as I did the night before that her body was perfection. It was also an astounding feat I was able to turn down her many offers to have her—all of her. My dick was seriously angry when I'd repeatedly refused.

There was a niggling in the back of my mind that told me to wait. I'd never been a romantic type of guy, never made nor needed declarations or promises before I fucked a woman. But this was Liberty. My Liberty. She was not a quick and dirty fuck. I wanted more and I wanted her to understand my intentions in a way she'd never doubt. Before I took her again, I needed her to know where I was at, and she wasn't ready to hear what I had to say about our future.

So there I was, in bed with a naked Liberty and her hand was on the move.

"Mornin', babe," I said and grabbed her wrist.

"You know, I'm starting to feel like a total hussy beggin' for sex."

Hussy, that's funny.

"Then stop asking."

"You're annoying."

"Because I won't give you my—"

"Gah. Why are men so crass?"

I rolled her to her back and in my haste to tease her, I didn't think. Her bare breasts were on display, her dark hair fanned out over the stark white sheets, the sexy column of her neck, her shoulders, all of that so enticing my cock swelled more and we needed to move. I twisted us back, then another roll, until I was off the bed and bringing her with me.

"Whoa. What was that?" she asked breathless.

"Time for a shower."

A slow, sexy smile curved her lips up.

Fucking shit.

She was going to be the death of me.

I grabbed her hand, pulled her into the bathroom, turned on the tap. But before I could turn, her hand was on my back. No, not her hand, her finger tracing my tat. Goddamn, that felt good. So good, I stayed still while she took her fill. I knew she was done when she pressed her lips to my skin. I waited some more, letting the scorch of her kiss warm my skin.

I shucked my shorts and pulled us into the shower. This, too, was torture—memories of us in Golan Heights assailed my mind. Both painful and sublime. But right then wasn't about sex or memories, it was about taking care of my girl and getting us out the door before what was left of my restraint snapped, my cock took over, and we spent the rest of the day with me buried deep and her mindless.

I tagged the body wash off the shelf, dumped a healthy glob into my palm, and braced as my hands went to her back. I concentrated on the bubbles rather than her soft, smooth skin as I lathered. Shoulders, down her spine, to her lats, and I dug my fingers in, massaging the muscles there, drawing out a low moan. Liberty dropped her head forward, jutted her ass back, and my eyes automatically lowered.

Fucking shit.

So close.

My cock pulsed and jerked, begging to close the inches that separated us.

I knelt and continued to soap her calves and thighs, bypassing all the parts I wanted to touch and taste.

I stood, fortified my resolve, and turned Liberty, reversing our position so her back was to the spray, grabbed the wash, dumped more into my palm, and repeated the process to her front. This time, I couldn't ignore all the good parts. My hands glided over her breasts, her nipples hardened, and without thought, I closed my thumbs and forefingers over them and pinched. Gently at first, until she gifted me with one of her sexy mews.

Torture.

My hands moved to her taut stomach, down to her hips, thighs, then I was so close to breaking, I pulled my hands off her. Staring down at Liberty, her eyes closed, face relaxed, so fucking beautiful my breath caught. I wanted this—every fucking day for the rest of my life I wanted to take care of her. Small ways. Big ways. Every way.

"You're good at that," she mumbled but didn't open her eyes.

"Glad you think so."

I reached for the shampoo and seconds later, I was massaging her scalp as she purred. An honest to God purr. Hell, yeah, I wanted this.

I tipped her head back to rinse the soap from her hair and she froze.

Every muscle tight.

Chest not moving.

Stock-still.

"Breathe, baby."

Liberty came unstuck and when she did, her fist came up and connected before I could stop it. Pain exploded in my jaw, the blow so powerful my teeth ached.

"No!" she shouted. "Don't touch me."

"Liberty," I clipped. "Baby, stop."

She didn't stop, her arms flailed, her eyes snapped open wild and raw.

"No, no, no. Don't touch me."

Christ.

Liberty thrashed. I slapped the water off, taking another hit, this time to my gut, and in an effort to stop her before she slipped and fell, I wrapped her in a bear hug.

"Stop, baby. You're safe. Come back to me."

Jesus, the woman was strong. Liberty squirmed, pitched, struggled, kicked her feet.

"Liberty!" My arms tightened as I jerked her roughly, trying to break through her terror. "Baby, come back."

She didn't stop. With no other choice, I pushed the shower door open. Liberty took advantage of her new freedom and clocked me in the temple with her elbow. My head rattled, my chin was taking a beating, and my jaw throbbed.

Of course my woman didn't slap and smack. No, not Liberty. She *fought*.

I got a slippery and struggling Liberty out of the bathroom. We shuffled to the bed, I dropped her on the crumpled sheets and stepped back. Now that she wasn't going to slip and fall in the shower, she needed space.

"I won't do it," she growled.

"Do what, baby?"

"I won't tell you. I'll die first."

Her words shredded me.

Sliced through me and pierced my heart.

Christ.

"Kill me," she taunted. "Do it. Just kill me."

Kill me.

Fucking Christ. What was left of my shredded insides splintered.

"Liberty. Come back. Breathe, baby. Breathe. You're in Georgia. You're home and you're safe."

"Just kill me," she cried.

The sound guttural, so painful it snuffed out the oxygen in the room, leaving nothing.

Raw.

Ravaged.

Wrecked.

Fuck this. I went to the bed knowing she was going to strike out, and when she did, I was ready for it. My hands moved to her face and I held her where I wanted and slammed my mouth onto hers. As I'd predicted, Liberty went wild—not her normal, sexy wild when I put my mouth on her.

Savage.

She clawed at my chest, raking her sharp nails over my skin until I was sure she'd drawn blood.

I pulled my lips off hers and begged, "Please come back to me."

I didn't let go of her face, keeping our faces close as I tried to break her free.

"Liberty, baby, come on. Please. Settle and look at me. Swear, you're safe to come back. No one's going to hurt you."

Her hands clawing at me slowed to a less frantic pace, but her nails were still dug into my flesh. I bit back a bark of pain as they gouged deeper.

Then I waited. I waited for what seemed like forever for her to blink. Some of the devastation started to clear but none of the grief.

"That's it. Look at me."

Her hands fell away but I didn't loosen my grip on her cheeks.

"There you are," I whispered.

Liberty's eyes flared. A whimper slipped past her lips and I felt that sound—down to my bones, I felt the bitter despair.

"You're...you're bleeding," she cried.

"Just keep looking at me and breathe."

I knew I was bleeding, the evidence of that was on her own lips where I'd transferred it when I'd kissed her.

"I did that," she sobbed. "I hurt you."

I dropped my hands, slid them under her armpits, and moved her farther onto the bed. I climbed in behind her and yanked the covers over us.

"Relax," I told her when her body went solid as I pressed my front to her back as tightly as I could, leaving not a centimeter of space between us.

"I...I did that."

"Liberty, please do me a favor. Take a minute and relax."

She took the time but didn't relax. We lay in silence for a good, long time, with her stiff as a board. Long enough that my phone rang and hers did, too. I heard several text messages beep but I didn't dare move away from her.

I couldn't.

"You should check our phones," she told me. "One of those calls is probably my dad."

Shit, she's right. I rolled just enough to reach over and grab my cell from the nightstand.

Three calls. Levi. Trey. Levi.

Two texts. Both Levi.

Levi's first message was checking in to see if everything was all right. That text was sent after I was officially thirty minutes late to work. The second message said I had ten minutes to check in before he started a search party. That was eight minutes ago.

I sent a short reply telling Levi we were fine, but Liberty had a rough morning, and that I would explain everything later. Before I could toss the phone back, Levi replied, demanding I call in within the hour.

Whatever.

I'd call him when I knew Liberty was safe.

"We need to talk," Liberty announced.

Her brittle tone told me I wasn't going to like what she had to say. Even still, I offered, "I'll listen to anything you want to say."

"That's not talking," she pointed out.

"No, you're right. Because right now, I'm going to listen as *you* talk through what just happened."

"We can't do this," she declared. And since I was ready for it therefore I'd braced, and the hit, that would've been painful wasn't as bad as it could've been but it still killed. When I said nothing, she continued. "I'm serious. I hurt you, Drake. I don't remember what happened but you're bleeding and I know I did that. You can't be around me. You're not safe."

I smiled, happy she couldn't see my grin. Likely it would piss her off, but it was cute she thought I wasn't safe. I remained quiet.

"You should leave."

I tightened my arms around her and teased, "Baby, this is my hotel room."

"Oh, right. I should go."

"You're not going anywhere."

"Were you not listening?" she snapped.

"I was. So now that you got that out of the way, talk to me about what triggered it." She went back to her solid state and I ignored it and pushed. "What was it that took you from me?"

"It doesn't matter," she whispered.

"Liberty, that's the only thing that matters. We need to talk about it so first we know what to stay away from or ease into and you need to get it out now before it festers. The wound is open, baby, now's the best time."

Stubbornly, Liberty went silent, and since there was nothing I could do but wait her out, that's what I did. I lay behind my woman and allowed my hand to glide over her hip, up her side, and back down. Over and over until I finally heard her sigh.

"I'm sorry," she softly murmured.

"Nothing to apologize for."

"Drake, you're bleeding. I hit you. I have a lot to apologize for."

"Fine, you can apologize by telling me what set you off."

"The water. I think when I tipped my head back and it splashed in my face it triggered a memory."

"You mean when *I* tipped your head back," I corrected. "In the future, I won't rinse your hair."

"Can I tell you something?"

"You can tell me anything."

I felt Liberty's lungs expand and heard the audible whoosh as she released her breath.

"I don't want you to leave me."

"Baby—"

"Please don't leave me. No matter what I say, don't do it. That's part of it, the PTSD." The left side of my chest tightened. That was the first time she'd admitted to me she had post traumatic stress disorder. "My therapist warned me, I'll disconnect and fight to cut myself off. She explained that I need to recognize and say it out loud. That I need to amputate those thoughts and to do that, I have to give myself the power and voice them. So, please, don't leave me. I know this is a lot to ask, but I'm asking. I don't want to lose you and I'm trying real hard to get back to myself."

She slayed me.

Humbled me.

Brought me to my knees.

Amazing. Christ, so fucking amazing and strong.

"Swear to you—on my life I will not leave you. I promise I'm gonna walk this path with you."

"Thank you."

"Baby, you don't gotta thank me for loving you."

Finally, my woman relaxed.

And it was another hour before she fell asleep and I texted her dad—Liberty was good but we were taking the day off.

Levi's response was simple: *Take care of your girl.*

But it said everything. He was acknowledging she was mine. And for a man like Levi McCoy, I suspected that was hard.

Though the man wasn't stupid, he'd already known.

If you're the man I'm walking my daughter to, then I got nothing but joy and appreciation.

I closed my eyes, held my woman close, and drifted.

40

"Come on, say it again." I laughed and holstered my Glock.

Then I looked from Drake to Carter, then to Brady.

Drake looked amused. Carter looked peeved—and he would because he just lost. And Brady looked his normal bored. Then my eyes went back to my man and I saw the bruise on his jaw and carefully concealed my wince.

None of the guys had said a word about it so I knew Drake had explained what happened, and while he was at it, probably told them not to say anything about it. So no one did. My mom and dad had both asked if I was okay and when I answered that I was, both had taken my word and dropped it.

Mom, faster than Dad. He'd given me a long, assessing look before he gave me a jerk of his chin and a smile.

He trusted that if I wasn't okay I'd say something, and if I didn't, Drake damn sure would.

"You win," Carter grounded out.

"Yep. I did," I jeered, earning me another scowl.

"You're the worst winner out of all of us," Carter complained.

"Well, let's see. I just outshot two former SEALs and a former..." I stopped because I didn't know what branch of service Brady came from. I assumed he was former SFOD-D like my dad and the uncles but I wasn't sure. "Former whatever Brady is. So I think I get to brag."

Brady's eyes came to mine and it was the first time I'd ever seen any humor in them. Though it was a teeny-tiny bit, it still counted.

"Think maybe I *let* you win?" Brady asked.

I feigned shock and shrugged. "Well, if you did, that's your mistake. I still win."

Brady shook his head and gave a ghost of a smile. "You're nuts."

"Actually, my therapist doesn't call it nuts, she says my brain is processing a traumatic event," I sassed.

I watched in horror as the shutters slammed down over Brady's emotions and his eyes turned pained and blank.

Oh, no.

Carter saw it, too. He actually flinched.

Drake, being as observant as Carter, therefore not missing it either jumped in. "Let's head back to the office. I'm starving."

We policed our brass, pulled down the paper targets we'd been shooting at, and started the walk back to the office.

Drake grabbed my hand and gave it a squeeze.

Yeah, he saw Brady shut down.

It had been three days since my episode in the shower. Three really awesome days. The only thing that sucked was that as the days passed, the time to go back to work drew closer. Part of me was ready, but there was a small part that dreaded going back.

I'd be close. Post was only a forty-minute drive. But I'd yet to talk to Drake about finding a place together, somewhere in the middle so neither of our commutes would be horrible. But he hadn't brought it up, either. He was taking things at my pace. He'd reiterated that when he drove me to therapy yesterday. He didn't come in, he waited outside in his truck. I appreciated him knowing without me telling him I needed to do it on my own. Even walking into my doctor's office.

Mom was right, Drake paid attention.

We'd gotten word yesterday that the special operations division of the DC metro police had found a bomb in Marko Kushnir's briefcase. Scarily it was the exact setup that Trey had said it would be. How Marko thought he'd get away with bringing an explosive device into a UN meeting was beyond me. But as Drake pointed out, ego made a man dumb. And Marko had an ego the size of Texas. Unfortunately, there'd been no sign of Roman.

That worried me.

Dad, Mom, and the uncles had doubled their efforts, even calling in a team they knew out of Maryland to help in their investigation. Brady, Carter, and Drake were pulled off the Roman hunt because Triple Canopy still had to keep the doors open. There was a SWAT team coming in to train next week and the three of them needed to get everything ready.

Drake wasn't happy, but he understood. At least that's what he told me.

Carter opened the back door of the office and held it as we entered. None of us were paying attention. As a matter of fact, I was contemplating how I was going to convince Drake to have sex with me since he still hadn't taken us there, though he was generous with giving me orgasms.

With my mind on sex and Carter grumbling about how he now had to eat a PB&J and how he was going to puke, no one saw it.

Not a single one of us was paying attention until it was too late.

The threat was upon us.

Everything happened in the blink of an eye, yet everything slowed.

A man grabbed Drake by the back of his shirt and pressed a gun to his temple. Brady disappeared around the corner. Both Carter and I drew our weapons and pointed them in the direction of the man holding Drake.

"What the fuck," Carter growled, his tone more deadly than I'd ever heard.

I quickly assessed the situation. We were in a tight space. The man moved backward, taking Drake with him.

Where the fuck is everyone?

Then my eyes hit the man's chest and I saw it.

A suicide vest.

No, no, no.

My vision blurred, memories of Lore threatening to invade my mind.

"Good to see you again, Moira."

My gaze snapped to the man and my body ached with phantom pains. I knew that voice. I'd never forget it. It haunted my dreams.

"Roman," I breathed.

"Ah, you finally say my name. I see now that's what was missing during our time together, you calling out my name as you begged for your life."

I heard the feral growl from Drake and prayed he wouldn't do something stupid.

My eyes went to his brown ones and they weren't warm and melty like they were this morning when we'd woken up tangled together.

They were lethal.

I knew I had a matter of minutes before Drake did something crazy. I begged him with my eyes to stay still, not to fight. I watched the tension coil tighter as he read my plea.

Brady would be coming up behind Roman through the reception area, blocking Roman from exiting the building.

Where the hell is everyone?

"I don't remember begging you for anything," I replied, hoping all of his attention came to me.

"You'll beg this time, bitch. You all will."

"That's doubtful, Roman. You've got one chance to end this with you still alive. Let him go and you walk out of here."

Roman smiled. The expression made him look maniacal—which scared the shit out of me.

Desperate men do desperate things. But men with nothing to lose are the most dangerous kind of men. I'd heard my dad say that, and watching Roman now with a gun to Drake's head, a vest strapped on, I knew my dad was right.

Roman was the most dangerous kind of man— he'd take us all out. Including himself.

"I got nothing left but this. *Nothing!*" he roared. The shout had to have pierced Drake's eardrum but he didn't move, didn't flinch. Just kept his eyes on me. I didn't know how that was possible.

"Carter, back up," I said.

"No, *Carter*, don't fucking move. After all, it was your fucking piece-of-shit father that killed mine. Finally I get what's owed to me."

Roman shifted and I raised the barrel of my Glock just a fraction to stay on target. Roman's free hand went into his pocket and out came a cell. His thumb slid across the screen and I didn't waste another second.

My focus sharpened and three red dots aligned. Then with a steady, practiced press of the trigger, I fired.

Drake moved with lightning speed, disarming Roman even though it was fruitless. Roman's body pitched, hit the wall, and he slid down.

The man was dead.

My world tilted.

A ripple of nausea rolled through me. There was commotion all around me. Brady came into view, Carter rushed to Drake.

"Saw the vest, hit the cell jammer on my way around."

That was good news.

My head was filled with chaos, but a different kind, it wasn't cluttering my mind, it was searching, scanning. There was something I needed to remember but couldn't.

Carter, Drake, and Brady were talking, I could see their lips moving, but I couldn't hear a damn thing.

Remember, dammit.

I glanced at Roman's dead body and felt a twinge of remorse. Blood spilled from his forehead and dripped on the carpet. His legs were folded unnaturally for the way he'd fallen. A phone laid next to him, and...

"The vest," I shouted and sprinted toward Roman, skidding to a halt as I bent to grab his ankles.

I pulled him down the hall to the back door with a super-human strength I didn't know I possessed.

"Brady jammed—"

"Lore always has a secondary power source."

Drake and Carter rushed me. Carter sprinted past, Drake stopped to heft Roman's upper body up. I heard the back door crash open—which was a good thing because I'd momentarily forgotten we were indoors and I would've smashed into it.

We were ten feet out the door with me running backward when Brady caught up. I knew he was about to take over. And I was okay with that. I'd made a promise to myself never to allow my need to prove myself put anyone in harm's way.

Brady and Drake would be faster.

The exchange of Roman's legs from me to Brady was smooth and flawless. Neither of us skipped a beat as I jumped out of their way and the men spirited Roman—who happened to be a bomb now— away from the building.

I watched with fascination as they stopped,

swung, and literally threw Roman. His body landed with a bounce. Both men turned.

Drake's face screwed up in fury and he shouted, "Run!"

Snapping out of my trance, I turned on my heel and ran.

Then my world exploded at the same time a very large body tackled me to the ground and covered mine.

It might have been minutes or maybe seconds. Suddenly Drake was on his feet and I was in his arms and he was carrying me. I glanced up, saw the angry set of his jaw, and smiled. My dirt-covered hand went to his face and I pressed my palm to his cheek. His eyes lowered to mine—no less pissed but no longer lethal.

"We need to stop meeting this way," I joked.

Drake shook his head, not amused in the slightest. Which only made me smile bigger.

My man took my safety seriously.

"I love you."

Drake's step faltered, his chest expanded as he drew in a gulp of oxygen. When he let it out, he smiled.

"I love you, too, baby. So damned much. But the

next time there's a goddamn bomb, you take cover. You do not stand around waiting for the show."

"Noted."

Then I burst out laughing and listened to Drake grumble about tanning my ass.

Yes. Please.

41

———

"Honey, we're gonna be late," Liberty whispered.

"Don't care." My mouth continued to work her neck, nibbling, biting, tasting.

Liberty's head tilted to the side, her leg hitched higher on my hip, and I knew she didn't really care about being late. I also knew she didn't care about me taking her again even though I'd just had her.

I hadn't allowed her to get up and clean up before I reached into the nightstand next to our bed and came back with a huge-ass diamond and slipped it on her finger. I didn't get the words out before she shouted *yes*, lifted her head, and kissed me.

"I wanna show my ring off." Liberty's hands slowly roamed my back. Something she did whenever she could. She told me she liked touching her tattoo. When I explained the tattoo was on my body, therefore mine, she smiled and said, "Same thing." I couldn't argue with that because she was right, I was hers—and she was mine.

And now that my ring was sitting at the base of her left ring finger, she'd be mine in a different way soon.

But I knew she was full of shit. She didn't want to show her ring off, she wanted to show her man off. We were due to her parents' house for a barbecue, this being the first time everyone would be together since I'd moved to Georgia. I'd met everyone except Nick, Meadow, and their kids.

And she'd been talking about it all week, how she couldn't wait for me to meet them.

They could wait.

"You think I'm gonna slide my ring on your finger and not slide inside of you, you're crazy."

Liberty started shaking with laughter and I paused to enjoy the feel of it. After I let that wash over me, I memorized it, even though I didn't need to. Liberty laughed a lot these days.

It'd been three months since Roman died. Two months and three weeks since we'd moved in together.

For the first week after Roman, we'd all watched

Liberty carefully. The fucker had invaded a place that had always been safe for her and we were all waiting for a sign that she wasn't handling that intrusion in a healthy way. But that day something had changed in her and it was fucking beautiful to witness.

First, when that asswipe got the drop on me, I watched Liberty slip into quiet professional. She didn't panic, she didn't freak. She assessed, processed, and determined her course of action. I had the barrel of that asshole's gun at my temple but I had my woman standing in front of me. And in that moment, I knew to my soul Liberty would have my back—all I had to do was wait.

And it's a damn good thing my woman's a good shot because her bullets zipped past my head with inches to spare.

Liberty remained calm and cool when the police, fire, and rescue squads showed. Thank God, Blake and the guys had left for lunch so they weren't there. But Lauren was, and unfortunately, she'd caught the brunt of Roman's wrath. He'd beat her unconscious. Levi, Jasper, Clark, and Lenox proved they were the men I knew them to be and had taken care of Lauren, her medical bills, and she'd recuperated at Reagan and Clark's house.

It shocked the shit out of me when two weeks after the attack, the shy, quiet woman showed up to work. Levi had wanted her to take another week of paid leave but she'd gone toe-to-toe with him and refused to leave. Lauren was a little bit of all right. She fit in at Triple Canopy even if she wasn't in-your-face tough—the woman had inner strength.

The night after everything went down, we were at her parents' house for dinner and it was like a switch had flipped. Liberty was happy and smiling while at the same time sad about Lauren, but what she wasn't doing was dwelling, second-guessing, or freaking out.

I thought she was just in shock. When I gently questioned her, she smiled and said, "I'm finally free."

It hit me then, she *was* free.

Free of Roman.

Freed from the worry he was still out there.

Yes, indeed, Liberty was finally free.

She had her control back.

"Drake," Liberty moaned when I pulled one of her nipples into my mouth and swirled my tongue over the tight nub.

When I was done, I let go and said, "You like my mouth, baby?"

"You know I do."

Yeah, she did. She loved my mouth—tits, neck, belly, between her legs, or on hers.

I drew in her other nipple, laved it with the same attention, and she started wiggling.

"You want something?"

"You know I do," she repeated.

I traced a path from her nipple to her throat with my tongue, pausing just long enough to give her a nip before I continued up her neck, pausing again just below her ear.

"Spread for me, baby."

I felt the tremble before I rolled between her legs, the tip of my dick notched into her wetness and she mewed.

"Tell me," I demanded.

Liberty righted her head and gave me her gaze, just like she always did.

Every time.

She gave me what I wanted—her eyes, then the words.

"Love you, Drake."

Christ, I loved hearing that.

I drove in, slid deep, and stilled. I knew she'd ask, I just had to wait her out.

"Please, Drake."

Fuck, but I loved that, too.

"Want your mouth, Liberty."

I watched my girl's eyes flare, the unusual amber color heated, and she gifted me with a blinding smile. She didn't give me her mouth, but what she gave me was better.

"I'm gonna be Liberty Hayes."

Christ.

I shoved my face in her neck, bared my teeth, and raked them across her sensitive skin until her hips tipped up in invitation and her nails dug into my back.

"You make me happy," I told her as I pulled out. "So damn happy." Then I drove home.

I didn't stop my pounding thrusts or my bites at her neck until she chanted my name between pants.

"Harder," she begged.

I didn't go harder but I slid my hand between us and started thumbing her clit.

"Oh, yeah," she purred.

"Give it to me," I demanded.

"Not yet."

"Greedy." I added pressure and speed at her clit. "You can't hold out forever, baby."

My taunt did exactly what I'd hoped and she clamped her pussy tight around my cock. She did this in an effort to make me go before her. She did it every time, and every time, she lost.

My girl was competitive—with *everything*.

But so was I.

"Baby, you know I love your pussy. Love it more when you tighten around me. But you know I'm gonna win."

I bit down on her shoulder, heard her whimper, and knew I had her. She was close, so close her pussy was clutching my dick, and her excitement was leaking out every time I surged in.

Fuck, she was killing me.

"Liberty—"

"I'm there," she announced unnecessarily.

Her back arched, thighs tightened at my sides, then her hand dove into my hair and latched on, yanking it as her pussy convulsed.

Thank Christ.

"Mouth," I growled.

Liberty tilted her head enough to give me what I asked for. Her lips parted and my tongue tangled with hers. The kiss was long, wet, and rough. The orgasm was better, best I've had, and that was saying something because every one Liberty gave me was the best.

Pure magic—every part of her.

But this time, I was pouring into my fiancée.

My present.

My future.

My fate.

I PULLED up in front of the McCoys' house and stopped.

"Gonna let you out here."

"Why?"

"Um." I glanced out the windshield. "I'm gonna have to park around the corner."

"That's okay, I can walk."

I looked back at Liberty and shook my head. "You're not walking a mile, babe. Hop down."

Thankfully, before she could say anything else and turn a pointless conversation into the world's dumbest argument, the Walker twins bounced out of the house, stopping on the porch and waving. The women weren't identical twins, but they might as well have been.

"I'll get out here," she stated, and I didn't bother to hide my chuckle. "What?"

"Nothing, babe."

"What? You know I can walk. It's no big deal—"

My hand shot out and I hooked her around the back of her neck, pulled her to me, and slammed my mouth on hers. She opened, my tongue plunged in, I kissed her quiet, and I did this for a long time. When we broke apart, her eyes were hazy and her lips swollen. The look complemented the freshly fucked glow she still wore. It was highly unlikely she'd be pleased to know she was walking into a family party with ten men in attendance—one being her father—and they'd catch sight of her and know.

"Be back."

"Okay, Drake."

I didn't have to park around the corner but it was still a hike. So by the time I'd made it into the house, everyone had seen Liberty's ring and they were all celebrating.

Levi, Blake, Jasper, Clark, and Lenox all knew I was going to ask her. I talked to Levi privately, then to Blake and Levi together. After I told them, I talked to her uncles. The men who meant the world to her. I didn't ask for permission but I did ask for their blessing. They'd given it without reservation and I had to admit, it felt fucking great being welcomed into the family.

My parents knew and were happy. My mom had

spent an hour on the phone with Liberty planning a trip out to Georgia.

That meant when I walked in, I was assaulted with a round of congratulations from the women, and pounding slaps on the back from the men.

I finally met Nick, Meadow, and their kids.

There was something to be said about this big, loud family. They loved hard and they did it openly. Within minutes, Nick had accepted me and talked to me like we'd been lifelong friends.

I was moving through the crush of people, trying to claim my woman, when I caught sight of someone outside.

What the fuck?

I changed direction and stepped out onto the McCoys' big back patio, where Carter was lounging back in a chair, beer in hand and smiling like an idiot.

"What the fuck?" I vocalized.

"Surprise," Liberty said from behind me and slid her arms around my middle.

"Yeah, what she said," Matt said.

I looked away from Matt and saw Luke, Logan, and Trey, all smiling.

Not at me, at Liberty holding up her left hand, wiggling her fingers.

"Holy shit!" Logan shouted.

"That's cold, brother. You put a ring on your woman's finger and didn't even call to tell us," Trey joked.

"You didn't tell them?" Liberty gasped.

"Baby, I asked you to marry me two hours ago. After you said yes, we had—"

"Don't finish that." She stopped showing off her ring because her hand was now over my mouth.

The table erupted in laughter. Carter groaned and closed his eyes. "I do not need to know that shit."

"Can I borrow Liberty a second?" Blake asked from the doorway.

My girl removed her hand and stepped in front of me. She rolled up on her toes but she didn't kiss me. Instead she said, "You make me really happy, Drake Hayes."

"You make me happy, too, baby."

"I can't wait to be your wife," she whispered.

When she was done giving me her sweet words, she pressed her lips to mine and I didn't give the first fuck her whole family was there. I kissed the hell out of my woman. And it was thorough.

EPILOGUE

Levi McCoy saw his daughter's fiancé fist her hair and lay one on her. It might have been forty years ago, but Levi remembered.

He'd never forget—not the moment he fell in love with Blake at the Tastee-Freez. Not him losing her. Not reconnecting. Especially not what it was like living without her.

So he got it. But that didn't mean he wanted to watch that shit.

He turned to find Lenox smiling at him.

"Feels good, doesn't it?" Lenox asked, but his friend wasn't looking at Liberty and her man.

Lenox was looking at his son, Carter. Delaney had wandered outside and was sitting on her husband's lap.

Levi's gaze moved through the rest of the room and took in his family. They were all there. A celebration. Though none of them knew what they were celebrating.

"Damn good."

"You ready?" Jasper joined their huddle and asked.

Neither Lenox nor Levi answered or they did, just not verbally as they made their way through Levi's house out to the back patio. They passed Delaney as she was coming back into the house. Clark, Jason, and Nick were waiting for them outside and Levi slid the sliding glass door shut.

"Need to talk to you about something," Clark started and didn't make the guys wait for the rest. "Nick's leaving the FBI and coming on board." Clark waited as the group congratulated Nick. Handshakes and smiles all around. Once the commotion died down, he continued. "Jason's giving the DEA six more months, then he's on board."

More handshakes, more congratulations.

"What about you?" Levi asked Trey.

"Me?"

"What's happening with your medical board?"

The man's face went hard and Levi knew why.

It's hard facing life when something important to you has been stripped away.

"I'm out," Trey grunted.

Matt, Logan, Luke, and Drake all sliced their gazes Trey's way. He obviously hadn't shared with the team.

"We want you," Lenox told him.

"My leg's—"

"Don't give a fuck. You can finish your rehab down here. When you're done with PT, we'll assess and you'll tell us if you want field work or not. Either way, we want you."

"Don't know what to say," Trey mumbled and Levi smiled.

"Say yes."

"Yes. 'Preciate the offer."

"Excellent." Lenox nodded and turned to Luke. "And you? Where are you at with your med board?"

"No clue. They're jacking me around," Luke answered.

"Good. Take your medical discharge and come work for us."

Luke jerked back, looked to Carter, then back to Lenox. "You serious?"

"As a heart attack. The four of us understand the value of a team and keeping it together. Matt, Logan, we'd like you to come down when your contracts are up."

Carter Lenox, Nick Clark, Jason Walker, Drake Hayes, and Brady Hewitt would take over Triple Canopy. All that was left for the original four to do was stack the company with good men for the five principals to manage.

"I'm in," Logan immediately answered.

"What's the pay like?" Matt smiled.

"Like you need money, rich boy." Trey laughed and threw a wadded napkin at Matt.

Good, light-hearted, and some not-so-light-hearted jabs were exchanged among the men.

Levi turned from the group sitting around the table and looked at his brothers—not of blood, but of bond. They'd walked through hell together, their friendship forged from blood and honor. Men he'd been proud to serve with but prouder to have built a family with.

"What's on your mind, Luke?" Carter asked as the men stopped busting Matt's balls.

"You know I'm mostly fuckin' blind in my left eye," Luke returned.

"Know that."

"I'm left-handed. Left eye dominant. I can't—"

"*You can't?*" Drake growled. "Since when do you

say I can't? You have a problem with your eye, Luke. But you didn't lose the use of your fucking brain."

Luke's jaw set and Levi understood that, too. Something no one talks about, something that all men try to push from their minds when they're in the field—what an injury will cost you. Not death, but injury. When you die in battle, you're celebrated. When you're injured, you get your walking papers. Some get medals and ribbons as if that's a consolation prize.

So, Levi knew exactly what Luke was thinking. The very organization he'd pledged his life to was going to turn its back on him. At least that's how Luke saw it.

"Luke," Levi called. "We have a place for you. Hope like hell you accept our offer. You and Matt make an exceptional team. Add in Brady and no fucking joke, our sniper course will be booked out for years. But something else for you to consider—you'll have your brothers with you. And something I've learned, my family's learned, when that shit you got in your gut starts to eat away at you, you keep your brothers close.

"Straight up, the five of you saved my daughter's life. There's nothing I can do to repay that debt. I could give you everything I own and it still wouldn't touch what I owe you. But I need the four of you to know, we're not offering you jobs because of what you did for Liberty. We want you because you each bring something unique to Triple Canopy. We want you because you've proven yourselves. We want you because you all are the best and you'll take Triple Canopy to the next level. We have to turn down contracts because we don't have the manpower to take everything that comes our way. Plus, we pay a fuckton better than Uncle Sam."

"I'm in," Luke agreed.

"Fuck, yeah," Logan cheered. "We stay together and get Church back. Only I guess he's no longer living his life like a monk so maybe he needs a new name."

Jasper growled beside Levi. He didn't like to be reminded his baby girl was no longer a girl but a woman sharing a bed with her husband. Though he was enjoying the hell out of his granddaughter.

"Good, that's settled." Clark clapped his hands and wrung them together. "Let's go inside. We have an announcement to make."

The men stood and each started to file into the house, but Levi hung back and waited.

Levi's future son-in-law stopped by his side, sensing he needed a word.

"She happy?" Levi asked.

"Very."

"Thank you."

"Told you before, tell you again, you don't need to thank me for loving her." Drake paused and a smile formed, then died when he looked back at Levi. "Don't know if it was you who made her the way she is, if it was her mom, the influence of Jasper, Clark, and Lenox, or if she was born tough. However that came to be, her being who she is, you need to know I see her. Past the tough, strong, determination —under all of that to the woman she is. Her soft heart, her compassion, the abundant love she has to give. And I need you to know I'll protect that. I'll keep it safe. And until my last breath, she'll know she is the best thing that's ever happened to me."

Levi swallowed past the lump in his throat, and he did that thinking his daughter chose well. She'd found herself a man who would give her beauty. And there was nothing more a father could ask for.

"Want you to have these." Drake reached into his pocket and pulled out a pair of dog tags. "She doesn't know I have them. I found them in the dirt in Syria and I've carried them with me everyday since. For weeks they were all I had of her."

Drake extended his hand and Levi looked down

at the offering, his chest burned thinking about why his daughter's tags were in the dirt and not on her where they should've been. "These aren't to remind you of what Liberty's been through, or how she made it through and found new strength. These..." Drake shook the tags, "are to remind you that I will always have her back. I will carry her when I need to. But more importantly, I'll proudly walk by her side."

Drake dropped the tags into Levi's open palm and left him to his thoughts.

These thoughts were no longer troubled.

The burn in Levi's chest turned to warmth, and he knew his daughter had chosen well.

CARTER LENOX LOOKED around the room filled with family.

Twenty-eight people—not including kids—elbow-to-elbow in Levi's living room and dining room, none of them caring they were crammed together, just happy to be together.

Pride swelled and his throat started to tingle.

They'd done it.

They'd created beauty.

"We got something to tell you all," Jasper boomed.

Now that they'd done the last thing they needed to do, it was time. The women were ecstatic. As they should be. They'd stood by their men as they finished their Army careers, started a business, put in long hours, worked hard, and grew that business so when they were ready they'd have something to pass to the next generation.

The future of Triple Canopy was secured so it was time.

"We're retiring," Clark announced.

The room went utterly silent. No one had thought the old men would ever step aside. Lenox understood why, but it was time.

"Nick's quit the FBI. He starts next week. Jason will be six months behind him," Levi started. "Carter, Quinn, Brady, and Drake are already there. Addy helps part-time. So we know the business is in good hands. Trey, Luke, Logan, and Matt will all start as their contracts are up. So we're stepping down and handing over what's always been yours to them. Of course, we hope the rest of you will follow and take your places when you're ready. But until that happens, we're confident we're leaving Triple Canopy in very capable hands."

Carter Lenox watched, and he did this with his heart full as his family erupted into celebration.

Hell, yes, they'd done it.

And retirement was gonna be sweet.

JASPER WALKER LOOKED around the table.

Brothers.

Not of blood, but of bond.

Once he was done with that, he glanced through the big windows into Levi's house and saw his family. They were all excitedly talking, celebrating, bonding.

His chest no longer warmed when he saw that, the burn had long ago settled into his soul. He'd done a lot in his life. But the best thing he'd ever done was marry Em. His black-haired beauty, whose musical voice and gorgeous blue eyes still hit him in the gut every time he saw her walk in a room or called his name. She'd freed him from the prison he'd locked himself in. It was because of her that he had all that he had—Jason, his girls, this big, loud family that loved hard and wasn't afraid to show it.

All of that because his wife gave it to him.

"What now?" Clark asked and poured himself a healthy shot of whiskey.

"Taking Lily to Hawaii," Lenox announced. "We leave next week. We'll be gone three weeks."

"Blake wants to go to Oregon. She's planned a whitewater rafting trip," Levi added.

Clark's gaze went to Jasper and he thought about his plans. Emily had already stocked their mammoth RV and wanted to take a few months traveling across the US. It would be a good trip, not because of the sights they'd see or the places they'd visit, but just the two of them together with nothing but miles in front of them.

But Jasper knew something his wife didn't know.

There was a storm coming, one that had been brewing for a long time, circling them and gaining strength.

Hurricane Hadley was gearing up to touch down and Jasper knew his baby girl well enough to know they all needed to brace for the F-5 that was going to take a bite out of Brady Hewitt.

Jasper was far from stupid. He'd watched his daughter dance around Brady doing whatever she could to get his attention. He also knew Brady wouldn't go there.

His money was on his daughter. Brady didn't stand a chance.

Since Hadley was fed up with the dance and was preparing to move in, Jasper needed to stay close. Not because his daughter would need him, but Brady would. The man was wrought with demons.

Demons his daughter could vanquish if Brady would allow it.

"Em and I will be around for a few months, then we'll head out West in the RV, take a few months and travel."

"Hadley and Brady," Clark surmised.

"Hadley and Brady," Jasper confirmed.

It didn't surprise Jasper his brother knew what was going on. Further, he knew Lenox and Levi saw it, too.

That was them.

Brothers.

The four of them loved their families, therefore they paid attention, and not just to the children who belonged to them by blood but all of them. Each man had vowed to always love and protect the brood.

They were sheepdogs watching over the flock.

"You got two left," Clark joked. "The rest of us are done. Now all we have to do is sit back and enjoy the grandkids."

Lenox tossed back the rest of his whiskey and shook his head. "When did we become old men?"

"Shit." Levi laughed. "Don't let this gray hair fool you, there's not a damn thing old about me."

Jasper Walker felt a lot of things, old was not one of them.

Clark picked up the bottle of Jack, refilled the empty glasses, and held his up. "To growing old."

"*A privilege denied to many.*" The rest of the men finished the toast.

Four shots were taken.

Four glasses slammed onto the table.

And four men grew silent.

"We have it all," Clark muttered.

"That we do," Lenox agreed.

And they did.

They had it all.

Blessed beyond measure.

Family.

SOMEWHERE INSIDE THE HOUSE, four women huddled.

Sisters.

Not of blood but of bond.

They were laughing as they watched their men commune. Something they'd seen millions of times. Something they'd been a part of and watched from a distance. Something they loved.

"What do you think they're talking about?" Blake asked.

"Do you need to ask?" Reagan smiled.

"Fighting, fucking, or killing," Lily and Emily said in unison.

Then the four women dissolved into a fit of laughter.

They'd each struggled. Fought for their happily ever afters, for their families. They'd worked to help their marriages stay solid and happy.

They each counted their blessings, for they were abundant.

Four women, the foundation, the roots that had grown the next generation.

Four amazing, strong women who had it all.

THE END!

Next up - Triple Canopy
Damaged- Brady and Hadley

ALSO BY RILEY EDWARDS

Riley Edwards

www.RileyEdwardsRomance.com

Romantic Suspense

Gemini Group

Nixon's Promise

Jameson's Salvation

Weston's Treasure

Alec's Dream

Chasin's Surrender

Holden's Resurrection

Red Team

Nightstalker

Protecting Olivia - Susan Stoker Universe

Redeeming Violet - Susan Stoker Universe

Recovering Ivy - Susan Stoker Universe

Rescuing Erin - Susan Stoker Universe

The Gold Team

Unbroken

Trust

Standalone

Romancing Rayne - Susan Stoker Universe

ABOUT THE AUTHOR

Riley Edwards is a USA Today bestselling author, wife, and military mom. Riley was born and raised in Los Angeles but now resides on the east coast with her fantastic husband and children.

Riley writes heart-stopping romance with sexy alpha heroes and even stronger heroines. Riley's favorite genres to write are romantic suspense and military romance.

Don't forget to sign up for Riley's newsletter and never miss another release, sale, or exclusive bonus material. https://www.subscribepage.com/RRsignup

Facebook Fan Group

www.rileyedwardsromance.com

facebook.com/Novelist.Riley.Edwards

twitter.com/rileyedwardsrom

instagram.com/rileyedwardsromance

bookbub.com/authors/riley-edwards

amazon.com/author/rileyedwards

ACKNOWLEDGMENTS

To all of you – the readers: Thank you for picking up this book and giving me a few hours of your time. Whether this is the first book of mine you've read or you've been with me from the beginning, thank you for your support. It is because of you I have the coolest job in the world.

Made in the USA
Coppell, TX
25 May 2021